I0613172

Alice Eddy Curtiss

The Silver Cross

a story of the King's daughters and Miss Marigold's tithes

Alice Eddy Curtiss

The Silver Cross
a story of the King's daughters and Miss Marigold's tithes

ISBN/EAN: 9783337256111

Printed in Europe, USA, Canada, Australia, Japan

Cover: Foto ©Andreas Hilbeck / pixelio.de

More available books at **www.hansebooks.com**

THE SILVER CROSS

A Story of the King's Daughters

AND

MISS MARIGOLD'S TITHES

BY

ALICE EDDY CURTISS

———

BOSTON AND CHICAGO

Congregational Sunday-School and Publishing Society

INTRODUCTORY.

THE stories which form this volume will be familiar
to those who were readers of The Advance a few
years ago, having originally appeared therein as
serials. They were then received with such marked
favor, and so frequently inquired for in this form,
that it seems fitting that they should be so preserved
as a memorial to their author. It is hoped that,
through their continued and wider circulation, she,
who was ever so ready to give words of comfort
and cheer not only to her immediate circle of
friends and acquaintances, but to a larger unknown
circle whom she hoped to reach, may still exert an
influence for good.

E. C. C.

CONTENTS.

THE SILVER CROSS.

MISS MARIGOLD'S TITHES.

THE SILVER CROSS.

CHAPTER I.

MARY was sorry when her brother decided to leave Berryville for the city. Not that she was particularly fond of Berryville, or indeed had ever taken it into her head to like or dislike any place where it happened to be her lot to live. Mary had moved a good many times in her short life, and she had never noticed that wages were better, or the price of bread lower, or the tenements where the family took up their abode less bare and dingy, in one town than another. To be sure, Ridgetown, with a drinking saloon next door and one across the way, was noisier than Grannis, where there were no saloons at all; but on the other hand there was the Salvation Army to make things interesting in Ridgetown, while Grannis had only an occasional fight between the Italians and Irish — and Mary certainly had no especial fondness for fights.

But Berryville had one gift which neither Ridgetown nor Grannis nor any of her various abiding places had ever brought to Mary before. Berryville had a

view of the mountains. Far away, blue and fair, they
smiled down on the smoky town, and little Mary
leaned on her attic window sill, to weave strange, wistful fancies about them when her day's work was done.
They were green near by, those beautiful heights, —
Mary knew that from her railway journeys, — green,
with tangled woods, and brown paths leading upward,
and the smell of pines in the air. Some of the girls
at the mill had lived on those wonderful slopes, in
little brown cottages that thrust aside the maples and
birches to peer down into the valley world below.
Mary asked many questions of these fortunate girls,
and learned many things in reply. Sometimes at
night she wandered in dreams along the fern-fringed
paths, gathered violets, listened to birds that sang like
angels, and saw the moon climb above the peaks — a
moon quite different from that which nightly did its
best to beautify the crowded neighborhood of Berry's
factory. Oh, it was quite another affair, that silver
boat, sailing softly up through the purple sea of sky,
with the mountain left behind like the shores of a
rocky harbor!

"Oh, I *wish* I could go there just once!" Mary
had sighed sometimes on waking; and it was always
a comfort to go to the window for a peep at the hills
in their morning glory, before she hurried to help Bell
with the breakfast. It was pleasant, too, to look

towards them sometimes over the crochet work that
filled her hands during the hours when Bell and Bob
were at work and Tommy and Jimmy at school.
Mary was too slow and weakly herself for spooling
or carding at the mill. Bell sometimes told people
that Bob's sister hardly earned her salt, with all her
bits of knitting work and her kitchen doings — but
then that was only Bell's way. Mary knew well
enough that no harm was meant, although, for her
own part, she generally worked harder after such a
speech, and resolutely turned her back to the sunlit
peaks, lest they should tempt her to idleness. And
Bell and Bob never knew that she cried a little, all
by herself, on the night when Bob engaged to go to
the city. If they had known it, what difference could
a few tears have made? Little Mary was the person
of least consequence in the family, and Bob was doing
a good brother's part by her. Why should it enter
any one's head to ask what she thought of the
removal?

So Mary put her small belongings together, helped
Bell with her packing, washed the children's faces
and mended their clothes for the journey; and went
back, quite alone, for a last glimpse of the distant
beauty which had been her secret comfort.

"Maybe the next one that has this room will like
'em as much as me," she said to herself; "and —

maybe — there 'll be something just as nice down to the city."

Which was just Mary's way of consoling herself for her small losses. She generally had a vague expectation that something was going to happen "around the next corner," which was quite astonishing, considering how few of her expectations had thus far been fulfilled.

It was a longer journey than usual, this time — away and away from Berryville and the far blue peaks; out through hill-pass and tunnel, and on across the level country beyond. The car was not very crowded, and for once Mary had a seat to herself. She leaned her head against the window casing after a time, and gave herself up to watching a girl who sat opposite her. Such a pretty girl! Mary almost forgot her vanished hills for the moment, in pleasure over the bright brown hair, the soft, rounded cheek, with its delicate rose tints, and the clear, gray eyes with their dark lashes.

"Dressed so pretty, too," said Mary to herself. "If I was rich I'd have a gray dress just like that, and wear gloves stitched with black, and a little bit of purple ribbon, too, against the gray. Only I would n't look like that, if I had all of 'em this minute!"

And Mary, who was not in the least sensitive over

her physical defects, drew her shawl over the crooked shoulders which made her unlike other people, and laughed softly, under her breath, at the thought of how she would look decked out in the fine clothes of the girl across the way. It was odd that at the same moment the girl herself looked up from her book just in time to catch the soft brightness left behind by the inward laughter as it died away. If Mary had only known it. there was a charm quite its own about her fair little wistful face when it was bright and interested as it was then. It caught and held the clear gray eyes until its smile was reflected in them, and each of the two girls became suddenly conscious that she had exchanged friendly glances with a stranger, and a stranger quite unlike herself. They looked away from each other immediately, but the friendly impression remained, and more than once during the next half hour the two pairs of eyes met again. Mary's full of pleased interest and the strange young lady's soft with gentle pity which could not offend.

At the end of the half hour something happened that changed the current of Mary's little life forevermore. Dear little Mary! How surprised she would have been if an angel had told her that she had come to the turning point of her existence! Such a little thing to be a turning point! Why, it was only the

tired mother who sat just before her, dropping asleep
from sheer weariness, with her baby slipping from
her arms! Mary loved babies, and there was nothing for her to do, while Jimmy and Tommy were
so comfortable with their ginger cakes, and their
mother nodding in her corner. What was more
natural than that she should lean over the seat to
speak to the drowsy woman, and ask her to set the
baby into her own lap?

"He'll be good! Oh, I know he'll be good!"
said Mary. "I can always make them good, only I
can't just lift him over!"

But here another voice broke in. The young lady
across the aisle — how strange it was! — had actually
started from her seat at the same time, for all the
world as if she too were a plain little cripple, eager
to help along in small ways because she could do
nothing else. There the two girls stood, with the
mother, startled and grateful, looking wearily up
at them, and the baby fairly wriggling up the
back of the seat to get at some new nurse not too
tired to be entertaining. It was the young lady who
settled it all.

"We'll take care of him together!" she said
impulsively, and sat down beside Mary with the
baby in her arms, and after that the girls were
friends in a moment.

But, oh, how that baby squirmed! He wriggled upright and threw himself forward upon Mary's neck with a whoop of glee. He straightened himself out and tried to snatch off the gray hat and clench his fists in the bright brown hair under it. He drummed wildly on the windowpane and shrieked with delight over the jumping mouse which Mary proudly constructed from a yellow-bordered handkerchief. Jimmy and Tommy drew near, strewing the seat with ginger-cake crumbs, which Mary brushed anxiously off, with a glance at the gray gown, and which were calmly ignored by the gray gown's wearer. People looked at each other and smiled, as a burst of rapid baby jargon resounded through the car. Bell sat up and stared in amazement at the sight of Mary's new friend and then leaned forward to ask her sister-in-law a question, so as to seem to be of the party. It was a very exciting time, while the baby's mother slept calmly on amid the crowing and struggling that went on behind her, until at last, with a sudden drooping of his flaxen head, the baby curled down all in a moment and dropped soundly asleep, with the yellow-bordered mouse in his mouth. His two protectors smiled at each other in triumph and drew long breaths of relief.

"How does she ever manage him? No wonder she's tired!" said the young lady in a whisper, and Mary responded feelingly : —

"I don't believe I ever could have held that baby all by myself, and what would anybody have thought of me after saying I'd take him!"

"You were so quick to offer," said the other. "I was watching you, or I don't know that I should have seen that she needed help. You seemed to take it right in, and you were quicker than I was, though I *am*"— She glanced down at the little purple ribbon that lay against the gray, and then up at Mary with a quick lighting of her face. "Why, I did n't think of it before." she said eagerly, "but maybe you wear the little cross too. Perhaps that was why! You don't mind my asking, do you? *Are* you — one of the King's Daughters? How lovely that would be!"

And as she spoke Mary noticed for the first time the tiny cross half hidden against the gray of her gown. She looked at it curiously as she answered.

"I don't know just what you mean," she said, hesitating. "The King's daughters? Do you mean — God?" She spoke under her breath, with a quick glance around in the direction of her sister-in-law. How surprised Bell would have been to hear little Mary talking of such things! "Do you mean God?" she whispered. "I — do try — only I'm such a little weakly thing, you know, and no account anyway, and I can't go to church because the seats make my back ache. Bell and Bob go sometimes — but when the Salvation Army preached in the street I used to listen out of our window, and I went to Sunday-school one year too, when I was pretty well, and I think about it all and I try — only *that* was n't what you meant, was it?"

The young lady looked at her in some surprise. The Salvation Army was not just in accordance with her line of thinking, and she hardly knew what to make of Mary's straightforward interpretation of her question. However, being an impulsive, enthusiastic girl, strongly attracted, moreover, by the sweet little thoughtful face beside her, she did not hesitate to draw the tiny silver cross into plainer view, and plunge into an explanation which brought the light to Mary's eyes and the rare color to her cheeks.

"The King's Daughters? Why, yes; it means that, of course — everybody that loves the Lord Christ and wants to do something for him; but, you see, sometimes people forget to do the little things, and the King's Daughters just try to do those, you know, — In His Name, just as those letters say on my cross. And the motto is what Mr. Hale wrote in his story — only you don't know the story, do you? But you must have heard the words sometimes,

" Look up and not down,
Look out and not in,

Look forward and not back,
And lend a hand.

" Well that's it ; that's what the King's Daughters
are trying to do ; and they have the cross because of
another story of Mr. Hale's, about some people who
loved Christ long ago, and kept this kind of a cross
for their secret sign, and were sworn to lend a hand
wherever they could ' In His Name,' and never refuse
to do a service when it was asked of them for the
love of Christ. Such a lovely story ! Do you like to
read? Why, see here,"— for Mary's eyes were eloquent in answer,— " I 'll just give you the one in my
bag. for I 'd like to have you read it, and it 's so
beautiful. I was taking it to my little cousin, but I
can get her another, and you shall take this to remember me by — and the baby." She laughed brightly
over the head of the sleeping child, and then in
answer to her companion's thanks and timid questions
went on with her story. ,

" Yes ; you see, the story was so lovely ; and it said
in it that there were so many people in this world
making a story all the time as they lived along, and
that by-and-by the test of everybody's life would be
whether they had lived for the love of Christ and in
his name. And people could n't forget it, somehow,
after they had read about it ; and the motto stayed in
people's minds so ; and then there was the other

story about Ten Times One, and everybody getting
ten more to live that way. Oh, I can't tell it all, but
after a while some ladies started the King's Daughters, and it is just people living ' In His Name,' and
trying to lend a hand, and they wear the purple ribbon
because it is the royal color, and the silver cross with
the three letters. to remind them; and everybody
tries to get ten more, and anybody can start a Ten
anywhere and choose what special thing to do. Some
of them visit sick people, and some start mission
schools, and some do cooking for poor people, and
some just try to make things pleasant around them,
and some do special things for the churches they
belong to. We had one at school for being polite and
making things comfortable for the teachers in the
class-room, and it was so pleasant! Why, we found
out about Madame's sick child that made her so cross
to us in the French class, and we sent flowers to her;
and after a while we got it arranged so that there was
some one to go and sit with her while Madame was
teaching, and it seemed to be of such comfort to the
poor woman! And I know of one lady that built a
whole beautiful cottage for sick people. and ever so
many are working in hospitals. Oh, there are so
many ways! But whatever else they do, every one
is pledged to be ready to lend a hand wherever it is
needed, and to be on the lookout for chances to help;

and whenever you see a purple ribbon like this, with
the little cross, you can be sure that the one who
wears it will do anything in the world to help you out
of any trouble, if you ask her In His Name. And
now that we're out of school our Ten are going to
help tired people, at home and everywhere else. It's
such a little bit of a thing, but there are so many who
are tired, you know, and we can't do great things yet,
any of us; so Kitty Holmes — she was the one to
start us — thought of this, and that was how I happened to take the baby. It was the first chance I've
had to-day."

How sweet and bright and joyous her face was!
Mary sighed wistfully, with a little tremble of her
lips. It seemed very beautiful, that glimpse of
another world than hers. The King's Daughters!
Just the right name for a company of girls like this,
fair and rich and happy, with hearts of gold that
wanted to help " tired people"! Mary was so often
tired herself, in body and soul! There were tears in
her eyes when she spoke again.

" It must make everything nice, living that way.
It'll be real pleasant to think about, and I sha'n't
forget it. Maybe some time I'll see somebody else
that belongs. I wish"—

She stopped herself hastily. How foolish it was
to wish anything about it! What had she to do

with the King's Daughters and their silver crosses,
except to remember them after this journey was over,
and think how beautiful it was that there should be
such people in the world! Did the King's daughter
beside her read all this in her face and answer,
straight from her heart, the unspoken longing? She
turned toward the crippled girl with her beautiful
eyes shining.

" You ought to belong yourself!" she said. " You
could! Why, there 'd be so many chances for you
every day, and you could get your own Ten to help
you. Oh, I should like to think about this journey
and remember that you started from now! We should
feel as if we were part of the same company, you
and I, even if we never saw each other again, and
there 'd be so many things for you to do, and I know
you 'd see them all the time! Oh, won't you?"

" Me?"

Mary sat up straight, with a sudden flush on her
thin cheeks. It all seemed to open before her in a
flash, the glory and beauty of this new way of living.

"Oh, could I?" she cried. "Could I? Just
there by the mill? I'd do anything! I'd help
every chance I had! Oh, do you suppose I could?"

Was it only a short two hours since these two had
first seen each other? Who could have believed it,
as their talk ran eagerly on, with the two lives, so

different in surroundings and opportunities, opening more and more to each other in the planning! The twilight was falling and the city lights beginning to gleam through the dusk before they had ended their talk. People began to gather together their luggage, and Bell leaned over the seat to hand Mary a bundle. The baby's mother woke and took the little fellow back with a sleepy " Thank you," and Mary felt with a pang that this golden time was past. But the girl in gray came back to her side after reaching down her bag.

"I 've brought you the book," she said softly; " and don't think it 's strange — but I 'm going to leave you my own badge. I want you to have it. I 'll write for another myself, and the girls will be glad when I tell them. I 'm so glad — if I was going to stop here I 'd find you again, but even though my home is far beyond, we sha'n't forget each other, and you won't forget about the King's Daughters thinking of each other when they pray, and asking help."

Then, before little Mary could answer with more than one flash from her startled, happy eyes, the fair young face was gone, and the new King's Daughter was limping down the car with her bundle in one hand, and in the other, clasped close and warm, the little book and the tiny silver cross, with its gracious letters, I. H. N.

CHAPTER II.

CONNOR STREET was certainly as ugly a thoroughfare as could be found in a day's ramble through the great city. There was not a pleasant-looking house, or a bit of fresh, green grass or garden ground along its whole dingy length. Tenements and tumble-down cottages jostled each other in dreary confusion; the sidewalks were always littered, the roadways deep in mud or dust, with great gaps in the pavement; there was not even a bit of picturesque ugliness to add interest to the scene. Crowds of children tumbled about the doors or sat on the curbstones, and night and morning the street was filled with men and women hurrying to or from the mills. A dreary place indeed; a place of work and worry and hand-to-mouth living, of tired bodies and worn hearts and ceaseless drudgery, ending only with the lives of those who dwelt there.

Yet on spring days even Connor Street had its drop of comfort. Straight through it poured the sweet sunshine, in a long lane of warm, golden light; the sky was deep and calm as the heart of a happy mother; here and there geraniums or early daisies

21

stood out on window sills to catch the pleasant air; more than one open door gave a glimpse of some bare little room that was a home in spite of its surroundings; and away at the lower end of the street one girlish face looked upward and around with joyous eyes and a smile that seemed to speak of some unknown delight just at hand. Ah, no! Connor Street was not all dreary! Sweet thoughts could flourish there as elsewhere, under airs from heaven. More than one unknown hero walked its broken pavements, and day after day pale little Mary, with her silver cross, slipped out of her door in the intervals of work and looked about her eagerly for some new chance to lend a hand.

Life - had grown strangely sweet and bright for Mary since that day on the railroad. There was a song on her lips often, as she sat at her knitting, and through her dreams of mountains and lovely country sights beyond her reach floated the bright face of the girl who had drawn her into the gracious company of the King's Daughters. Will she ever know, I wonder — that happy-hearted girl — how much has grown out of her afternoon's talk? Even Bell and Bob and the boys had noticed the difference in Mary's face since that day. They had never seen her so bright and active or so anxious to serve them all. Bell had actually shown pleasure over the girl's attempt to brighten the little living room by means of picture-cards on the walls and new half curtains at the windows, made, while the "lady of the house" was absent, of very gay and crisp lawn from the five-cent shop around the corner. Mary had worked very hard to earn the extra twenty-five cents which had made these curtains possible, but Bell knew nothing of that, and the delight in her face when she came into the room on the day they were put up was more than payment for an aching back. Poor Bell! She was assuredly one of the "tired people," and she would have been such a neat housekeeper if it had not been for the mill and Mary's lameness and the boys whom she and Bob were determined to "bring up educated" so as to give them a better start in life. It was a real comfort to her to take her place in this new home, as fairly well-to-do — and what else could the neighbors judge her with those fresh-frilled curtains? She patted Mary's shoulder with real affection as she pointed them out to Bob, and it was with great pride that she brought in a pot of pansies next evening to grow in state between the flying pink and blue muslin.

And if Bell was happy, Mary was happier. She even put a special little thanksgiving into her prayers, for this first happy thought, and the very flapping of the curtains grew into a part of the song that was

always singing through her heart in these days:
" Make tired people happy!" " Keep things pleasant about us!" Such a blessed song to be set sounding through Mary's little world! There were so many
tired people in Connor Street! The very house was
full of them. From Bridget Flanigan in the basement, with her jolly, warm-hearted brood of seven,
to the fierce-looking man in the attic, who wrote for
the papers and had been pointed out as some myste-
rious being called an " anarchist," there was never a
face where Mary had not seen the look of weariness
and discouragement which was just what the King's
Daughters were to drive away.

" Of course it's only the littlest kind of things I
can do, such a crooked, little, lame thing," said Mary
blithely, patting her tiny cross; " but when it comes
to darning Bob's socks real even, so's they won't hurt
his feet, or picking up the Flanigan babies when
they tumble down right outside the door, or telling
the other Flanigans how to play ' Miss Jennie Jones'
to keep 'em contented, or, for that matter, giving a
' Good morning' to most anybody that looks a little
down, why, I can do such things as well as anybody,
just as the young lady said, and if I do them, maybe
I'll get some better chances as I go on."

It was a pleasant consequence of all these happy
thoughts that Mary's pale little bright face was com-

ing to be well known among her neighbors. People looked up involuntarily as they passed the window where she sat at work, and her shy smile sank into many a work-worn heart like a bit of stray sunshine. There were not many really happy faces in Connor Street, perhaps because there were not many who held in their hearts, like a secret treasure, the knowledge that through any one of those passers-by might some day come a blessed chance to lend a hand in the King's name.

" Life seems to go easy with that little thing," was the general verdict of Connor Street ; a verdict given with an inward glow of kindly interest, quite unusual in those hardworked men and women. Faces lighted up with friendly smiles, in response to hers, and many a greeting was called out across the pansies in the window. The old organ grinder who lived around the corner grew into the habit of passing through, just for the sake of a nod and smile from the lame little knitter. He was crooked and lame himself, poor man, and Mary's tender heart quite longed for a bit of comfort for him, even before the evening when he looked forlornly up in answer to her greeting, and showed the empty tin cup which usually held his gathered pence. It was raining that night, and his gray hair hung down straight and lank about his tired face.

"No luck!" he said. "People all in a hurry! Hard times!"

He rested his organ on the sidewalk and leaned upon it, looking up, with a vague longing for sympathy, which Mary somehow read and understood. Her hand went involuntarily to the little cross, as was growing to be her habit.

"No folks at my place!" went on the organ grinder, more forlornly than ever. "All the others, they have wife, children! Hard times for me, this world!"

He made the sign of the cross and looked up, beyond Mary and the lighted window and the curly heads of Jimmy and Tommy peering over their aunt's shoulder. When his eyes came back to the empty cup a snow-white pansy lay in it, and Mary was nodding a rather timid "Good night," and calling softly, "Better times to-morrow," as she disappeared into the room.

Bell was somewhat scandalized that night by the robbery of her pansy-pot, but Mary's pleading eyes and the memory of the new curtains stopped her little lecture before it had fairly begun, and a glimpse of the old man's face as he turned the corner quite won her over. Warm-hearted Bell would have stripped every pansy from its stem for him after that little picture, and Mary often remem-

bered it afterwards — the tired, drooping figure, bent
under its burden, the rain falling on the gray head,
and the brown face lighted up with a sudden brightness above the little white flower. Since then more
than one pansy had been dropped into the tin cup.
The organ grinder was quite a familiar friend, and
Mary had already, after much thought, sowed various small boxes of earth with flower seeds, which
were already springing into tiny green shoots along
the window sills with promise of abundant blossoms
later on.

Old Anselmo and the Flanigans might be said to
rank together as chief among Mary's new friends.
The Flanigans were a perpetual source of entertainment. From her window on the first floor she could
overlook all their gambols and scuffles about the basement door, and before she had been a week in the
house, had learned the names and peculiarities of
every one, from Nora, the small elder sister, who
kept house in her mother's absence, and Patsey, the
big, red-haired boy, who was understood to be the
" livin' picter of his poor daddy," down to Biddy and
Peggy, the twin babies, who were dragged about by
their elders through thick and thin, taking part in
every scrimmage, sharing in spoils of peppermint
stick and penny apples, when such rare windfalls

came the way of the young Flanigans; paddling in gutters and creeping after street sights; and coming blithely up through every emergency with a rosy immunity that was apparently their fairy birthright. Lucky babies indeed were the Flanigan twins in their untrammeled energy, and shortsighted were the strangers who wasted a moment's pity upon them. Their brothers and sisters would have hooted at the idea that Biddy and Peggy were poorly off. Biddy and Peggy! Why, were they not the pride of every sandy-haired Flanigan in that basement? Even Mike and Peter stopped kicking each other's shins when Peggy embraced the flying heels with a consciousness that nothing would hurt her; and the occasion when Rosy lost her temper and knocked over Biddy's milk was the only day on record when a Flanigan had been sent to Coventry by the family, from morning till night, without even a whispered word of sympathy to sustain the culprit under the motherly whipping which followed Bridget's return from the mill. Oh! they were a merry set, these happy-go-lucky Flanigans, and yet even to them life had some drawbacks. The basement was damp in the first place and rents were high, and there were no boys of Patsey's size wanted in the mill, and papers were " nothin' to spake of for a growin' bye wid six to the back of him," as his tired mother

informed her sympathizing little neighbor while she
sat on the doorsteps one Sunday afternoon. Nora
would have gone into the mill instead if she had
only been tall enough.

" There 's no knowin' *why* the blissid saints c'u'd n't
have granted me a *wan*, big enough to turn to, whin
the father o' thim was took," said Bridget, with a
sigh ; "but it ain't for me to be groanin' over that,
while the last one o' thim 's well, an' the twins like
two lady apples, bless their swate faces ! " and Bridget
seized the treasures one in each arm, and hoisted them
into her lap together for the Sunday hugging which
was almost her only chance of petting them. " I
tuk Nora wid me own hands," she went on, " up to
the mill, and I axed the overseer wid me own lips to
foind a place for her. ' Arrah, *that* slip of a girl !'
says he. ' She don't look ten year old !' ' She 's
thirteen next month,' says I, turnin' me eyes on her
to give her the hint to sthretch up like, an' she niver
takin' in what I was m'anin'. an' shrinkin' in more
nor iver wid his eyes on her, that shy is Nora!
' We can't take a child like that one,' says he. ' Not
if her father was run over by the railroad a dozen
times instead o' wan ! It 's ag'in the law,' says he.

" ' Ochone !' says I, ' thin it 's a black, cruel law it
is, to be after takin' the bread out o' the mouths o'
fatherless childher,' says I, ' bad 'cess to it !' An'

says he, very short an' sharrup, ' You be off to yer worruk, Mrs. Flanigan, an' send that child home; an' it 's a cruel woman,' says he, ' that 'u'd put a slip like that one into the mill.' An' says I to him, says I, ' Hunger 's worse nor worruk, sorr, an' cowld 's crueler nor a half-crazed mother wid her man underground an' seven to fend for, an' may the saints presarve ye from the likes!' I says; an' come away wid the tears a-sthramin' down. An' sorry a bit of help have I had from wan of the childher, miss dear, they 're that small, barrin' Patsey wid his papers, an' for all I can see, Nora nor Rosy ain't bigger nor they was last winter, an' whin they 'll get to worruk the Howly Virgin only knows!" And Bridget trotted the twins violently on her knees, with an audible sob for the close of her story.

Nora came around and stood behind her with a discouraged look on her small, sharp face. Nora would have given her most precious treasure at that moment to be taller; even the battered doll, sole relic of the prosperous times of her babyhood; the only doll ever possessed by a member of the household.

"I 've growed some, I know," she said wistfully. " Seems to me my dress looks shorter. I was askin' Rosy last night jist, an' she thought so too."

Bridget let Peggy slide off her lap, and pulled down Nora into her place.

" Sure, 't ain't your fault, honey," she said with a little laugh and squeeze. "You 're the drop o' me heart, wid yer stirrin' ways, mavourneen; and afther all, what 'u'd I do widout the likes o' you at home, to look out for the young ones? No, it 's the will of heaven, that 's what it is, as Father Malone was sayin' to me only a week past, about the masses for your poor father's sowl! ' It 's the will o' heaven, Bridget Flanigan,' says he; ' an' you kape up a good heart an' worruk a bit longer, an' I 'll wait for the money till you 're able for it,' says he, that kind is Father Malone."

Mary leaned farther out from her window with a thought plainly growing in her eyes.

" Why, Mrs. Flanigan," she said, " I could help some; I just know I could. Nora 's so bright, and she does things so sort of quick and handy; I 've noticed her ever so much with the children. I might have thought of it before, just as well as not, only you never told me about it all. I can teach her to crochet things the way I do. There 'll be plenty of work for her at the store where Bell found me mine, and they give you out the stuff if it 's orders, or I could lend her a bit of worsted and a needle to start with. There 's edging and such, you know, and there 's baby things and mittens and so on. It don't pay quite like mill work, but it 'd be something, and

it would n't be long before Nora could do more than
I can, with my back so sort of weak. I 'll begin
to-morrow if you like."

It was good to see the flash of joy that lighted up
Nora's homely little face, and was reflected in double
brightness upon her mother's.

" Tache the child all thim ilegant doin's what I 've
seen you fussin' over avenin's?" cried Bridget.
" Tache her *thim*, Miss Mary, dear? Oh, I 'd pray
to the howly Mother for ye from now till the end o'
me life! Nora, darlin', do ye hear? It 's laces an'
baby socks an' ilegant rickrack ye 'll be doin' intirely,
an' what 'll we iver be doin' to pay ye, miss, dear?"
The poor woman fairly burst out crying, with her
face buried in Biddy's carroty curls. " I 've been
that worried about the riot an' the clothes, to say
nothin' of what they 're all to be afther 'atin', with
thim growin' appetites, an' only me two hands to kape
'em," she sobbed; " and now ye 'll be afther putting
the brightest wan o' the lot in the way of helpin',
an' it won't be Nora that don't make the most of
her chance, will it, mavourneen?"

But Nora had already rushed up the street to tell
Rosy of her new prospect, and was beyond hearing.
Mary's face was as delighted as Bridget's, as she
leaned on the window.

" Oh, I know she 'll do beautifully," she said.

" And she can work at it every day, as long as she
wants to ; for after the boys are at school I 'll just
take my work and bring it down to your room, if
you don't mind ;" for a vision of Bell's clean kitchen,
with the seven young Flanigans running in and out
of it, rose like a sudden nightmare before the eyes
of her sister-in-law. " I 'll come down there when
the housework 's done up, and that don't take long :
and then we 'll work together, Nora and I, and maybe
Rosy, too, and we can keep an eye on the children at
the same time, and see that nobody gets into our
place, too. It 's real handy, is n't it ?"

" Indade thin, it is," responded Bridget fervently ;
" and it 's meself that 'll be afther tellin' the childher
to kape the place dacint for the likes o' ye. an' it 's
meself that 'll be grateful to ye for the least glimp
o' yer eye to 'em, miss, for it 's sore at heart I am
to l'ave 'em run wild this way, though they 're good at
heart, the childher, if I do say it ; an' they 'll mind
ye, miss, from the twins up to Patsey, or I 'll know
the reason !" And Bridget glared round upon her
clustering household like a Roman matron.

The children nodded an emphatic assent. There
was not one of them who did not love Mary already,
and Patsey decided on the spot to spend his next
afternoon at home, instead of making off to the
circus to peep under the edge of the tent with the

Kennedy boys from the next block. Patsey knew enough of Miss Mary's ways to understand that keeping an eye on the children meant stories, and if stories were to be told Patsey preferred to be on hand. Stories were better than the circus any day, especially when one was not financially in a position to see anything except between people's legs.

" Miss, dear," said Bridget solemnly, in Mary's ear, as she rose to go into the house, "miss, if you could anyways get a holt of Patsey, so 's to give him some thoughts of makin' a man of himself, it 'u'd be doin' more aven than puttin' Nora in the way of earnin' her own livin'. He 's a good bye, Patsey, but thim Kennedys is the fear o' me life, wid their gittin' him off an' beguilin' him into spendin' his paper money ; an' he 's that fond of stories an' that interested whin things is goin' on, that I see in his face that this maybe 'u'd be the very thing to fix him ; for I can't bear it," said Bridget, with another little sob, "I c'u'd n't bear it to have poor Patrick's first bye a-goin' wrong ; an' *why* I should tell ye all the throuble of me heart there 's no tellin', acushla, an' you such a little, young thing ; but out they come at the sight o' ye, dear, an' my heart 's the lighter for it, bless ye !"

She followed the children down the steps into their low room, and Mary was left with her new work opening before her in a pleasant vision.

" Such *beautiful* chances! " she whispered. " I
was always sorry for children that had to have their
mother go to mill. And Nora and Rosy are so
bright. I can tell them all about ' In His Name'
to start out with. And — why, yes ; if everything
turns out right, I can get Mrs. Flanigan and Nora
and Rosy, all three, to be King's Daughters too, and
then there 'll be four of us." She leaned her head
on her hand and fell to dreaming pleasant dreams,
which lasted until Bob and Bell came home from
their Sunday walk with the boys and it was time to
get supper. There was reading aloud after lamplight, for Jimmy was well on in his classes at school
and his father and mother were fond of having him
exercise his learning at home.

Mary had brought out her little book as soon as the
family were well settled in their new home, and they
were listening to it every evening with great enjoyment and some bewilderment over the unaccustomed
characters of troubadour and peasant. To-night,
through all the pretty story of Aucassin and Nico-
lette, Mary listened for sounds from below and
pictured to herself the seven freckled-faced, happy
children nestled down for their night's rest, with
their mother telling her beads beside them and
thanking the Virgin for the burden lifted from her
heart.

"I'm so glad!" sighed Mary, as she fell asleep herself later. "It's better than Berryville here, even without a mountain anywhere. I'm glad we came to the city!"

CHAPTER III.

"NOW, then," said Patsey energetically, "look y' here! The last one's done, and sure they're ilegant."

The other children gave a whoop and came crowding around him. Nora wrapped her work in her apron and Rosy dropped the broom. Mike and Peter and the twins began a lively dance about their brother. Two pretty, blue-eyed little girls came shyly up to the table, and another with soft golden hair leaned in at the open window to see better.

"Ain't they beautiful!" was the general cry.

Perhaps the most pleased face of all was that of our Mary as she drew her chair closer to Patsey and looked at his work. There they lay in a line, nine small crosses, cut by his busy fingers from bits of shingle and covered close with smooth tin foil that gleamed in the sunshine "just like true silver," in Rosy's admiring language. There were the letters too, I. H. N., cut fair and plain with the point of Patsey's knife, and there were the bits of purple ribbon, cheap and "sleasy," but of the true royal color. The badges for Mary's "Ten" were all complete.

"Ain't they the daisies?" remarked Patsey proudly. "Sure, I'm rale glad you thought of it, Miss Mary, for all it's took so long to get them crosses even. A boy likes to have a bit to do when he is n't doin' anythin'. Next time you want a job turned off jest spake to Patsey Flanigan ag'in!"

"Oh, they're beautiful!" said Mary delightedly. "Just what we wanted; and now we'll put them right on, those that are going to wear them. Here's Nora's, and she's lending a hand every day with the crocheting, and so's Rosy with the tidying up the room and keeping the children straight. Why, this room's twice as pleasant as it was before you started out lending a hand. Then here's the one for your mother; and she says she'll find many a chance in the mill, helping out the girls and speaking a pleasant word as she goes along, — though seems to me she's always done that anyhow, — and that's four to start with. I don't know but Trudel's big enough if she'd like to wear one."

Trudel, the fair-haired girl at the window, clapped her hands by way of answer.

"Oh, I should like that!" she cried eagerly. "It is good to belong to things! The father let me carry the red flag one time in a procession and I liked that, but this would be better. This would be for all the time."

She spoke with a pretty foreign accent, though in good English, and she was better dressed than the other children. Mary looked up at her, smiling a little doubtfully.

"I suppose your father gets pretty tired with his speeches and writings and things," she said meditatively; "and I suppose you could keep things pleasant up in your rooms, for one thing. Then there's old Mrs. Wills right back of you, and you could give her a shoulder up and down stairs sometimes, if you wanted to, or bring up a pitcher of water now and again. It's real hard living up on the top floor when you ain't strong. I've tried it. Do you think your father wouldn't mind if you belonged?"

"The father never minds anything if I want it!" said Trudel decidedly, with a little pucker of her soft eyebrows. "Why should you all think him cross? He is *not* cross, and he does more for me than the other children's fathers. Last Sunday he took me down the river in the excursion boat, and often I go to the concerts with him. He is good, my father. Of course he will let me wear what I please."

' Oh, I didn't mean that," returned Mary hastily. "Of course I didn't mean that he wasn't good. Only I wasn't quite sure; and a body doesn't want to get things settled too much. But then, I don't suppose he'd care; Father Malone let Nora and Rosy belong."

" Yes ; an' he says you was n't the kind of heretic to hurt a fly, after he come in to talk to ye about it that day," put in Rosy with triumph. " He says you 'd make a good sister, if you was a Catholic. Maybe you 'll be one yet. Father Malone says so, an' he says it won't hurt nayther one of us to wear the little cross an' make things pleasant as much as iver we like ; so of course Trudel can too."

" And I 'll help ever so much ! " cried Trudel, who was already tying her purple ribbon in its place. " I 'll bring my book of tales down and tell you what ' Ashputtel ' means in English ; and I 'll be good to Mrs. Wills, too, and I won't run after Tessy on the stairs to make her tumble down. You shall see how much I can do ! "

Tessy, the elder of the two little girls at Mary's knee, looked up with a smile at the last promise. She was a timid-looking little thing, with a look of appeal in her soft eyes. Her little sister leaned against her in a confiding way and smiled when she did. In fact, Tessy and Dolly always did everything alike.

" Could I be it, too? " said Tessy wistfully. " I could try, and I 'm seven, you know."

Mary stooped and kissed the little upturned face. Tessy and Dolly were the dearest of all the small flock which had gathered about her in the last few

weeks ; motherless children, with a bewildered young
father who loved them and had no idea how to care
for them. They came from the " second floor back" ;
and Mary had watched until late one evening to catch
their father on his way upstairs and ask him to let
the little ones come down to Bridget's room next day
instead of being locked into their own during his
work hours. He had stared at her in amazement,
the stooping, pale-faced little creature, who asked
so calmly for the care of Tessy and Dolly.

" It's hard on children to be shut in all day,"
Mary had said. " I used to be sometimes, when I
was little, and I can remember. Besides, Bridget's
willing, and some of the others in the house come
in here too, and it's no trouble, and they could run
up for their dinner at noon, and Nora Flanigan would
see that the room was locked up all right after it,
she's that steady, and it's so hard on my back going
up the stairs. And I like children — and — it's lonely
being locked up all day."

" It's good of you ! " the young man had answered,
leaning on the stair rail, with a puzzled expression.
" It's *real* good. I don't know 's — I ever had anybody think of bein' so good to them children before.
I did n't like to have 'em run the streets, Doll 's so
little and Tessy's such a baby in her ways. Why,
yes ; I 'd take it awful kind if you 'd let 'em come,

I ain't hardly known what to do with 'em since their ma died — nor before, either," he added under his breath as he went on upstairs.

So Tessy and Dolly had come creeping down to the home of the light-hearted Flanigans, where they learned many astonishing games, looked on at more than one rough-and-tumble fight and reconciliation, aided in the general "tidying up" which Rosy undertook day by day now, under Mary's interested eyes, and even tried to repeat these energetic doings in their own room, causing their father to open his eyes in astonishment and remark under his breath, "Makin' that bed up straight, an' settin' the supper out square, an' tryin' to sweep, as sure as I 'm a sinner! I swan if I don't believe that Tessy 's takin' after my own mother instead of poor Martha! If they should turn out like her after all!"

And Tessy and Dolly related in an exalted manner next day the wonderful fact that " pa " had gone out again immediately on his return home and bought them each a stick of pink-and-yellow candy as a reward for their efforts.

"I could try real hard!" repeated Tessy now. " Pa says I 'm gettin' to be a little woman. Could n't I wear one, please? I do know about lendin' a hand, even if 't ain't to anybody but Dolly and pa."

So Mary fastened the cross to the child's shoulder

with an inward feeling that Tessy might be too small, but that only a hard-hearted mortal could resist that pleading voice.

"I 'll tell you what," she remarked after a moment's hesitation : "you ain't a bit big, you know, Tessy ; but you 're a real good little girl, and so 's Dolly, and I 've been thinking you might have that one between you, and one wear it one day and the other the next, and both try to think of ways, you know, and then it would be like one bigger girl, if you both helped each other."

A very foolish and childish speech indeed, which would have set Bell into fits of laughter over Mary's simple-mindedness, but which sent Tessy and Dolly skipping about the room in a mild imitation of the gambols indulged in by the Flanigan children in moments of abandon.

"And now there 's six of us!" cried Nora, flying back to her chair and working at her edging with redoubled zeal. "O Miss Mary, dear, there 's only four more left to find; an' sure, old Mis' Wills will be afther takin' one, for she says you 're the only rale lady on the strate, wid your kind ways, and she tould me only yesterday that if there was more like you it 'u'd be a happy world for us all."

"And see here!" broke in Patsey, growing red in the face as he brought out some long-pondered idea,

" *I'm* a-goin' to have one too, an' so's Jimmy! We talked it all over whin he was a-comin' from school. Tommy he ain't up to it yet, nor Mike and Pete, but we're a-goin' to belong, and then whiniver there's anything hard on hand, why, there'll be Jimmy an' me. Jim read me a bit o' that book hisself, out on the steps, an' 't was mostly men in it, an' we're a-goin' to belong an' be the King's Sons. Why couldn't we? There might be a bit o' fightin' in the way, fer instance, wid folks that was ag'in the society, an' thin where 'd ye all be widout a bye or two?"

Where indeed? The perplexed leader looked at the boy with an astonished smile. Boys among the King's Daughters! What would the young lady in gray have said to such a proposition? But Patsey was fingering a badge with an expression of entire confidence in his argument. His own work, too, and he had tried so hard to make them the right shape! What could Mary say?

"Jimmy never told me," she faltered.

"No; he left that to me," said Patsey grandly, "me bein' the biggest of the two. He's had to stay afther school, I doubt, or he'd 'a' been here by now to git his badge. Oh, we'll keep up to it, Miss Mary; never fear. We've been round already pickin' up the bannany skins them Kennedys flung down to make people tumble. *We're* a-goin' to make things pleasant, sure enough, an' many 's the time you 'll bless the day there was two King's Sons along wid ye."

" And — you 'll really and truly have the motto and everything?" said Mary dubiously. " I don't know 's I ought to — but I don't see why not; and after all we 're just off by ourselves so, and it would n't do any harm, I guess. Well, you can then, but the other two I 'll just keep myself. I don't believe *they 'd* better be boys."

" Sure, no!" assented Patsey. " *We 're* a-goin' to be the only boys in it, Jimmy an' me, an' niver another will we let into what them letters is fer. An' ain't we up to fun though, upsettin' the mischief of them Kennedys, an' they niver guessin' who it is, I 'm that managin'? It 's the best thing! an' Jim 's a-goin' to read me the whole book, considerin' I ain't great on fine print. Oh, you jist wait till you see how we 'll work it!" And Patsey went exultantly across the room in a series of somersaults, to the mingled terror and delight of Mary's gentle soul.

" And you must remember that even if we are all by ourselves here," she said, after a little, " that we 're only a part — the smallest little part of a great big company that 's doing — oh, wonderful great things! so much that the little bits of ones we can do ain't anything at all, and we must try to do just the very best we can, so they would n't be ashamed

of us if they ever found out we had one here — only
they won't, you know, of course; and we'll just try
all the harder for that, because it's so lovely to be
part of it all. And " — Mary's voice trembled with
shyness, but she went bravely on — " you know I told
you what the young lady said about how they prayed
for each other, so I suppose we'd better all just say,
' God bless the King's Daughters, and help them to
lend a hand,' when we say our prayers, hadn't we?
I should think that would do."

The Flanigans nodded assent from Patsey down to
the twins, who wagged their carroty curls because the
rest did; but Tessy and Dolly looked up with a look
of doubt, and Trudel spoke out clearly from the
window sill : —

" I don't know any prayers. The father does not
like such things. Will this one all alone do? I
wouldn't mind saying that!"

A harsh voice from behind interrupted her.

" Prayers? What do you mean? Who is teaching
you such evil stuff? And what is that on your dress
— a cross?"

It was Trudel's father, the fierce, dark-browed man
from the attic, feared by every child on the street
except his own. Even Mary started at sight of his
scowling face. He had caught Trudel by the shoulder
and jerked her to her feet.

"What are you about?" he demanded again. "Do
you suppose I will have that thing fastened to you?
Take it off!"

The children inside the basement room huddled
together in fright, but Mary came out to the window
and Trudel stood her ground bravely.

"It's nothing but a badge," she said, with a little
catch in her voice. "It's a society — a society for
making things pleasant, and I want to be in it."

"Not with that sign!" roared her father. "Do
you think I will have you led away by any of their
priest-ridden notions? Take it off!"

He snatched it from her breast himself as he spoke
and flung it harshly on the ground, causing Patsey to
dash out of his corner with flashing eyes at the insult
to his handiwork. Trudel burst out crying, and Mary
came quite close and spoke out timidly, yet clearly : —

"But, indeed, it isn't anything wrong, Mr. Müller.
It's only the King's Daughters that try to help people
in His name, and it was to make us all helpers here,
for Christ's sake, that was all; and Father Malone
himself said it was no harm and Mrs. Flanigan and
the children might belong. It was only to make
people happy. I never thought you would mind if
Trudel wore it or I wouldn't have given it to her;
but it was no wrong!"

Müller turned on the girl a look of black scorn

that made her shrink and tremble. People were generally kind to little Mary and no one had ever looked at her in that way before. He lifted his foot and set the heel of his heavy boot upon the little shining symbol at his feet, crushing and grinding with all his force.

" *That's* what I think of your cross and all belonging with it!" he said malignantly ; "and that's what it's coming to before long, in this world that's getting beyond priests' fables! If a wretched little humpback like you wants to amuse herself with it, keep out of the way or you'll get crushed down along with it. And you remember this : leave my child alone ; and never ask her here again with your canting, false, hypocritical ways! I'll not have Trudel taught such things!"

Mary was quite pale with the fright and surprise of his words. The tears sprang to her eyes as if from a physical blow, but she drew back without a word, only reaching quietly out to pick up the poor little broken cross, as if it had been a wounded thing which she could help.

" Shut the window, Patsey," she whispered. " Don't let the children hear such talk."

But Trudel stopped the boy by flinging herself on the ground in a passion of sobbing.

" Oh, I wanted it, I wanted it!" she cried. " It

was all so pretty and pleasant and I was going to do so many things and Miss Mary is so sweet and good and I want to come here with the rest! Father, you should not have broken it! You should not!"

"Come!" said her father sternly, lifting the sobbing child, with another scowl at the frightened little author of the trouble. "Come you with me, and never shall you enter this place again!" and then, as he carried her away, Trudel, with one mighty effort, called out above his shoulder: —

"But I will! I will! I *will* make things pleasant, and nobody can stop me from that; and I will say the prayer too; yes, and you shall see that I am a King's Daughter all the same!"

Poor little Mary! she had no heart to laugh at the incongruous outburst. Her heart was very heavy as she left the basement and went up to get tea ready for Bob and Bell. Jimmy and Tommy looked at her in wonder, until they had heard the version of the story given by Patsey, and been roused into a fury of indignation by learning that "that mean, oid, blackfaced Müller had called her a humpback!" Patsey, Jimmy, or even small Tommy himself would have fought Müller single-handed on her behalf, from that moment on.

"If we could anyways jist leave the bananny skin that Kennedy dhropped fur *him!* an' make sure that he'd smash his ugly nose over it!" muttered Patsey, and Jimmy and Tommy nodded in dark silence.

Not one of the three guessed that Mary's grieving was not for the taunt to herself, but for Trudel's disappointed little heart and for the crushed and broken cross.

It was a saddened face that bent over the flower boxes in the window when the "hands" were passing home from the mill. It was growing to be Mary's custom to watch there evening by evening now that the flowers were coming into bloom, and all along the line of toilworn figures, faces were lifted and good-nights called out, as the mignonettes and petunias dropped into the hands of those who "looked the tiredest." It was wonderful how those flowers grew! Let Mary pick as many as she might, there were always more by another morning. It was as if the seeds had been blessed by the fairies, or by some good angel who loved the gracious order of the King's Daughters. The pleasant office brought comfort with it to-night, though to Mary's eyes there had never seemed so many drooping forms or weary looks before. Long after she had given the last blossom, except the one that was saved for Anselmo, she stood smiling down, with the same sort of tender trouble in her face, and a new thought of all the sin and sorrow and grief that could never be touched or helped by her feeble, girlish hands. Some one coming swiftly up the street stopped short with a curious look of mingled pity and reverence at sight of the bent little figure in the twilight.

" She ain't more than eighteen or so, and it's a city, and them boxes ain't anything to our garden to home ; but I swan, if she don't look something like my old mother !" murmured Jack Winter to himself. "Poor thing ! if it's along of them crooked shoulders she gets her ways — I would n't mind — most — havin' Tessy an' Dolly grow up crooked too. Though, after all, I suppose 't ain't that. It's that little cross the children was tellin' me about. Well — I 'm glad there *is* such folks in the world ! "

He watched a moment until the little figure turned away into the lighted room, and then went slowly upstairs to find his own supper ready, and Tessy and Dolly dancing gleefully around it, crying, —

" We belong to the King's Daughters and we 're both of us half of one ! "

CHAPTER IV.

THE summer had settled down, hot and breathless. The houses in the beautiful city avenues, where Mary never went, were for the most part closed and silent. Excursion trains and steamboats were crowded day after day with people in search of fresh air and green fields or woods. Even among the factory workers were many who found their way out of the close streets to gather wild flowers or enjoy the river coolness ; but the Connor Street mill was not among those which closed on the Saturday afternoon, and Bob and Bell, with eyes fixed steadily on their life object of " giving the boys a chance," would neither go to Sunday excursions nor spare the money for the cheap moonlight water trips, which might come within their means.

"Dimes put by for a rainy day are better than dimes dropped in the river!" said Bob sturdily, and Mary accepted his words with her usual sisterly conviction that Bob must be right.

Nevertheless Mary would have liked to get away from Connor Street during those burning weeks. The thought of the country kept coming back to her, bringing with it all sorts of broken memories, treasured from the few occasions in her life when her old longing had been gratified. There was the day, before her father died, when he took her to the beach, carrying her in his arms quite close to the blue water with its dashing breakers. The sand had been yellow, and the wind wild and soft, and there had been children running barefoot through the curling foam.

"I suppose it's always cool by the seaside," thought Mary, looking from the blazing sunshine on the sidewalk to the brick walls that seemed to gather and reflect the heat until Connor Street was like one long furnace.

Then there was the picnic to the woods, during that summer when Mary was "well," and went to Sunday-school. Should she ever forget the tree with mossy roots, where she sat and watched the stronger children playing "tag" and "I spy"? There were the railroad trips, too, with their glimpses of quiet villages and outlying farms; and, dearest of all, there were the mountains as she had seen them from her last home. It was strange how these pictures rose before her tired eyes, and how her heart swelled toward them. The old dreams of mountain heights and moonlight wanderings came back night after night now, and there was not even the far-off outline against the morning sky to comfort the girl's beauty-loving eyes as she awoke. Connor Street had no lovely sight for Mary. There was nothing to be seen from her bedroom window but the bare courtyard behind the tenement, a place so dismal and stifling that even the children chose the street in preference. It was far pleasanter in the other room, where the window boxes made at least one spot of loveliness, and where Bell's brisk ways were like a tonic in themselves.

" Wouldn't it be kind of nice, Bell," said Mary, one morning, over the breakfast cooking, "real kind of nice to wake up these days and find yourself out in the country, with everything green around you, and not a sign of a pavement or a house anywhere, and birds " —

But here Bell dropped her iron spoon and surveyed her sister-in-law with such astonishment that Mary flushed and stopped talking. She had actually been growing confidential. No wonder Bell was surprised.

" You *do* beat all !" said the latter young woman emphatically. "I wonder if crooked folks always have such queer notions. What do you think of such things for, when you can't get 'em? You always was possessed after the country. No, I'd hate it, I'm sure ! Nothing going on, and nobody to change a word with. Here; the hasty-pudding 's done, if you'll hand me that dish."

Mary said no more about her secret desires, and

Bell forgot them the next moment, as was natural. The thoughts, however, stayed on unspoken, and had, I think, not a little to do with the fact that Mary's face grew paler, her step slower, and the dark circles under her eyes deeper, through all those summer weeks. If it had not been for the children, she might really have grown homesick for Berryville; but the children were always there, and filled her days to an extent that left no room for homesickness. Mrs. Flanigan's living room was often quite full now, during working hours, for there were other mothers who were glad and grateful to find a place for their little ones while they toiled for them at the mills. Lame Johnny Morris was carried to Bridget's bed every morning, instead of being left alone in his mother's room next door, and two or three babies were usually scrambling over the floor, cared for in a haphazard manner by Mary or Nora or Rosy, frolicked with by all the swarming boys and girls, and handed out at noon and night to tired-looking mothers on their way home from work. Patsey and Jimmy, as " King's Sons," kept the small army in order with much enjoyment, when they happened to be present, and the whole company were accustomed to look with sympathy on one small apparition that came and went outside their circle — poor little Trudel, whose father still forbade her to enter Bridget's room, and turned upon Mary, whenever he met her, a sneering frown that made her shrink and tremble as if from a blow.

But Müller was only one black cloud in a happy sky, and the daily gathering went pleasantly on. Not one of those who knew of it had ever heard of a Day Nursery, and no one thought of the arrangement as anything remarkable. Mrs. Morris and Mrs. Saunders and Mrs. Jones were relieved, the children were a rollicking fraternity, and Mary was happy with them; that was all. As for the use of the room, was not Bridget Flanigan herself a King's Daughter, and the most good-natured of Irish souls besides?

"Begrudge thim babies and that poor little gossoon that ain't another year for this world," she remarked to Bell, who sometimes manifested a little neighborly interest in Mary's friends; "begrudge thim a bit of flure, or the space of a few hours to lay in me poor old bed? Not Bridget Flanigan, Mrs. Bennet! 'The more the merrier,' says I, and the saints bless the swate face of her that thought of it!"

"Well, it's all right," responded Bell, with some natural surprise over this fervent prayer for insignificant little Mary, "it's well enough; but all the same Mary knew better than to fetch them all up into *my* rooms!"

"Arrah! your rooms, wid the flure like the driven

snow, and the bits of curtains to the windys, and
the flower garden of yer own betune thim," cried
Bridget, with Celtic flattery. "An' where's the babe
in arms that would n't be afther knowin' betther than
to let that raft of childer in there? Sure, Miss Mary
showed her sense to bring 'm down to me own place,
that's only fit for the loikes of thim, even wid all
the cl'anin' that Nora and Rosy carries on since
she's afther t'achin' thim! No, no; aven Biddy and
Peggy 'u'd have sense to kape out o' here! Look at
'em there, starin' in at the dure loike owls and niver
offerin' to cross the sill." And Bridget gathered her
sagacious infants under her arms and bore them away
to the lower regions, leaving Bell smiling with that
conscious superiority that is so pleasant to all our
souls.

Only two of the children, accordingly, ever ventured to follow Mary into her own home. Towards
Tessy and Dolly, with their quiet ways and soft
footsteps, Bell relented, and the two little girls
often crept in, to sit smiling quietly about them or
putting up now and then small, carefully washed
fingers to touch the green leaves that overhung
Mary's window boxes. Bell never sent them away
or spoke harshly to them. She had even been known
to stroke the soft hair that fell over Tessy's forehead, Tessy being the more timid and quiet of the

two mouse-like creatures. Mary wondered and re-joiced in secret at all this. She had never had a suspicion that deep in Bell's sensible soul lay a longing wish for a little girl like one of these — a gentle, clinging, "pretty-behaved" daughter, to be all her own, as no son could ever be.

There was another visitor in the living room during these summer evenings. Jack Winter and Bob had formed an acquaintance as they went to and from work, and the young man often stepped in with his little girls to talk over the day's doings. Mary used to watch his strong, broad-shouldered figure, against the light, and contrast it with Bob's stooping one. Jack did not look like a man who had grown up in factory life. It was quite a pleasure to hear him tell Bob that he had always lived in the country until his marriage. Mary leaned forward to listen when she heard this wonderful piece of news. It was the next thing to being in the country herself to talk to some one who had lived there. The girls from the moun-tains had generally laughed at her questions, but Mary would have liked very much to ask them over again now, if Bob and Bell would not have thought her foolish. Were there green fields as far as eye could see, at Jack's old home? Was there an orchard? Were there woods near with birds in the trees? and were there wild flowers, to be had for the picking, all summer? It was with a little thrill of disappointment that she drew back in silence under Bell's laughing eyes.

"If Mary is n't dropping her work to hear about where Jack came from!" remarked Bell. "There never was such a crazy thing about the country! If she lived there once she 'd know better, would n't she, Jack? I tell her it 's because she 's different from other folks. I guess you would n't go back there for a pretty penny, would you?"

Jack looked at the little figure in the corner with a slight knitting of his black brows. He had seen the words rise to Mary's lips and die there. In fact, Jack Winter saw much more of the most unimportant member of Bob's household than one would have thought possible. It was because she made him think of his mother, he told himself, that he liked to watch her unobserved.

"I don't know," he said slowly. "I don't believe I 'd say that I would n't go back. I 've thought a good many times that I 'd like to see that place again. The city ain't been much of a place for me."

"You don't say!" said Bell, with amazement.

"We sold our little place when I married Martha and come here to settle," went on Jack. "Martha was dead against the country. She 'd come out there to visit her aunt. I was a sort of a fool over

Martha. She was a real pretty girl. Smart too, if it had n't have be'n " — He stopped suddenly with a glance at the two little girls.

" She was dead against the country," he continued, " and mother, she 'd just died, and I was lonesome, and wanted to get more money, so I sold out — 't was only a little smitch of a place — and come here. But it was n't much of a change for me. I 'd be better off there. I 've laid awake nights sometimes planning how I could get back, but when a fellow gets to a place he 's likely to stay there. I always liked the country.

" Do *you* like it so much? "

The question came so suddenly that Mary started in her chair.

" I always wanted to see it, to be in it," she said timidly, with a deprecating look at Bell. " I never really was in the country to stay. Seems to me 't would be nice this hot weather."

Jack nodded.

" I 've thought of it a sight just lately," he went on. " Sometimes I can just about smell them sweet peas that we always had by the back door, and I 've seemed to hear the brook down in the field, running along on the edge of the hill. It was the coolest water! There was ladies' eardrops growing there. Did you ever see any ladies' eardrops? Red and yellow, you know, with a little hook like, on the tip, to hang 'em up by in your ears. My sister Tessy used to hang 'em in her ears. She died when she was eleven. Tessy 's named for her."

A faint color came and went in Mary's face. If Bell only would not laugh at her!

" Were there many birds?" she asked, half under her breath.

" I should say so!" Jack sat up straighter, his own eyes kindling. " Crowds of 'em! Bobolinks and thrushes and robins. My! you 'd like to hear 'em sing! I could whistle like a lot of 'em when I was a boy. Never could get a bobolink's whistle though. There ain't nothing like that! Quails and whip-poor-wills was the easiest. Ever hear a quail? This is the way they call."

Even Bell and Bob looked interested as the soft pipe was heard.

" Kind o' pretty, ain't it?" said Bob condescendingly.

To Mary the sound seemed to come from a dim, unknown world of unimagined loveliness. She listened with parted lips and wistful eyes, but even Mary had no idea of the picture that rose before Jack Winter's eyes, causing his throat to swell and his heart to stand still, at the old familiar whistle. To the others it was only a clear, soft note, heard in a close, city room, on a summer evening, amid sounds and odors from the street without. Jack Winter saw a long, grassy hill, sloping away under gray, falling twilight; mossy stone walls overgrown with woodbine; crowding daisies, white in the summer gloaming; a low-roofed house with day lilies on either side of the doorstep, and great, spreading chestnut trees above a small, bent figure in the doorway, leaning out to watch the boy coming up the road, a figure with soft white hair and a gentle, smiling little face.

"Jack, deary," she was calling, "supper's waiting." And clear, wild, and beautiful, from out the shadows, came the quail's far-off cry.

The young man brushed his hand across his eyes as if to clear away a mist.

"I'd like to go back there," he said simply. Then, looking up at the girl who had brought back the old-time vision, he went on abruptly: —

"You'd ought to get out to where there's trees and water and so on, you're so fond of 'em! You're looking sort o' peaked along back too, for I've noticed it. Why don't you go out to the park now? It's real pretty, and there's flowers for you by the yard."

Every one looked at Mary, who blushed with embarrassment as usual. Nevertheless there was a certain novel pleasure in the discovery that somebody actually thought about her looks.

"It's so far," she said. "Bob and Bell take the boys sometimes Sunday afternoon, but I can't walk that far. It's most two miles from here, they say."

"Them open street cars would be easy as a carriage," said Jack. "They'd land you at the gate, and you'd be right in among the flowers in no time."

"Street cars for five cost something these hard times," said Bob, with an uneasy glance at his little sister. Bob was really fond of Mary, and would have taken her to the country every week if he had known she wished to go, and if it had cost nothing.

"Don't you feel well, Mary?" he asked, with rough kindness. "I might fetch you home a box of liver pills. They'd last a long spell and set you right up."

Mary murmured her thanks with sincerity. It was good of Bob, even though she did not need the pills.

"I'm all right, Bob," she said somewhat nervously. "I was only talking. I'm real well this summer, seems to me."

But Jack Winter shook his head. When an idea took possession of him, he was slow to be turned from it.

"Now, look here," he remarked meditatively, "I'm going to lay off to-morrow. I've been promising the children I'd take 'em off for a picnic this long time. Tessy, she's done a sight up in our place since they've be'n wearing that badge of your'n, and

I believe in encouraging them. Besides, I always did like to get out there under the trees. Now, you just come along with us. I'd like to take you real well. You've done the children lots of good. Will you? It's only three blocks to the car, and you could walk that, slow, could n't you? Come now!"

Could Mary believe her ears — or Bob and Bell either?

"That's right down good-natured in you, Jack Winter," said Bob enthusiastically. " Why, of course she can go, if you don't mind. I never thought she cared about it myself. Three blocks ain't anything, Mary. Stay all day, did you say? Now won't that be a spree?"

" You can get dinner ready before you start," said Bell, with interest. " Take a bite of lunch along too, and you might put in some of them cookies you made yesterday. It'll be real nice. Why don't you say something, Mary?"

For Mary had been too astonished and happy to speak, except with her eyes. It was like a bit of one of her own dreams. All night long she thought of it, and watched the stars in the intervals of slumber, as a child might have done, to make sure that there was no fear of rain. When she slept she dreamed of boundless fields of grass, with quails piping on all sides, and a brook quite hidden among wonderful

flowers which she knew were ladies' eardrops; and
when she awoke in the morning her heart was flutter-
ing like a bird, with happiness and expectation and
gratitude for Jack's kindness.

"He don't care a bit about my being lame," murmured Mary joyously. "And I can ask all about
the country, and I can sit on the grass and look at
pretty things all day long. It ain't only King's
Daughters that do kind things!"

What a day it was! Were there ever such shadows
swaying and trembling across the emerald lawns at
the park? Was there ever a sky so blue or sunlight
so soft? Was ever water so sweet and clear as that
in the little lake where the white swans fed? It was
something to treasure up in one's mind for always,
that golden time! Mary could never be quite certain
whether the morning or afternoon were more beautiful, or whether the long sweet pea beds were really
prettier than the marvelous pansies. Connor Street
could never seem quite so close and bare again, with
the knowledge that such beauty lay close at hand, in
easy reach of stronger people.

"The real country can't be much better," sighed
Mary, in the fullness of her content.

But the pleasantest time of all the day was the still
hour before sunset, when Tessy and Dolly were dropping pebbles into the lake, and Mary sat on the bank

listening to Jack's story of his dear old home. It
was strange how simply and freely he talked. Mary
could not understand how any one should care to talk
to her so long. If she had known that the young
man was looking to her with a half-wistful hope, as
the one being who might bring his little girls to his
dimly formed, half-unconscious ideal of womanhood,
she would have wondered still more.

"Their poor ma!" said Jack slowly. "Well,
she's dead and gone, poor Martha, and I wouldn't
say a word against her, only for Tess and Doll. She
took to drink, you see. It was kind o' hard on us all.
Sometimes they had her up in court toward the end.
She got wild for it. I didn't know what I'd do with
the children. Couldn't bear to have 'em come up so.
When I'd think of my mother I'd be just about wild;
she'd have felt so to have her grandchildren brought
up that way. And I won't deny but what I did get
hard on Martha; and downhearted. Did seem as
if there was no end to it all, and I got to takin' a
drop myself now and then to throw it off, and that
only made things worse. It seemed as if I couldn't
get out of it all, even when Martha died last year and
I moved into Connor Street, away from the old place.
But I've quit now. Lately it's all come back to me
someway, about mother and everything. I want to do
my best by them children, and I don't mean to drink

any more, for I won't deny but what it's too much for
me. I wa'n't brought up to it like some folks, and I
can't stand it. I've be'n awful grateful to you for
takin' Tessy and Dolly in, and it's sort of seemed to
put a new heart into me. I was sort of dumb before.
Got it in my mind that they'd turn out like Martha,
whether or no, and there was n't no use trying; but it
does seem as if they was getting to be more like
mother! And I was thinking if there was anything
you could teach 'em — I ain't much on prayers and so
on, especially since Martha took to drink — but if you
could tell 'em about them things sometimes — mother
used to tell me stories — there was Moses and Goliath
and the rest. I told 'em about Goliath myself last
Sunday. Well, I know it's a queer thing to be asking
a girl like you to take an interest in other folks' children, but they told me about that there cross of your 'n,
and I says to myself: ' It won't do no harm, seeing
the young ones belong to it too.' Well, you 're real
good to all them children. I 'm glad there 's such
folks in the world. I was sort of dumb before they
begun to go down with you."

It was almost dark when the happy little party
reached home. Jack carried sleepy Dolly in his
arms and Mary limped beside him, holding Tessy's
hand. She had brought away from the park a host
of happy memories, a great content, and a sense of

friendship and eager sympathy such as even her service-loving soul had never felt before.

"I never, never had such a beautiful day before," she whispered to herself, as she went into her room. "What a lovely world it is, just a little way off from here!"

CHAPTER V.

A LONG whoop of delight rang through Connor Street. From right and left came rushing feet and shouts of laughter, mingled with cries of "Grandmother Tipsytoe!" and "Hurrah for Queen Victory in her stars an' garters!" Some one began to sing "Glory, hallelujah!" and a score of shrill, small voices joined in. The street was alive with fun and mockery.

Bell and Mary turned from the washing of the tea things and hurried out with the rest.

"Such a bedlam!" scolded Bell. "And if there is n't Jimmy in the midst of it! Jimmy Bennet! Come here this minute, or I'll come after you. Let that woman alone"

Other sharp voices were calling in the same manner to "Jack," or "Willy," or "Sue," and here and there a mother's flying form was seen to dart from one of the houses, catch a small rioter by the arm, and drag him backwards. But the other children danced and shouted only the more for these interruptions, and the figure in their midst looked around her with frightened, bewildered eyes. It was a very old woman, bent and tottering; so old a woman that it

was a wonder in itself to see her in the street. She
leaned on an immense umbrella as she walked, and
her thin gray hair was flying wildly in the evening
wind. Her feet were bare and thrust into ragged
slippers and she wore a very gay and dingy double-
gown, which flapped about her curiously. In one
shaking hand she carried a basket, from which
peeped out a bunch of turnip tops. Mike Flanigan
had danced up to her and was poking a dirty finger
under the cover to see what more it held.

"Inions and three pertatys," he shouted. "Sure
it's a banquit the old lady's makin' fur. Give us
an invite, mum?"

The whole howling band took up the word and
hopped about the trembling creature like an army of
small imps. She looked at them piteously, putting
up her under lip like a child.

"It ain't pretty," she whimpered. "You had n't
ought to act so. I want to go home."

"Home to the banquit!" hooted the children.
"Take us along; give us a turnip. Hurrooh!"

"I ain't used to children," sobbed the poor old
creature. "There's too many of you. 'T ain't pretty
to make such a noise. Oh, why don't Sarah Jane
come!"

"It's a shame!" cried Bell, rushing down the
steps. "What on earth took Bob off just the time
when he might do some good? Jimmy Bennet!"

But a more effective champion was before her. Mary had caught Patsey Flanigan as he rushed out of his mother's room to see what was going on, and the boy sprang past Bell, almost knocking her over in his hurry.

" I tould ye there 'd be fightin' some day !" he cried gleefully, as Mike spun into the gutter and the Kennedy boys found themselves a scrambling heap in the middle of the road. " Ah, ye bletherin' goose, be off wid ye ! Here, Jimmy Bennet ; what are ye about wid this crowd? Take the old woman up to Miss Mary while I send these ones flyin'."

Nothing could stand before such an impetuous attack. In five minutes the crowd of children were flying in different directions, the Kennedys muttering vengeance from their own corner, and Patsey stood proudly victorious on the doorstep, surveying the field of action.

" Ain't you glad you 've got a King's Son to help ye out?" he asked, with a broad smile. " Jimmy, you missed the fun, bein' in wid 'em ! Don't you go in wid them Kennedys no matter what they 're after, an' ye 'll be all right. Now then, who 's the old woman an' what 'll we do wid her?"

Here a very small and discouraged boy came slowly up to the door, rubbing his eyes forlornly.

" It 's my granny, " he explained. " She jest got

up out o' bed an' grabbed the turnips an' things an'
walked of. How was I a-goin' to stop her, when she
just went right along? She's bigger'n I be, an'
they had n't oughter expect me to keep her in bed. It
ain't fair, an' ma'll be after me with the slipper, too,
as quick as I go home. Besides, they scared me most
to death." And the little fellow burst into a doleful
wail, which was echoed by his partner in misery, as
she sat on the upper step with her face buried in her
hands.

"I was a-goin' on a picnic — a moonlight picnic,"
sobbed granny. "Sarah Jane, she keeps me right
to home and 'tain't right. An' now there ain't no
moon nor no grass to sit on, nor no nothin', 'n' I want
to go home. The world ain't what it was."

"You'll have to take her, I guess," said Mary.
"I suppose the boy knows the way. It's real good
of you, Patsey. Say, Bell, can't Jimmy go along
too? He did n't mean any harm. Let her take your
arm, Patsey. Poor old thing!"

"And you tell them Kennedys that if they set the
children off any such way again, I'll send your pa
after them," cried Bell to Jimmy as the comical
little procession took up its line of march, granny
glancing about her in the same frightened manner,
and her small guardian weeping aloud wrathfully,
under the anticipation of maternal injustice. Heads

of scared children were thrust out at them all along
the street, and tongues were extended and noses
wrinkled in derision wherever Patsey's eyes fell, but
the "King's Son" was serene in his triumph and
walked on with head in the air. The sudden excitement was over, and Connor Street relapsed into
peace.

Mary sat on the steps and leaned her head against
the doorpost to wait until the boys should come back.
She was tired that night, but there was an under-
current of happy thought beneath her idle watching
of the comers and goers in the growing darkness.
Only when Müller came stamping up the steps she
drew back hastily with a startled face, to let him pass.
He looked down at her with his usual sneer.

"You ain't been talking to my girl again?" he
demanded. "She talks of you too much. I will not
have it. If you let her come to you when I am away,
you shall suffer. Do you hear? None of your cross
for me or mine — curse you!"

"She never comes," said Mary under her breath,
shrinking farther into the shadow, while Müller
laughed harshly and went on.

"It is well that I frighten you!" he cried, from the
stairs. "I know what tricks you would play else,
you Christian liar! You are all alike."

Then his heavy steps went tramping on, and Mary

heard a faint little cry of welcome as he reached his own room. She remembered vaguely that Trudel had not been downstairs that day, and that one of the children had reported her as ill.

" Poor little thing ! " thought the pitiful King's Daughter. " I 'd be real good to her, if he only would let me. Dear, dear ! how dreadful it must be to be like that."

A puff of cool wind came up the street, and the girl leaned forward to enjoy it. Her thoughts stole away from Müller and Trudel and even the poor old woman who had just gone, and went wandering down pleasant paths of their own, where there were only kind faces and friendly words to greet her. The last few weeks had been very pleasant ones to Mary. She could not quite remember whether she had ever been so happy before. Since that day in the park a new experience had come into her life, nothing less than the experience of friendship. Mary was used to having people kind and pitiful toward her ; used to the careless love of little children and the half-grateful, half-patronizing affection of their mothers ; but this was a very different affair. Jack Winter *talked* to her ; told her of his work and planned with her about the children's future ; told her stories of the country, and sometimes spoke, half under his breath, of the higher thoughts which now and then came to

him in his busy days. She knew all the sad story of
his city life and something of the temptations which
had come to him through it. In fact Jack's old asso-
ciation of the young girl with the dear old mother
still lingered in his mind and had its own influence
over the character of their companionship. Bob and
Bell " took it kind " in him to be good to Mary.
They remarked on his considerateness in taking a
little walk with her now and then, regardless of being
seen with a " crooked thing like her," and when one
night he actually brought in a bunch of pink-and-
white asters from the market and held it out to Mary,
with a little laugh, they were as pleased as if it had
been a gift to one of themselves— more pleased, in
fact: for what would Bob or Bell have done with a
pink-and-white bouquet in a paper frill?

" He 's real good and kind to Mary, and she 'd better be thankful she took up with the young ones." said
Bell and Bob ; and Mary echoed the sentiment in her
heart.

She was thinking over some of these things as she
sat a little later on in the summer evening, looking
down the street, perhaps watching unconsciously for
Jack. He was very late that night, and Tessy and
Dolly had gone to bed without waiting for him. Old
Mrs. Wills had stepped in to see them, on her way to
her own room above — good old Mrs. Wills, who wore

the cross of the King's Daughters at her apple stand, and did many a kindly deed " In His Name " as she went about her daily work.

"Funny he ain't come home," she called over the stairway to Mary. " He ain't be'n out this way for nigh six months, I guess ; not hardly since you come here, anyway. I hope he ain't got into one of them saloons. He used to, once in a way, you know. Oh, well, it is n't my affair, I suppose, and the children are all right, anyway. Coolin' off a bit, ain't it, Mary? Time, I should say. This has been a summer ! "

Later and later ! Mary leaned out again and again, watching for the boys she told herself, but with eyes open as well for a sight of the familiar, broad-shouldered figure, with its swinging stride. The saloons? Oh, no ! Jack had quit drinking. He had told her so on that beautiful day by the sunset-lighted water. He had begun to go to church with Bob and Bell. He was growing back into the old boy nature that had been left behind him with the green hills where the quails piped in the summer twilight. Oh, Jack would never stop at the saloons again !

" And the King's Daughters did help him about it a little bit," said humble-minded Mary, smiling out into the dark.

What was that sound from down the street? Some one shouting, singing ; other voices in a confused clamor that came nearer and nearer. The scuffle of many feet and a noise of quarreling. She sprang up, ready to go into the house out of the way of the drunken brawlers. Such scenes were not uncommon in the factory region, and yet Mary always trembled before the ugly sights and sounds. Why should she pause now to look back once more? Two figures were flying like the wind in advance of the shouters — boyish figures, panting with haste and excitement. Bell came hurrying out at the sound of their rushing feet, and Mary clasped her hands in involuntary fright. Oh, what was it? And why did Jimmy and Patsey come flying so?

The boys rushed up the steps, gasping and breathless.

"The children!" cried Patsey. "Tess and Doll! Oh, get 'em out! Get 'em down! He's crazy drunk and he's comin' straight here! He'll half kill 'em this way!"

The wild cries and shouts came nearer as Bell turned and ran swiftly up the stairs.

Jimmy had broken down and was sobbing with excitement, but Patsey went on with an eager story as he leaned against the door, still panting for breath.

"We stayed round a little to see what he'd do," he cried. "We heard the men talkin'. They got him in at Rooney's place, a lot of 'em, because he'd sworn

off, an' they said they 'd make him drunk, an' they
kep' him goin', an' he 's be'n there ever since he quit
work. They says he never got so wild before, once,
an' they 're all laughin' an' goin' on! Oh, my! He
never got like that! Why don't she bring them children down?"

The rough crowd outside were almost at the door
now. Mary gave a gasp of relief as Bell flew down,
with Tessy clinging to her and Dolly, still asleep, in
her arms.

"Come back in our room," she whispered. "Come
right back in here, every one of you! Let them men
get him upstairs. They 'd ought to be locked up,
every man of 'em. Here, Mary, I 'll put the children
right in your bed. Curl down there, Tessy, and go to
sleep again. Nobody 'll hurt you. Oh, why don't
Bob come home?"

They gathered about the closed door to listen, as
the loud-voiced band burst into the house. Could that
be Jack's voice, thick and broken, breaking off in the
midst of a wild song to swear as he stumbled on the
stairs? Mary did not know that her face was white
and drawn, that tears were dropping slowly down her
cheeks. She only felt at her heart a dumb pain, that
made her lean against the wall for support. Was
that Jack? Was that her friend — the one who had
been kind to her?

They could hear him stumbling about the room upstairs, crying out fiercely for the children, and knocking over chairs and table, while his companions stood laughing around the door. One or two were almost as excited as himself, and went reeling about the landing, filling the house with their tipsy singing.

"I did n't think he 'd miss them so soon," whispered Bell. "I 'm most afraid he 'll come down here. If he does "—

Some one came up the steps outside, at the moment, and with one glance at the scene within went swiftly away again. No one noticed him. The riotous troop were rushing down the stairs, with Jack at their head, crying out that he would find his children and brain those who had stolen them. Bell and Mary shrank together. They had heard him kick open the door of the room next his own. Oh, what would happen when he came here?

"Let me in!" shouted Jack, with a furious oath and a blow on the door.

Those inside looked at each other for one breathless instant. Then Patsey fled to the inner room, drawing the younger boys with him.

"We 'll drop 'em out the back window if he gets in," muttered Patsey bravely, with his teeth set. "I ain't a-goin' to have them poor little things hurt."

"Let me in!" shouted the furious voice again;

and Bell dropped helplessly in a chair with a burst of frightened tears. Oh, where was Bob?

But Mary stood up, pale and still, with her trembling lips and her poor bowed shoulders. He would break in in another moment. Should she wait, or open the door to him herself, and let whatever came come to her? After all, Jack was her friend. It could not be that he would harm her! How frightened Bell was! It would be better to have it over — perhaps she could keep him from harming the others. "In His Name," whispered Mary in her heart, and opened the door.

"Where!" — shouted Jack, with his arm raised to strike down whoever stood there. His face was flushed and excited; his eyes glaring. The men behind sprang forward with confused cries. But Mary looked straight up into the angry face with her grieved, pleading eyes.

"Jack," she said.

The man's arm dropped by his side. He stared wildly, drawing back a little, almost with a look of fear.

"What — what — it ain't *mother?*" he stammered.

"O Jack! O Jack!" cried Mary again, with a little sob. She could not say more, for the swelling at her heart, but she put out her hand and took his, to lead him in. His companions began to fall back.

The white-faced, trembling little figure seemed to have struck a silence among them. One muttered something like an apology, and another turned back to stop the loud singing which was still going on in the stairway.

In the moment's hush that followed, steps were heard outside, and the door was filled with new faces. Mary uttered a little groan at the sight of the blue uniforms. For Bob had hurried away at the sound of fighting, and it was with two policemen that he came home for the second time. His face fell when he saw who was the cause of the trouble.

"I would n't have believed it," he said between his teeth, as Jack was led away. "I'd never have believed it!"

Bell rocked herself in her chair and sobbed; the boys came out, to talk excitedly; and neighbors crowded in with indignant comments and sympathy; but through it all Mary sat silent and trembling, with Jack's face before her, half-sobered, still wearing the look that he had cast over his shoulder as he left the house; a look of shame and anger and despair that haunted her the long night through.

She was tired and languid next day, with little heart to join in the gossip of the house, about the evening's excitement. There was the same dull pain at her heart through all the hours of work, and it was hard to sit quietly down with her knitting in the evening and hear Bob talk of the trial and the fine that Jack had paid and how he had been " let off easy " because it was his first offense. Where *was* Jack? She longed to see him, if only to forget that horrible face of last night. He had been so very kind to her. Poor Jack!

CHAPTER VI.

THERE was a step in the passage, and a somewhat faltering knock at the door. Every one started and looked up quickly, as if expecting to see Jack himself standing before them. But it was only Annie Morris, the bright-faced girl who worked next to Bridget in the mill, and who had pinned the little cross upon her shoulder in the first days of the Connor Street "Ten." The mill was such a good place for the King's Daughters! Mary sometimes almost envied Bridget and Annie their "chances." Why, they had kept Mrs. Wilson's loom between them for a whole fortnight, when she was laid up with her sprained wrist; kept it and turned the money over to her and welcomed her back to her place with a hearty good will that was a medicine in itself. Mary was always glad when Annie dropped in, which was not often, with her blind, old mother sitting solitary in her attic across the way.

To-night she was in haste and only beckoned Mary, with a smile and good evening to the others.

"I want you to come out to the steps with me," she said. "There's something I want to speak to you about. It's real pleasant out, to-night, anyway. You can come, can't you?"

Bell would have kept them to talk over the last night's excitement, but Annie would not sit down.

"I'll be over again," she said briskly. "Mother'll want me soon now. and I can't stop. Come, Mary. It's something special."

"Some of their lend-a-hand doings!" said Bell, with a touch of impatience, as the door closed behind the girls. "They're always at it."

"And a good thing for the rest of us if they are," rejoined Bob, with something of a growl, which caused his wife to lift her eyebrows in silent amazement, Bob not being given to taking the part of champion.

But outside, in the dark street, Annie turned and looked Mary full in the face.

"What do you suppose I wanted?" she said. "Jack Winter stopped me just now, when I was going in at our house, and asked me to call you out. I wasn't a-goin' to, after the way he went on last night — why, they said he came near knocking you down, only the policemen came in time; but he's all broken up, Mary, and ready to drop over it, and he said he spoke to me because I belonged to the King's Daughters, and he knew I wouldn't say no; and what could I do then? He said he *must* see you before he saw the rest, and he's waiting over on our steps — there's nobody else out to-night — and I just *had* to go and get you. There! now you can stay or

not, just as you choose, only he's about wild, he's so
cut up about it, and I'd just speak to him, seems
to me."

"Why, of course," said Mary simply. But she
clung to the railing as they went down the steps, as if
she were not quite sure of herself. Her face was
very pale as they crossed the road. Jack Winter,
watching it in the lamplight, felt a miserable sinking
of the heart. He had been straining his memory all
day to recall just what had taken place the night
before. Mary's eyes were all that came back clearly
from the confused remembrance — eyes full of fear
and pain. What had he done to bring that look into
them? It was with a groan, almost a sob, that he met
her in the doorway.

"It's like you to come," he said brokenly, and
then, as Annie went on into the house and Mary sat
silently down beside him, he broke out into eager
questionings.

"I didn't — O Mary, I didn't hurt you? I've
tried to remember till I'm 'most crazy with it. I
didn't — touch you? All I can remember is opening
a door — and there you were, like mother herself.
O Mary, do tell me!"

Mary turned towards him, her fear dying out in a
rush of pity.

"No, no!" she cried. "Why, Jack, I was sure

you would n't when I opened the door. It was n't *you*, anyway. It was those dreadful men. Why, Jack, of course you would n't harm me. Oh, are you crying? Jack, Jack — don't!'"

But Mary was crying herself, with sorrow and sympathy.

"You have n't got any call to be sorry for *me*," he groaned. "It's them children — and me trying to be a good father to them. I never thought I'd touch a drop again. I did n't know what I was about, hardly, after the first glass. It must have been mixed stronger than any I ever had on purpose. The fellows said they'd make me drunk. And I was fool enough to think 't was their friendship. I'll never speak to one of 'em again. But — do you suppose it's any use? See here, Mary, have you giv' me up? Do you believe there ain't any use in me trying? If you have" —

"But I have n't — Why, no, of course I have n't!" cried Mary, with a swift gathering together of hope and courage. "I could n't think that. Anybody as good and kind as you are! Why, nobody ever was so kind to me, hardly. You won't ever get that way again, now, you see."

But the young man shook his head with a heavy sigh.

"That's what I thought before yesterday," he said

slowly. "I ain't so sure to-night. It takes the heart right out of me. They'll be after me again — and there's places on every corner — I did n't take it in how hard 't would be. I did n't know it had got any hold of me. I 'm clear discouraged, Mary; and what on earth I 'll do with them children " —

A thought was rapidly taking form in the mind of the tender-hearted little comforter beside him. She sat quite depressed for a few minutes, while Jack poured forth a flood of gloomy forebodings. Then as he paused, looking at her in surprise and doubt at her silence, she spoke out with an effort.

"I 'll tell you what I 'd do if I was you."

"What?" said Jack eagerly. Her face had grown suddenly bright and resolute.

"I 'd just go away," said Mary decidedly. "I 'd go away this very night out into the country, where there ain't any of those men around and where there ain't places to drink on every corner, the way you said. I 'd leave the children with Mrs. Wills; she 'd be glad enough to keep 'em in her room, for a little money, just to pay for what they 'd eat; and I 'd help look after 'em too, and we 'd all take care of 'em. And when you 'd found a place somewhere, some farm or other, why, you could come back for Tessy and Dolly. You 've got money enough to keep 'em while you 're gone, have n't you? Bob says you get good wages. Why, I should think it would be splendid, when you want to live in the country so, anyway. We 'd all miss you here. You 're real good to us all, Jack. But we 'd take good care of the children, and you 'd be safe then, don't you see? And maybe 't would only be just a little while till you 'd get a good place and come back for them. That 's what I 'd do."

The young man looked at her with a new light in his eyes. It was singular, the influence which this pale, childish little creature had gained over him during one summer.

" I believe I will," he said, lifting his head. " I 'll do just what you say. And if you ain't discouraged, why, I won't be. You 're awful good, Mary. I won't ever forget it, how good you 've be'n to me and the children."

A little later the two crossed the road again and went straight in at the door of Bell's sitting-room together. Bob and Bell stood up in surprise at sight of Jack. I cannot tell what their reception of him might have been if Mary had not been there, but Mary's face was so eager and wistful and appealing that Bell herself was softened. Jack found no hard judges that sorrowful night. When, after a long talk and the laying of many plans; after Mrs. Wills had come down to arrange for the care of the children;

after Tessy and Dolly had been kissed in their sleep,
and Jack's satchel packed by Bell's energetic hands;
after the last good-bys were said, and Jack had
started down the street in the deepening night, the
load of hopelessness seemed already lifting, and a
new strength beckoned from those unknown fields to
which he was going.

"The Lord help the poor boy," said Mrs. Wills,
wiping her kindly old eyes. "It's a hard life his
has be'n, and he'll have the more credit for gettin'
above it. There! I'm an old goose to cry, but I'm
right down sorry for Jack Winter, for all he give us
such a scare last night. You'd ought to have heard
Trudel Müller scream when they bu'st in that way.
Did you know she was awful sick to-day? Don't
know what's the matter with her, but I hear her just
ravin' in there. I'd go ask her pa to let me help if
he war'n't so sot against church folks. Seems if he
could n't abide the sight of me sence I tried to get
Trudel to Sunday-school. Well, good-night."

Poor little Trudel! They knew "what was the
matter" next day, when her father came stumbling
down the stairs, his fierce eyes brighter than ever, his
brows drawn with anxiety and trouble. It was Sunday, and Bell and Mary sat together where they could
look out across the petunias and mignonette into the
sunny street. Jack's little girls were with them;

Tessy in Bell's lap, Dolly leaning on Mary's knee and listening with wide-open eyes to the reading of a Bible story. If Mary had been alone with the children, the story would probably have been told instead of read, but Mary had no idea of venturing on her own rendering before her sister-in-law. Bell approved of the reading, and sat very upright and intent, with an air of duty performed, and an occasional correction in pronunciation, for Bell had been to school until she was a well-grown girl, and felt herself quite qualified to instruct ignorant little Mary, who had almost picked up her education by herself. The room was still and bright and pleasant in its Sunday trimness, and the fragrance of the flowers floated even beyond it into the bare hall. It was all very quiet and comfortable. Every one was startled when Müller's hurried knock sounded at the door.

"Come you here" — he said abruptly, beckoning to Mary as Annie had done the night before; and then, as the girl hesitated in surprise, he spoke again, with a stamp of his foot. "Come you here, you lame girl. Make haste, and leave those children behind you. I must speak to you, and I cannot leave my child for long. Stupid girl, do you suppose I mean to hurt you?"

Bell set Tessy on the floor and went with Mary into the hall, closing the door behind them. She might

scold and snub "Bob's sister" herself, but she had
no idea of leaving her to be scolded by any one else.
She faced the German with a sort of defiance in her
comely countenance.

"You may as well be a little more polite, Mr.
Müller," said Bell decidedly. "It's no wonder the
girl's afraid of you. What do you want?"

"Want?" cried the man, with an impatient frown.
"I want *her*. Trudel calls for her day and night
since she fell ill. The girl has bewitched the child;
and now the doctor says there should be a woman
there. I want her to come to Trudel. Do you hear?
The child may die! The fever— Will she come?
No? I thought so. Trudel cried, · Call her and she
will come.' Of course it was not so. I shall go
back, then, and I shall lose the child."

"But wait, wait!" cried Mary. "I will go. Oh,
yes, if she wants me and you will let me come. Poor
little thing! Is she so *very* sick? Only — only — is
it something catching? I'll go, but"—

The man gave a great harsh laugh that made the
women tremble.

"Yes!" he exclaimed. "Yes, you will go if there
is no danger. It is scarlet fever, then. She may die.
She raves and cries of '*Mary! Mary!*' and her cross
and the lying tales you told her, and the doctor says
there should be a woman; and what woman is there

to come? Oh, yes, if there were no danger, you would go! She said, 'Call her, for she will come for the sake of her cross!' But you will let the child die. Oh, it is just as I told the doctor. He is waiting for me there, and I must go back! You are what I thought you, you poor little coward! She cried out in her raving that you would come for the sake of Christ, and I came, though I hate you all, for her sake."

"But oh, stop!" cried Mary again, as he turned away. She was frightened at the despair in his face. What did it matter that he had cursed and scorned her? Mary had quite forgotten everything but that he was in trouble. "Oh, it was n't that I was afraid," she cried eagerly. "Why, of course I'll come with you, only there are so many things. I was thinking — there's Tessy and Dolly, and if Mrs. Wills did n't have them, she would help you take care of Trudel — I ain't much good working, you know, with my back — just wait one minute. O Bell, what can we do? There 'd ought to be somebody to help him."

The man stopped on the stairs and looked down at the two, with a half-wondering hope dawning in his haggard face.

"I'll have to stay up there if I go," said Mary. "I could n't bring it down to the children. And there's the work — Bell, what shall I do? It would

be for a good while. There's Mrs. Wills would help
him, if it was n't for her apple stand, and Nora would
do up your housework, I know, to help; or Rosy —
they 're real trusty, Bell. But there 's Tessy and
Dolly. And O Bell, he said for the sake of Christ!"

" You go right along," said Bell in her most matter-
of-fact tone. She had no idea of letting excitement
run away with her. " You go on, Mary, and I 'll fix
things. Of course we ain't going to let that child
carry on after you that way. I 'll take Tessy and
Dolly myself in your room, and the Flanigan children
can turn in, as you said, and as for Mrs. Wills, Patsey
and Jimmy 'll keep that apple stand, and do as well
as anybody. I 'd trust them with a bank, either of
'em, though Jimmy did run after that scarecrow last
night. You go up, Mr. Müller, and don't run any
more risk of carrying the fever round, and Mary 'll
be along in a jiffy. I 'll send your nightgown and
things by Mrs. Wills, Mary, when she comes in, and
you can use her room, you know, and come back when
the doctor says so. Don't you go to getting tired out,
either. I 'll see to Tessy and Dolly. The King's
Daughters comes in real handy this time, and no
mistake. That man 'll find out there 's some good in
Christians after all," concluded Bell, with a little
chuckle of irrepressible enjoyment.

Mary threw her arms around her sister-in-law's neck
for the first time in years.

" You ought to be a King's Daughter yourself," she cried impulsively. " You're so good, Bell. You know just what to do."

" Well, why shouldn't I know? " assented Bell, disengaging herself from the embrace, with a pat on Mary's shoulder. " And as for being one — well, if you'd ever invited me, I would have, 'most any time, only I suppose I *am* kind of sharp and cornery for that sort of thing. I'll put on that other cross of yours, though, if you want I should."

Mary gave an actual gasp, in her astonishment. *Bell!* The tears sprang to her eyes, between remorse and happiness.

" I never knew you'd want to ! I was afraid you'd think 't was silly ! " she faltered, in confused accents. " Why, Bell ! It's just too lovely. Now I don't care about the fever or anything. You'll just know better than any of us what to do — and it's in my workbox on the table, and oh, dear me ! I never could find just the one to give it to, and I'm so glad I don't know what to do ! "

Bell smiled, somewhat condescendingly, but very affectionately.

" I'll get it on then, right off," she said. " You're a good little thing, Mary, and that's the truth. I'll be glad to have it on, too, for — well, I suppose folks *don't* always feel like asking things of me very much,

you know, with my ways and all, and it's just as well
to have something that 'll sort of show 'em I 'm willing
to do for 'em, if they tell me what they want. I ain't
quick to see things to do, but sometimes I 've felt sort
of bad because folks did n't know enough to ask me.
There! you go along upstairs, and I 'll keep things
straight down here."

The strange doctor, waiting for the woman whom
Müller had gone to fetch, looked up in surprise as
Mary came limping in. He had never seen a brighter,
more joyous face. It was not strange that Trudel
had wanted her, he told himself, watching the happy
light in the gray eyes, as he left a few instructions
for the one who should nurse the child.

" You 're a lucky man to have such a pleasant little
friend, Müller," he said, as the father followed him
out to the stairhead. " She 'll soothe the little
thing, you 'll see. Steady and quiet and not afraid.
Hope the old woman 'll do as well. Pity this one
is n't stronger."

Trudel was clinging with both arms about Mary's
neck, when the man went back. Her eyes were burning, and she was crying out in her hoarse voice, half
in German and half in English, broken words about
the sun and the heat and the bad dreams she had had.
She turned impatiently from her father, as he bent
over her, and clung closer to Mary. The girl looked
up at him with her soft, quiet eyes.

" You 'd better go and lie down, Mr. Müller," she said gently. " You must be tired out, if she 's been this way all day. I 'll stay by her, and Mrs. Wills will be in soon, and you won't need to do anything till you get rested. Maybe I can get her to sleep."

Müller went into the next room and threw himself on the bed there, with a dull wonder amid his trouble. What manner of creature was she, this girl with her pale face and happy eyes, who cared for his comfort and pitied his child, and called her friends to help him, in the name of Christ? He could hear her, through the half-open door, singing softly, in a weak little quavering voice, or answering Trudel's fevered words in soothing accents. It was all very puzzling.

"I will never call her humpback again," thought the man ; " no, nor liar. It means something to her —the name of Christ."

A little later he heard another step in the outer room, and reaching forward saw Mrs. Wills' gray head stooping over to the sick child. How lonely and frightened he had been an hour before, and what blessed rest had come to him in the midst of his anxiety, from these two whom he had hated ! His mind was full of new and strange thoughts as he dropped asleep.

That night, while Trudel's fever ran high, and her delirious cries and tossings were filling the watchers with alarm, her father sat with bowed head in the corner of the room, looking and listening, in prayerless anguish. She was all he had to love — poor little Trudel. What should he do if she should leave him? If only anything would quiet her!

"Talk a bit — say over something kind of soothing, Mary," he heard the old woman whisper. "She gets stiller at the sound of your voice, dearie."

Mary looked over her shoulder doubtfully at the silent figure in the corner. Trudel's golden head was on her arm, and the child's crimson cheek was pressed against her pale one.

"Everything's burning — burning! There isn't any cool anywhere!" moaned Trudel. "Mary! Mary!"

'There's things out of the Bible that I say to myself when I'm tired hot nights," said Mary hesitatingly. "I can't think of other things — Do you suppose he'd mind?"

Müller raised his head half angrily.

"Don't be a fool," he muttered. "What do I care now, as long as you get her still?"

Mary's voice, low and clear, sounded through the sick room. The old, old words, "with healing in their wings":—

"'The Lord is my Shepherd; I shall not want.

"'He maketh me to lie down in green pastures: he leadeth me beside the still waters. . . .

" ' They shall hunger no more, neither thirst any more ; neither shall the sun light on them, nor any heat. . . .

" ' As the dew of Hermon, and as the dew that descended upon the mountains of Zion : for there the Lord commanded the blessing, even life for evermore.' "

How strangely the sentences fell in the hushed air ! The gentle voice went murmuring on while Trudel's cries grew fainter, and her tossings less violent ; while the dark-browed man stared dully from the shadow. and the homely face of the old woman took on a look of devotion and tender awe at sound of the " good words."

On and on through the long night went softly the murmuring voice, and when in the gray dawning the sick child lay asleep in Mary's arms her father still listened vaguely to the grave, soft accents, half breathed, half spoken : " Even life for evermore."

CHAPTER VII.

THE fever had come and gone. Trudel was out again, thin and pale, with her frocks grown remarkably short, and her wrists pushing their way out beyond her sleeves in a way that caused her father to lift his eyebrows in dumb amazement. Life had apparently fallen into its old channel throughout the house, but there was a great change in the anarchist and his child. Trudel followed Mary or Mrs. Wills about from morning till night, clinging to them like Tessy or Dolly themselves, listening to Mary's stories with her bright head against the lame girl's knee, or sitting in the September sunshine at Mrs. Wills' apple stand and making change with a child's delight in being busy.

Patsey had made another cross to take the place of the broken one, and it hung from Trudel's shoulder with no denial from her father. Müller had quite lost his scowl when he spoke to Mary or her friends, and when one Sunday a comrade of his own remarked disapprovingly on the fact that Trudel was trotting off to a mission school, with her hand fast locked in the wrinkled palm of the apple-woman, he turned upon the man so fiercely that further comments were stopped forever.

" She shall go where she likes and do as she likes! "
roared Müller. " How do I know? It may be that
women need such things. At any rate those people
are no liars. They came to save the child for me, for
love of their Christ, and they shall teach her what
they will. She will come to no harm with those two."

So Trudel enjoyed her new friends and was happy;
sang her Sunday-school hymns about the house
with a true German love of music, and went gayly
down to Bridget's room with the other children, when
they came together again after the separation.

How pleasant it was to be back among them all!
Mary's heart overflowed with pleasure and with love
for every one of the eager, affectionate band. She
racked her brain for stories and games and songs to
entertain them; chattered like a child herself about
all the small changes that had taken place in her
absence, and turned a dozen times a day to drop a
soft kiss on the forehead of Tessy or Dolly, who were
sure to be ready for it, close at her elbow. Their
father had not yet been heard from, but his friends
were in no surprise or anxiety. None of them were
addicted to letter-writing on their own part, and Jack
would be sure to come back, in good time, for the children. In the meantime the two pretty little creatures
were petted and made much of by all the house, and
blossomed out in the kindly atmosphere like a pair of
small, sweet twin flowers under spring sunshine.

Mary's thoughts were often away with Jack, under the hot, sultry sky of these September days. The warm weather lasted on unaccountably that year, bringing illness and death in its slow passage through many a close court and crowded street. Mrs. Saunders' baby had been carried to the potter's field while Trudel was ill, and wan-faced Johnny Morris had grown so thin and hollow-eyed that the tears sprang to Mary's eyes as she saw him again. How she wished for the power to gather all these little ones together and carry them far away from the city to the quiet meadows and orchards where Jack had gone! She hoped that it was a pretty place which he had found for Tessy and Dolly. It would be so pleasant for them to grow up in the country! If there might only be a brook for them, with shelving stones along its banks, like those where Jack and his little sister had played long ago. Mary quite pitied the other children who had no such bright prospects before them.

There came a day when the hot, moist air seemed to settle down over the earth with a deadly weight. Even in the damp basements there was no coolness to be found, and many a weary household spent the livelong night in the streets or on the housetops waiting for some merciful breeze. Even Bell looked languid the next morning, and almost lingered after the factory whistle, before going to work.

"The way the dust flies in that weaving room is enough to make a saint mad!" she said fretfully, looking back at the door. "I wish I was you, Mary. Whoever saw such weather as this?" There was a lump in Mary's own throat as she washed the dishes and made the beds. She had hardly ever been so tired, it seemed to her.

"If there'd only be a storm!" she thought, looking out at the brazen sky between the houses. "Summer's sort of dreadful when it lasts like this."

She took up her work, wearily, and went down to Bridget's room, where the children were already waiting. Jimmy and Tommy were at school, but the Flanigans, except Patsey, were in full force, with a touch of the general fretfulness to temper their usual good nature. Johnny was there too, whiter than ever, his transparent hands lying listless on the bed covering, and Mrs. Jones' baby was wailing forlornly in Trudel's lap. The air of the place was dank and musty. For a moment Mary felt like bursting into tears and flying back to her quiet room to shut out everybody, and rest by herself. Then her hand went to the silver cross and she came forward with a little smile.

"Pretty hot, is n't it?" she said, dropping into a chair. "Well, I should n't wonder if there'd be a storm soon, it's so heavy feeling. Trudel, give me the baby, and you might tell us one of your fairy stories. Johnny 'd like it, I know."

The hours slipped slowly by. Johnny dozed and woke and dozed again, smiling faintly over such parts of Trudel's tales as reached his ears. The baby fell asleep and was laid on a pillow in the corner, and Biddy and Peggy settled down to their own naps on the floor. How heavy the air was! A storm was surely coming, and, indeed, the air grew suddenly darker, and a dash of raindrops was heard on the sidewalk outside.

"Rain!" said Mary joyously. "Now it 'll be cooler!"

She went to the window, to look out thankfully, but drew back startled at what she saw there.

A great black cloud was spreading rapidly over the heavens; such a cloud as Mary had never seen before.

"It 's awful black!" said Nora in an awestruck tone from beside her. How lurid the air was! Surely this was no common thundershower. She caught her breath involuntarily, while the children gathered around the window and looked up with terrified eyes as the storm burst suddenly. A wild rush of rain swept through the street; there was a crash of thunder, and then a tremendous roar that came through the gathering darkness like a trumpet blast. Mary's heart stood still with terror. She sprang from

the window, huddling the children into the corner of
the low room.

"It's the end of the world!" shrieked Nora.
"It's all come to onct and we'll be killed. Mother!
mother!"

"Get down on the floor behind the bed!" cried
Mary, wringing her hands. "Cover your eyes up!
Oh, what is it? What is it?"

She tried to push the bedstead closer to the wall,
out of the way of the rain that came through the
open window in a whirling flood. The darkness had
settled down so thickly that she could hardly see
Johnny's white face on the pillow. The long roar of
the wind was sweeping around them, filling earth and
sky, to her frightened ears. It had all come in a few
moments, like some horrible dream. What was it?
where was she? A shout from outside answered
Nora's scream, and Patsey leaped through the window, his eyes staring with fright. The crash of falling chimneys came with him. Flying *débris* was
hurled past the window, and shrieks from the street
pierced the fearful voice of the whirlwind.

"It's a tornado! Everything's falling down!
We'll be killed!" cried the boy, rushing toward Mary
with outstretched hands. Then, with one terrible
crash, the roaring blast seemed to descend upon them,
tearing life and thought away in its whirling wings.

Mary could never tell how long the sounds of crashing timbers and falling walls went on about her, or whether they were hours or minutes that passed while she lay half stunned, with the cloud of flying plaster blotting out every sight from her eyes. The children's voices, raised in frightened sobbing, called her to herself at last, and she put out her hand vaguely, with a dull wonder where she had fallen and what was about her. She was lying on the floor among broken timbers and rubbish from the walls; above her stretched a long beam which rested against the angle of the wall and formed a support for a mass of crossing boards and fragments of plaster, piled so high that Mary's eyes closed in sick horror at thought of what would happen if that uncertain prop gave way. She was just in the angle between beam and floor, where it would be impossible to move without danger of bringing down the whole ruin. Beyond the bed, she could see the children, already beginning to stir and creep about in their fright. There was a little more space above them, but how long would it be before they were all buried together?

"Keep still right where you are, every one of you!" she cried sharply. "If you move about, you'll bring everything down on us! Get in the corner close to the wall, where that beam slants, and then keep still. I can't get there. Nora, you and Rosy and Trudel must just stop crying and keep hold of those babies. Are you all there? Is anybody hurt?"

She counted the little heads as they cowered back at her word. Nora, Rosy, Trudel, Mike, and Peter, Tessy and Dolly, and the three babies — how was it possible that so many were alive? There was only room for the little group to crouch together. If she could only keep them still! Mike was moaning with an injured arm and Tessy's face was cut and bleeding, but the rest were apparently unhurt. But above them, over the edge of the bed, hung the nerveless, waxen hand of little Johnny, from under a pile of broken plaster, and Mary knew that the child had gone, all in a moment, from the wasting pain of his earthly life to the land where the inhabitant shall not say, I am sick. And Patsey — She turned her head with a heartsick fear. Some one had been moaning beside her for a long time, it seemed to her. She had been too dazed and bewildered to think who it was, but now her full consciousness came suddenly back. It was Patsey, half buried under the broken boards, a streak of blood across his pallid face, his lips white and pinched, his eyes dull with pain. Mary gave a little cry at the sight.

"O Patsey! O Patsey, dear! And I never saw!"

The boy reached out his hand painfully, trying to draw her nearer.

"You was lookin' after the young ones!" he gasped. "It did n't matter. I 'm glad they ain't any of 'em killed. I come back to help — I wisht you 'd get hold of my hand. It gets so dark."

His eyes closed and a sharp cry of pain cut short his words. Mary burst into a flood of tears. She looked up and about her; at the cowering children, kept from death by the slanting beam; at the timbers, that must be moved if she crawled from her place; at the dying boy, whose hand was seeking hers.

"Oh, what shall I do?" she sobbed. "O Patsey, dear, I can't move to get there! You can't see; but it 's all held up some way, just over me, and I don't dare stir for fear of bringing it all down on the children. There 's ten of 'em, Patsey! Oh, I would n't care a bit for me; but there 's ten of 'em, and all their mothers, dear, and they can't one be saved unless we all keep still. See, I can't reach you, though I 'm reaching my hand as far as I can! Oh, what shall I do?"

Patsey looked toward the children with the ghost of his old debonair look of leadership dawning in his eyes.

"It don't matter," he said slowly. "It 's all right, Mary. You young ones — did you hear? You mind her an' kape still, or I 'll" —

His voice failed again. There was blood on his

lips; his matted curls were damp about his forehead A sharp pang of pity shot through Mary's heart. She forced back her tears to comfort him.

"Have you got the little cross, dear?" she said. "Take hold of that, Patsey. It'll be like the hand of the Lord Jesus, that's close to you though you can't see him. Don't be frightened, dear; you're the King's son."

"It's all right," he whispered. "I ain't no baby. If you could say a bit of prayer."

"We'll say it together," said Mary, beginning in a voice which she would not let tremble. "Our Father" —

The children joined in one after another, amid their sobbing. But Patsey's voice sank into silence with the first words, and before the prayer was finished he lay quite still and peaceful, with the shadowy smile lingering on his face, and his rough, brown hand still clasping the silver cross. A great rush of grief and fear swept over Mary's heart as she saw that he had gone.

The other children were all so little, and she felt so young and helpless and frightened herself. Could it be true, this horror that had come upon them? Was the whole city swept away? A tornado? Why, such things only came on the prairies! If she might only wake and find it all a dream! If she could only crawl over to Patsey and close his glazed eyes before his mother came! If she could have touched his hand before he died! But the other children were still safe, and she must think of them.

"Don't be scared," she said. "Things ain't going to fall any more, I guess. Somebody'll be along to take us out pretty soon. You just keep still, and don't jar the boards and things, and you'll be all right. Listen! The wind ain't blowing now. It was all in a minute! You can hear the folks running along the street! It won't be long."

Yes, there were hurrying feet above them, and voices that called and shouted amid the falling rain. The factory whistle was blowing an alarm, as if for fire. Men and women were gathering in crowds, and the lifting away of the *débris* was already beginning. Mary heard words about the row of houses that had fallen, and one man called to another amid their work that they had been condemned months before and the landlord was responsible.

"A perfect heap!" the man cried. "There'll be more than one life for him to answer for! Good land! Keep folks back! We need room!"

"Help! help!" cried Mary, in her feeble voice. "There's children down here! Oh, do get us out!"

But the sound of work went on for what seemed like an eternity on either side, while no one heard her

call. The children sobbed and sobbed in their corner.
Rain was dripping and trickling about them. It was
hard to breathe in the choking air.

"They have to take things as they come," explained
Mary bravely. "They'll get here pretty soon. I
suppose folks can't get through. Don't cry, Tessy!
You must be brave, you know. I'd get over by you
if I could. We've just got to be patient, that's all."

Hark! there were voices nearer, and footsteps
pausing close above their prison. Bob's voice, crying
"Mary! Mary!" and Bridget's and Bell's. "Call
out! Call out loud!" cried the girl, with a great
heart-throb of thankfulness; and the children's shrill
voices were lifted in a wavering shout, answered by
eager words from above.

"We'll get you out! We'll have you safe soon!
We've just made a way. Mary! Mary! is any one
killed?"

And then came a long wail from mother lips, and
Bridget threw herself on the pile of rubbish, trying
vainly to make a way to her boy's side. Mary trembled and moaned as she listened to the crying above
her: —

"The father an' the son! the father an' the son!"
over and over again. She looked at the children in
their narrow shelter. They might be drawn out one
by one, if she herself kept quiet till the last — but

what would come to her with the moving of that strangely-balanced pile? She shut her eyes, with a little prayer. They must be saved at any rate. How many there were to miss them — and two were gone already.

"It don't make so very much difference about me," thought Mary, lying very still under the edge of the great beam. "They're all straight and strong and with folks that can't get on without them. It don't matter for me."

She steadied her voice once more, with an effort, and called clearly up to Bob : —

"Over in the corner by the street, close up. They're all down there under that long beam. You'll see 'em soon, if you work careful. Nora and Rosy can help the others up, if you make a way, only you'll have to be pretty careful about stirring things."

Steadily, carefully, the work went on. Light and air were coming from the corner, while Mary lay watching the trembling ruins. How long the time seemed! She spoke now and then in the same steady voice, sometimes a word of encouragement to the children, sometimes a direction to the unseen workers. Once or twice a board or a bit of plaster slipped and fell. They had almost reached the supporting beam. What would happen when it was moved? Could the children be drawn out from under it? No; they were too small to be reached from above in that way. She shut her eyes again, drawing a long breath. It would all be over very soon now.

" You 'll have to move the long piece in a minute," she cried resolutely. " Don't you mind, Bob! Get the children out, anyway, only if you could do it sort of easy — because I 'm just under the end — but get 'em out, *anyway*, you know. Nora could hand up the babies first " —

There was a sudden pause and outcry among the workers. What was this — this outbreak of excitement — this burst of words? Was it her name they were calling so? Even Bridget had stopped her wailing, for the moment, to join in the outcry. She could hear hurrying feet drawing nearer and recognize one voice and another of those who were gathering. How strange their words were !

" Mary ! Mary ! She ain't down there at the very middle ! Good Lord, what 'll we do? Why, it 's little Mary ! It 's the King's Daughter with her cross — it 'll all fall in a heap when that 's stirred ! Yes; the one that drops the flowers out, the one that helps folks — oh, my ! oh, my !"

Why, this was some one whom they loved and honored and could not spare ! Some one who must be saved, at whatever cost. They were sobbing aloud, those women, and talking wildly of how they loved her! She could hear Müller crying out: "She faced the fever for my child, and I 'll die in there too, but I 'll get her out!"

Could it be that they all cared for her like that? The sweetness of it flooded her heart with a wonderful gladness, in the face of death. Why should they think of her so?

"Why, it don't matter for me like other folks, you know," she tried to call. "Oh, do take the children to their mothers! They 've been so good; and maybe it won't hold this way much longer. Do take them out and never mind me!"

Nobody noticed her. A newcomer had just reached the spot, dashing through the crowd with a force which carried him to the very corner where Bob and the rest stood in helpless consultation. The girl cried out in surprise at the sound of Jack Winter's well-known voice. How had he come at this time? And what a home-coming it was for him!

"Jack!" she called shrilly. "Jack, take Tessy and Dolly out! They 're all safe yet. Oh, *can't* you get them to save the children? I 'd rather be killed a dozen times than wait this way!"

Jack's voice came back to her strong and distinct. He had knelt down and was speaking with his face

close to the opening made by the rescuers. The
other men gave place instinctively, before the light
in his face.

"He's got two children in there!" said an awe-
struck voice.

"You keep still, Mary!" called Jack steadily.
"Don't you be afraid! I ain't a-going to let anything happen to you. I'm coming down myself.
Keep back there, Müller; it's my place! I've got
more down there than you, and if anything happens
there's them that'll look after Tess and Doll. Hand
me that crowbar! I'm the strongest here and I can
hold it up best. Now, then, hand up them babies
that's small enough to go through. That's it! Now
you straighten back against the wall, the rest of you,
and give me room to slip down. We'll have you safe
in a minute. One board off — there — Müller, when
I get it braced, help the young ones up; I'll give 'em
my knee to step on — yes, I can do it! Don't be
frightened, Mary, I'll get you out!"

Mary, lying with face against the wet ground, felt
her heart stand still with a sudden wild hope. Was
she going to be saved after all? Was the beautiful
world not left behind her? Her eyes swam and
dazzled as Jack slipped slowly into place, kneeling
with his iron bar beneath the broken rafter. It had
not stirred, so careful were his movements. O Father

in heaven, were they saved? Through a dark mist she saw the children creep out to where they could step upward and be lifted to the open air. There was not a sound to welcome them. It was in the midst of a great silence that Jack's voice reached her again, low and strained.

" I can steady it a bit longer, Mary. Creep out careful, if you can. Don't give 'way now, when you're all but safe! That's it! Easy— I can't help you, but I can keep it up — just a bit farther — Müller, be ready there, for she's all but gone. Reach up your hand, dear, and they'll catch it — there!"

A long, wild cheer filled the street as Mary was lifted out. A dozen men leaped forward to help Jack to follow her. Women sobbed and laughed and clasped the rescued children, and Müller and Jack shook each other violently by the hand, with tears in their eyes. But Mary herself lay white and unconscious with her head in Bell's lap, and knew nothing of it all.

THERE was the fragrance of roses in the air; far-off roses, very faint and sweet. It mingled with Mary's dreams and floated back with her as she came slowly into waking consciousness. Where could it come from? The girl lay with closed eyes wondering dreamily, before she looked about her. It seemed as if the last night had been very long. She could dimly remember some terrible excitement which had passed away and left a confusion of other memories — faintness and fever and people crying about her — Bell's face and Bob's and others whom she did not know. Some one had put them all away, and sat down beside her, laying a cool hand on her head while some one else held a glass to her lips and told her to go to sleep. The hand had been very soft and pleasant; not like any hand that Mary had ever felt. Somehow the roses made her think of it again. Yes, and there had been a gentle face beside her; a lady's face. Who could it have been? And where was she? Not at home — Why, home was gone! The storm rushed back upon her memory with sudden terror. She opened her eyes and glanced about her for some familiar face. Where was this? The room was white and still and fresh; the bed soft and snowy; such a bed as Mary had never known. A little table stood beside her, and upon it, in a glass, were the roses which had sent their dewy breath to meet her as she came to thought and life again. How beautiful they were, drooping toward her, pink and creamy, amid their russet leaves! There was another bed in the opposite corner from her own, and a sleeping child lay there, with a tousled, sandy head turned toward her on the pillow, and the traces of tears on his freckled cheeks.

"Why, it's Mike!" said Mary aloud, in her puzzled wonderment.

Some one who had been sitting at the window rose quickly and came to the girl's side. Mary felt the flush of pleasure rise to her cheeks as the newcomer bent over her. Where had she come from — this stately woman with the shining gray hair and the dark, beautiful eyes? It was all like some pleasant dream, and Mary smiled up into the stranger's face without asking what it meant.

"Are you better, little sister?" said the lady, smiling down in response.

And as she spoke Mary saw that she wore on her breast a little silver cross.

The girl sat up in bed with sparkling eyes, unheeding the strange weakness that made her tremble as she moved.

"Oh, it was you that was so kind last night!" she cried. "You had your hand on my head when I was so dizzy and frightened. and you sent the others away. How good you were! and you've got on the King's Daughters' cross— Oh, was it because of that?"

The lovely lady smiled again, and sat down at the bedside as Mary sank back on her pillow.

"Because of that that I called you sister. and was glad to help you? Why, of course, my dear," she said. "I belong to a Ten whose work is helping the sick, and I had come down to the hospital to do what I could, when you were brought in. You don't know how glad it made me to see the cross fastened to your dress, and know that I was to have a chance to help one of ourselves. Have you rested? You seemed to be sleeping so sweetly!"

Oh, Mary was quite rested! She lay in the same half dream, a little bruised and languid, but very peaceful, looking about her with happy eyes, while her new friend moved in and out, bringing breakfast, and talking quietly, in her low, pleasant voice.

Yes, there were many of the King's Daughters in the city, only Mary had never happened to meet one of them before. There was work and to spare for them all just now, among the poor people left homeless by the storm or lying wounded in the different hospitals. It had been only a narrow path that the

whirlwind had taken, but it was through the poorer
portion of the town. where slightly-built cottages and
rickety tenements, such as Mary had known as home,
had fallen an easy prey to the force of the wind. A
few had been killed, many were injured more or less
seriously. Household goods were scattered and more
than one poor woman was mourning her ruined dwelling place, as Mary knew that Bell must be mourning
hers. Poor Bell! Her little sister thought with com-
prehending sympathy of all the treasures which were
lost; of the clock which Bell had brought from her
old home at her marriage, and the blue dishes which
she had worked after hours to pay for. It was strange
that she should have forgotten it all in the rest and
pleasure of this quiet place!

"Did you see Bell — that's my brother's wife?"
she asked timidly. "Did she feel very bad about the
dishes and things? She thought a lot of those
dishes!"

The lady smiled once more, this time with something of amusement in her face.

"I don't think anybody thought of dishes much,
last night," she said. "Your sister was so thankful
to have you safe and to know that her children were
not in the track of the tornado at all, that she seemed
to be very happy, except for thinking of the poor
little fellow who was killed."

Patsey! Mary's eyes filled with tears as his face
rose before her, white and dying, with the fading
smile in his eyes. How far away all the pain and
fright and grief had seemed, and how it all came
back with the freshening of her mind!

" Poor Patsey!" she sobbed. " Did you know?
He was a King's Son. Did it do any harm? He
wanted to be so much, and he made all the crosses.
I couldn't help letting him and Jimmy be in it.
And he was so brave! Did you know?"

The older woman was crying too, before the story
of Patsey's death was finished, yet the tears of the
two were not all sorrowful.

" ' And the armies that are in heaven follow Him,' "
said Mrs. Graham softly, " ' in fine linen, white and
clean.' The brave little soldier has seen the great
Captain before this."

Mary only answered with a tender, half-wondering
smile. To think that little red-headed Patsey should
be among those glorious armies! It was so beautiful
that she could not weep for thinking of it! She
would tell Bridget that verse some day. It must be
very nice to know how to say such things! Mary
felt a little thrill of pride to think that she also was
an insignificant little member of the noble Sisterhood
of the Silver Cross.

" I suppose there 's lots of 'em just like her," she

thought, following the stately figure with her eyes, as Mike awoke and Mrs. Graham went to make him comfortable. " Lots more, just as beautiful and good and sort of splendid as she is! How much good they must do! Well, anyhow, I'm glad there's a little place in it for folks like me, that can just help along a wee bit!"

Bell came in a little later and sat by Mary's bed, talking in a subdued, gentle way, unlike her usual brisk style of conversation.

" Yes; they found the little cross shut tight in his hand, and they just left it," she said. " Mrs. Flanigan's going to have it buried with him, and 'twas about the only thing that seemed to do her good, when Nora and Rosy told her about it. I was real glad you happened to think of having him take hold of it, Mary. It seemed to be a sort of comfort, some way, and the priest he talked beautiful about it, if he is a priest. They're real good sort of people, anyway, Catholics or no Catholics. Yes, I was glad you thought of that. See here, Mary, did you know there was a piece in the paper about it? There was! One of those men was a reporter, and he heard them all going on about you, and he just wrote a piece about it. Bob, he bought two papers to keep, he was that pleased. It said you were a heroine!"

And Bell surveyed her sister-in-law with respect

and curiosity, as if expecting to trace some new feature in her astonished, blushing face.

"That was what it said," she went on. "A heroine; and it told a lot about you. I was real took aback when Jack Winter brought it in. 'Mercy to me,' said I, 'what on earth'll she say to having herself in the newspaper!' And he said: ''T won't do no manner of harm to her nor anybody else to have folks know there's such people in the world!' He does set store by you, Jack Winter does. He's coming in to see you this afternoon, too. He said he guessed they'd let him, and he wants to thank you about the children. You don't care, I suppose, seeing he got you out. He's got a splendid place on a farm, and he's going back next week with — the children." Bell stopped herself, with a conscious look, as if she could have added more.

"Oh, I'd like to see him!" said Mary softly. "I want to thank him, too. I'm so glad he's got the place. We'll miss them though, won't we, Bell? I don't know how we'll get along without Tessy and Dolly."

"They're real, sweet, pretty-behaved little things," said Bell heartily. "I will say that I wouldn't mind being step-mother to 'em myself, so there!" with which remark, delivered in her most warlike manner, Bell withdrew to pursue her business of house-hunting, leaving Mary to look forward eagerly to Jack's visit and plan for a long list of questions concerning the new home.

"But, oh, dear me! I'm getting real selfish," thought the girl. "It does seem as if I could n't bear to have them all go away. We 've had such nice times together, and nobody was ever so kind to me as Jack 's been." And Mary resolutely turned away from the thought of parting with her friends, to tell stories to Mike and picture to herself all the beauties and advantages of that blessed country life to which the children of her love were going.

The sun was beginning to sink in the western sky, and a long golden lane of light lay across the floor of the room, when Jack came at last. He stood at the bedside quite silently for a moment, looking down at the pale little gentle face on the pillow, with something like a mist in his honest eyes.

"I 'm so glad they let me in," he faltered, after a minute. "I was 'most afraid they would n't, and seemed as if I could n't stand it not to have a chance to talk to you — to tell you " —

"And oh, there 's so much I want to know!" said Mary eagerly. "Do sit down, Jack, and tell me all about everything. Bell said you were going next week — And I wanted to tell you — Only I just can't. Oh, there 's so much to say!"

Jack drew up a chair and seated himself, with his eyes still on Mary's face. He was a little flushed and embarrassed, and there was some hesitation in his manner as he began to answer Mary's questions.

Yes, he really had found a good place where he would have a chance to make himself a pleasant home for the rest of his life. It would be just the place for the children, and there was a brook and a little brown house where they would live, with a tiny garden of its own and a climbing rose vine about the door. There was an orchard near by too, and (here Jack straightened himself and grew more animated) there were rows upon rows of beehives, which he was to help take care of.

"And such fields of white clover for them!" said Jack with enthusiasm. "I always did like bees. We had half a dozen hives when I was a boy, and I know I can do the work well. The boss is real pleasant too, and he's got a mighty nice wife. She asked me all about the children — and any folks I might have. She would be a good friend to anybody. It's a real cosy little house too, Mary. Two rooms downstairs and two up, and I've got enough to buy what furniture we'll need. It seems like a new start, where I can get into what I always wanted to be — And I hain't touched a drop, Mary, since that night, and there ain't any temptation to it there, for it's a place

Jack drew up a chair and seated himself with his eyes still on Mary's face
Page 124.

where they don't have saloons, and I 'm glad of it.
And O Mary! I did think of you when I see the
mountains out of the back door of that little house.
For they 're there, only a few miles away, all green
and pretty with pine trees and big gray rocks and all,
and says I to myself: 'If Mary was here, they 'd be
always on hand, and she 'd look off at 'em when she
was washing the dishes up, or getting the dinner, or
setting out on the porch Sunday afternoons, telling
stories to Tessy and Dolly; and when there was n't
too much to do, why, I 'd hitch up and take her up
there in the wagon, and we 'd set round on the pine
needles — you don't know how nice and warm and
sweet-smelling pine needles are to set on — and look
off over the valley and down to the river.' Would n't
it be nice?"

"Yes," said Mary, a little faintly, with a wistful
look in her soft eyes.

"And the bees," pursued Jack, looking at her
guardedly from under his eyebrows. "You would n't
mind bees, I know, for they don't sting if folks don't
bother 'em, and the hives are so lively with them all
buzzing in and out, and you could set in the garden
and watch them getting their honey and listen to
them. It 's a regular kind of song, I think, kind of
sleepy sounding and nice. I just thought, 'Mary 'd
like these bees!' There ain't so very much to do

round 'em in winter, but there's enough to keep me busy, and me and the boss took to each other right off. I 'most *know* you'd like it all, Mary. And I'm going to be the best kind of a father I can to Tessy and Dolly, you know; take 'em to church regular, and Sunday-school, and all. It's a new start, sure enough, and it's all along of you, Mary, for I'd never have got started right again if it had n't be'n for you. I'd sort of hate to feel as if I was n't going to see you again."

Here Jack drew his chair a little nearer with a worried glance over his shoulder at inoffensive Mike, lying wide-eyed and quiet in his bed, intent on a picture-book, but casting now and then an interested look upon his friends across the room.

" A body could talk better if there was n't anybody round!" he muttered. " I — well — do you think it would be a nice kind of a place, Mary?"

"Oh, yes!" said Mary again, with a sigh. "It'll be beautiful, Jack. I know you'll always be glad, and the children will be ever so much better off."

Jack nodded. " Yes, of course," he answered absently. " And — see here, Mary, do you think I'm likely to be pretty steady now? *Seems* to me I am. I never did get like that only that one time, and I'm going to try to be just like mother'd want me to be all the time — and you. Do you feel as if I was pretty trusty now?"

Mary laughed, and then grew earnest under his appealing look.

" Why, Jack," she said, " I should think you'd know! You're about the best friend I ever had, and there isn't one of us all that'll ever think about that night again. It makes me real proud to think how soon you got over it and broke right away from those men so that it wouldn't happen again. I wish you wouldn't think about that!"

" Honest, now?" said Jack, with a pleased look and a sudden flush in his brown cheeks. " Well, then, I know one thing—I won't ever go to disappointing you, Mary!"

There was a silence. Mary was watching her friend with half-amused curiosity as to what might be on his mind and why he hesitated and lingered so strangely in telling it, when Jack suddenly lifted his head and delivered himself in a burst of hurried words.

" There ain't no manner of use trying to get at it the right way," he said. " I wasn't going away till I'd got it settled one way or another. Bell, she said she didn't know what you'd say, but she thought 't was all right herself. I've just thought about it day in and day out, while I've be'n away. I don't see how I'm ever going to get along without you, Mary, anyhow. I never did think so much of any-

body in this world — there! And that was what took
me down there after you, yesterday, more than anything else. And you always did want to live in the
country, and if you'd go along — or I could come
back for you, you know, after you'd had a chance to
get all right again, and that Mis' Graham says it'll
only be a few days — and I'd take the best kind of
care of you, and you wouldn't have to work a bit
more than I could help, and that wouldn't be as much
as you do now — and there wouldn't ever be so much
as a stick of wood for you to carry into the kitchen —
and Tessy and Dolly, they'd grow up just like you!
There! I know you ain't had it in mind, but if you
just *could!* The very first minute I laid eyes on the
mountains out that back door, I said, 'Mary'd just
like this, if I could anyways get her to come.'"

But there Jack stopped short, for Mary's face had
grown so white and startled that words failed him
altogether.

" I wouldn't want to ask too much of you," he
went on after a moment, with an effort. " I know I
ain't fit for you Mary — rough-spoken and all that,
and always getting my foot in it one way or another;
but I think a sight of you, and I'd be good to
you all my life. I would n't have bothered you
to-day, only I thought maybe you'd be wanting time
to think of it, and there's only over Sunday I can

be here, and I just couldn't wait. The doctor, he
was n't going to let me come up, first off, and I just
said I 'd got to. He asked if I was any relation, and
I said, Not exactly; and he wanted to know if we was
engaged, and I felt so sort of desperate that I just
up and said, ' Well, no, we ain't, if you must know;
but we 're goin' to be before I come away, if I can get
half a chance to ask her and she 'll let me! There!'
And he burst out laughing and wished me good luck,"
continued poor Jack, with a comical effect of talking against time, while Mary recovered herself. " I
thought I 'd come at it kind of gradual, but I have n't.
Seems as if I could n't say a word of what I laid out
to — only — I 'd be a better man all my days if you 'd
come, Mary, and I 'd make you happy — I 'most know
I could make you happy. Seems as if I could n't get
along, unless you 'd come with me."

"O Jack! O Jack! *Me?*" whispered Mary. The
faintest rose color was creeping into her face. Her
eyes were wide and bright and wondering, and her
breath came and went tremblingly. Was it another
dream, this strange overwhelming joy that was taking
possession of her? Could it be that such a gift had
come to her, little crooked Mary, with her plain face
and limping gait?

" Are you sure?" she said, paling and flushing,
still with that half-frightened gladness in her eyes.

"Why, Jack, I never knew you cared for me that way. I never thought anybody could — why, when I ain't like other girls — Oh, are you sure you mean it all?"

"It's just because you ain't like the rest of 'em," said Jack sturdily. "I don't believe there ever was anybody else just like you, anyhow. It's 'most *too* good, to think of having you belong to me. What do you want to be like other people for? It ain't them I want. Besides you 're just as sweet and pretty as you can be, for all you don't know it. Being a little crooked ain't anything. Why, nobody thinks of that. I 'll tell you what, Mary," broke out Jack, in a burst of poetry never seen in him before, "you 're just like one of them white petunias in your window boxes; most like a little lily reaching up out of the green, with little fine lines down in the middle of it and that faint kind of sweetness that the other petunias don't have. And the other girls are the pink and purple and striped ones, that are pretty enough — but, dear me! I 'd rather have one white one than a basketful of the rest. There!" Jack stopped short, in confusion at his unwonted style of conversation, but Mary's soft eyes, smiling through their mist of happy tears, drew him on almost unconsciously. "And I ain't any more fit to have you than Connor Street was for them window boxes," he went on;

" but the posies did grow there, you know, and made folks think of country sights and pleasant things, and sort of rested everybody that laid eyes on them. And if you 'd let me have *you*, to grow that way — well, you know what I mean — grow your way where I am, you know — why, you don't know how you 'd be helping me along, Mary. I 'd try to be fit for it — as fit as I knew how to be — for you — and your cross," he added, under his breath, with a glance at the silver symbol where it lay on the table at the bedside. " Will you, Mary ? "

And Mary put out her trembling little hand for all answer, and laid it in his, her pale face quite transfigured with the inward gladness.

The forgotten Mike put a stop to further romance by suddenly exclaiming, —

" And see here ! you won't go and be married till my arm gits well, will you, so I can go to the weddin' ? An', Mary, may n't I come an' see you, out to that place where the bees is ? "

Afterwards, in the calm of the September sunset, Mary lay thinking it all over, with her eyes on the rose-flushed sky, where the moon was sailing softly up in a sea of pale blue, and the evening star was sending a single, long, trembling silver ray from the heart of the crimson glory. There had never been so beautiful a sunset ; Mary was quite sure of that.

What a lovely world it was that lay in evening peace below that celestial splendor! A line of some unknown poem, quoted long ago in a daily newspaper, floated through her mind as she watched, and she murmured it over again and again like a whispered song : —

" Like the love of the Redeemer shown on earth and sky."

Were there really pain and suffering and mourning, somewhere out of sight, in this beautiful earth — our Father's earth? To-morrow it would come back to her and she would take up her life-work, with eyes wide open to all the burdens waiting for a helping hand, " In His Name." There would be Patsey's mother to comfort and Mike to amuse through his convalescence ; tired women to be cheered and children to be taught and loved, in the midst of work and care and weakness ; all this and more lay in the shadows ready to be taken up with a brave, sweet strength, through long years of Mary's quiet life. But, to-night, everything was bright around her, and the future stretched before, fair as the green hill country of Jack's story, and sweet as the climbing roses which were to blossom about her door in the summers to come. A deep hush of awe and thankfulness filled her soul; the voices of friends and neighbors were in her ears as she had heard them when death seemed close upon her, calling her name in broken words of love and grief; Mrs. Graham's serene, fair face smiled upon her from the window-seat, with blessed promise of coming friendship and inspiration; Jack's eyes were looking into hers, and the pretty, curly heads of Tessy and Dolly were glancing in and out among the flowers of the little garden which was to be her own. Oh, how was it possible that God had given so much to her?

"And it all began with the little cross," said Mary softly.

The crimson cloud-wreaths paled to gray and floated lightly up across the clear, far azure. The white radiance of the moonbeams flooded the room; a little breeze stirred gently in the maples outside the window, as Mrs. Graham began to sing in her low voice a lullaby song about the wind and the birds and the angels watching by the beds of sleeping children.

"It was all from the little silver cross," murmured Mary again.

She was weary, even amid her happiness, and no formal prayer or thanksgiving came to her lips as she fell quietly asleep. But I think that the heart of the great Father was open to gather up all the love and praise and tender purpose that lay behind the whispered words which were Mary's last thought that night: —

"God bless the King's Daughters and help them to Lend a Hand!"

MISS MARIGOLD'S TITHES.

MISS MARIGOLD'S TITHES.

CHAPTER I.

THE END HOUSE.

L IVING 'S as interesting as a storybook!" Miss
Marigold was wont to declare, looking from
her gay little garden up the sunny length of Beech
Street. It was a commonplace street enough to eyes
of thoughtless passers — that row of brick cottages,
with small, green courtyards, brightened by an occasional bed of geraniums, or made gay with gypsy-
kettles of flowers, set primly in the very middle of
what were called by courtesy, " the front yards." In
reality there was plenty of variety behind the same-
ness of those ordinary house fronts. Hearts as light
as thistle-down and as heavy as lead beat near each
other, year by year ; songs and laughter rang all day
long through one dwelling, while perhaps only next
door were grinding care and haunting sorrow that
made life a weariness and labor a burden almost too
great to be borne. The Willises, at No. 56, looked
down from a height of scornful single-blessedness on
the ridiculous Browns at 58 with their ubiquitous and

137

adored twin babies. Mrs. Edwards, in whose veins
flowed the blood of the Pilgrims, looked on day by
day as M. Dubois shuffled out to market in his flowing
gown and velvet cap, and the young Edwardses had
even been known to stand strangling with laughter
under his window while he taught his classes of
" young gentlemen and ladies desirous of acquiring
the Parisian accent." France Hayward, with her
shining hair and rosy, dimpled face, lived side by
side with Patty Winthrop, who lay from morning till
night near her window, wearily watching the stream
of life that flowed by beyond her reach. Every house
was the center of some little world of love and hope
and work, and no day brought the same story to two
hearts from one end of the street to the other; but
nobody thought of that, except little Miss Marigold,
smiling out on the world like a gray-haired baby,
and declaring over and over again that it was all as
interesting as a storybook.

Miss Marigold's house was the one exception to
the respectable uniformity of the Beech Street dwell-
ings. It was a pretty little place, small and old-
fashioned, but set in the midst of a garden which was
the delight of every child on the street, so bright and
crowded and fragrant was it. How Miss Marigold
managed to make so many flowers grow in one small
patch of ground, no one knew; but there they were,

set in close ranks, like a compact little army —
larkspurs, pinks, four-o'clocks, pansies, sweet peas,
and roses, with mignonette in abundance, a round
bed of sweet white petunias, a row of tall lilies,
and a mass of honeysuckle and morning-glories
along the house, while, at the farthest end of
the yard, lines of hollyhocks lifted their long
spears of delicate rose-color, white and crimson.
There was a rustic seat in the midst of all this
brightness, and here Miss Marigold was accustomed
to sit on summer afternoons, with a book of poetry
surreptitiously laid under her apron, and a rheumatic
dog curled lazily at her feet. People used to cast
curious glances over the fence, at the trim little old
maid among her flowers. If they met her eye, they
generally turned away with a smile such as one gives
to a pretty child, for never did happy baby look
about it with eyes sunnier and more confiding than
those Miss Marigold turned on the world as she sat
in her garden at the end house. France Hayward
always insisted that she was like a flower herself,
a slender sweet pea, light of motion and bright of
face, looking up to the sunshine from a bower of
greenness.

"Talk of pretty girls," said France, leaning over
the fence from next door, "there is n't any girl in
the street so pretty. Rosy cheeks may be all very

well with yellow hair like mine, but I'd just like to
know where you'll find anything so pretty as rosy
cheeks with gray curls and a baby's eyes looking out
of the middle of it all. Miss Marigold, I hope when
I'm as old as you are, that I'll look just like you."

Whereupon the little old maid would blush and
laugh and answer deprecatingly : —

"I'm sure, my dear, it's very kind of you, and
if I did n't know it was *only* you, I might be quite
vain, though to be sure, it is n't the way a woman of
my age ought to look, if I've really got eyes like a
baby. I suppose it's because I've never been about
much in the world and never had much chance to
study and improve myself, as I hope you'll do with
a will, while you can, my dear. Youth never comes
but once, and folks ought to make the most of it."

"Suppose there is n't anything to be made?"
France would answer with her blithe laugh, yet with
a shadow in her eyes that belied the careless words.

Then Miss Marigold always shook her head thoughtfully, with her eyes looking very far away into some
world where the girl could not follow her.

"There's *always* something to be made, France.
If it were n't for what I got out of my young days,
I could not get anything out of these. Only it seems
to me, if I was back there now, I'd make more out
of them than I did. It's like the walks I've taken

Miss Marigold, "I hope when I'm as old as you are that I'll look just like you." See page 140.

sometimes, when I 'd pass by the flowers, except here
and there one, and think I 'd pick loads when I came
back, and perhaps I 'd go home another way after all,
or else find that some one had been before me and
there was nothing left when I was ready to pick. It's
always best to take things as you go along, in this
world. I know that much, though I 've never had
any experience in life to speak of."

In fact, Miss Marigold had lived all her life in the
little old house at the end of Beech Street. There
had been a time when it had been full to overflowing
of young life and frolic, when Miss Marigold had been
" little Prissy," the pet and plaything of a half dozen
light-hearted brothers and sisters, and when the flowers
had had no chance to grow in the garden because
of the dancing feet that made it their playground.
Little Miss Marigold, sitting alone with her sweet,
childlike smile, looked back on the old days with a
strange, wondering awe at thought of the older
brothers and sisters who had died as children and
left her, the youngest, to grow old by herself. She
said their names over to herself often, lingering
lovingly over the syllables that no one else on earth
spoke now ; Ruth and Hannah, and Will and Asa,
and Ellis — they were all lying together in the grave-
yard on the hill. The fringe of pines above them
could be seen from the parlor window of the house

where they had lived. It seemed only a little time since the epidemic that swept them all away had left Prissy a lonely, wondering child in the home that never seemed quite to wake up after that stillness settled down upon it. A little time — and yet she knew that it was forty years.

" I 've gone beyond 'em all." said Miss Marigold, with her eyes on the rocking pinetops. " To think how I used to look up to Ruth, and now I 'm an old woman, and she was n't as old as France when she went away. And Will, that thought so much of me and used to carry me about the yard because I was so little and light ! It 'll be strange when I get home to have those happy things meet me, and I an old woman, though a happy one, thank God ! "

But she never talked in this way to others. The far-off childhood, and the youth that had brought its own bright, breezy lights and shadows, were shut away safely in her own heart, like a green pleasance, of which she alone had the key, and into which very rarely was any one else invited. But in quiet moments " when the heart 's at rest and the world away," Miss Marigold slipped into that fair, silent spot, and walked there among the lilies and roses of long ago. If others caught the fragrance that floated from them over the high walls, she never knew it.

Father and mother had gone to join their children

in the home land long since, and in the end house now lived only Miss Marigold with one maid, "more for company than for help," as she told the neighbors, "for of all dumb creatures, Phebe is the dumbest."

In fact, as Mrs. Scrubbs, from around the corner, remarked: "There's idiots born so, and there's idiots that make themselves so. There's idiots by nature, and if so *be* there's idiots by grace, Miss Prissy Marigold's that kind to stick on with that gump of a Phebe because she knows she'd bring up in the Home for the Friendless if she sent her off."

But Miss Marigold and Phebe held on their way in spite of criticism, and though it was a queer partnership and many a time came near to dissolution, the end house had remained under their rule for a long time now, and seemed likely to continue in the same way for years to come. Phebe was a tall, mealy-looking girl, lank of figure and puffy of face, with hair of the faintest flaxen hue and a general air of mental depression, which gave one no idea of her capabilities in the line of breakages, or her positive genius for misunderstanding orders.

"You really *never* heard of a girl," Miss Marigold had been known to say, in mild despair, "who'd be quick enough to think to pour the vinegar over the currants, and set the cucumber pickles to strain in the bag, just in that minute when I stepped to the

door to speak to the fishman! But there! It is n't
her fault. She's born so!"

"I suppose I be!" Phebe had answered dolefully,
after more than one such utterance; which reply
always had the effect of extinguishing Miss Prissy's
flickering wrath, and producing in both mistress and
maid a manner of remorseful kindness toward each
other for the rest of the day.

But if Phebe was good for nothing, Miss Marigold
was not, and no house in Bentonville was kept in
better order than the little one at the end of Beech
Street. It was a picture of dainty comfort, from the
dimly-lighted best parlor, with its great chintz-covered
sofa and shining mahogany tables, to the dining room,
where the windows were draped with honeysuckles,
and the sitting room, bright with flowered curtains
and made homelike with Miss Marigold's great cushioned chair and the light wicker workstand that was
always overflowing with other people's sewing. There
was a little set of bookshelves in this room, and on
them was arranged an odd collection of books, where
Doddridge's Rise and Progress stood side by side with
Thaddeus of Warsaw, and Edwards on the Affections
looked sternly down on Rob Roy and Guy Manner-
ing. One whole shelf was filled with poetry of every
description, from Thomson's Seasons to Spenser's
Faërie Queene in three volumes, pushed as far as pos-

sible to one side and half hidden under a brilliant scarf of India crape, which Miss Marigold, in a burst of æstheticism, had draped about the shelves. Miss Marigold always explained carefully that these "poetry books" had belonged to one of the long-dead brothers, leaving it to be inferred that she herself was quite indifferent to such frivolous reading. Cowper and Pope were occasionally found upon her workstand, and she took pains to remark in the hearing of such young people as visited the end house : —

"They are very improving books, my dear, and I always make it a point to read them now and then. If your mamma should wish it, I could lend you either of them to take home. Young people nowadays miss a great deal by not knowing such books."

Hypocritical Miss Marigold ! when perhaps under your work at that very moment lay one of the three brown books from behind the India scarf, and you only waited for the retreat of the youthful visitor to open the cover, with a feeling of half-guilty delight, and slip away into the land of enchantment, with Una and Britomartis and the Red Cross Knight !

Every household has its center; some little nook or corner that holds the key to the life of the whole place. The center of Miss Marigold's abode was found not in the silent parlor or fragrant garden, or even in the sitting room, with all its flowery chintz

and heaped up workbasket and secretly loved bookshelves. Upstairs in Miss Marigold's own chamber,
where visitors never came, were tokens of an inner
life known to few among those who met her from
day to day. Here were her little pictures of the
vanished ones, hung in a little cluster on the wall
opposite her bed, and over them, placed there with
secret misgivings as to its orthodoxy, was a cross of
phosphorescent paper, set in a frame of tender purple,
from which it gleamed white in the daytime, shining
through the dark in misty brightness when Miss Marigold woke in the night. " It's like the love of God
itself," she would whisper at such times, " coming
out bright when everything else grows dark."

Everything was white in this little room ; the old-
fashioned bedstead with its dimity curtains, the mat-
ting on the floor, the cover on the table by the
window, where stood a curious box of carved ebony,
oddly out of harmony with the New England simplic-
ity of its surroundings. Miss Marigold's Bible lay
beside it, and close to the window stood a small splint-
bottomed chair, where she sat often in the early morning or evening, looking from the holy pages out across
the town that went sloping away from Beech Street,
roof below roof, with cloudy treetops between, until it
ended at the blue river with the bluer hills beyond.

Night after night, when Miss Marigold came up to

bed, after she had read her chapter and said her
gentle prayers, she turned the key of the ebony box
and opened it with loving hands, smiling down on it
like a child with some happy secret. There were two
compartments within it, lined with faded silk and
carved round about with the same strange eastern
figures which covered the outside. In the one lay a
bunch of withered roses, a shell, bright as if the
colors of the dead flowers had crept into it to live
there in immortal beauty, and, laid softly over them
both, a crape handkerchief of pale blue, sprigged
with dull gold. Sometimes the little old maid touched
them with tender fingers, or lifted them out and laid
them softly against her cheek — the delicate old cheek
that France Hayward thought so pretty. Oftener
she only looked at them with that quiet smile.
In the other compartment lay — money. A miser
was Miss Marigold, to turn it out so often, counting
it over on the cover of her Bible? Never miser
laughed over his hoard in that merry, triumphant
way, or figured up projected expenditures in the light-
hearted fashion with which Miss Marigold counted and
planned.

"There's the cup for old Margaret." she would
say, standing in her long, white nightgown like an
elderly mediæval saint, with a half-eagle in her hand
instead of a lily, "and here's enough and to spare

for a bit of beef for broth to take in to Mercy Sparks to-morrow. And the missionary collection coming next Sunday, and if it is n't a mercy that I did n't spend my last five dollars on those Ruggles children, instead of making over my blue gingham for 'em, that was as good as new, and gave their mother an idea of work besides! And I declare, if here is n't a twenty-cent bit down in the corner! I can just get a dozen of lemons to send down to the hospital by the Flower Mission to-morrow! It 's wonderful how it counts up!"

A pleasant sight was it to see Miss Marigold on these evenings, and still more when she could open her purse and add a bill or a bit of silver to the treasured hoard in the ebony box.

How she turned it over in her hands, and looked at it with eyes full of pleasant dreams as she laid it in! How her face glowed as she locked the box and turned away to the great white bed; and how softly her voice sounded through the silent room as she murmured over the little prayer that always came to that childlike heart before it slept: —

> "Now when I lay me down to sleep,
> I give my soul to Christ to keep,
> Wake I at morn, or wake I never,
> I give my soul to Christ forever!"

Happy Miss Marigold!

CHAPTER II.

"MISS Marigold! O Miss Marigold! Please wait!"

It was France Hayward, running out of the yard, with her bright hair flying about her face, and her market basket swinging in one hand. Miss Marigold had just passed the door on her own way to market — trim and dainty to behold — in her gingham gown, with a knot of violets in her belt. She waited, smiling, as the girl came up.

"I wanted to come with you," said France, pulling on her gloves as they walked up the street together. "I've just been watching for you for the last half hour, and then came near missing you after all, with Win and Polly tumbling downstairs together just at the last minute, and mother's hands in the bread, and nobody to pick 'em up but me. If I could ever prevail on those infants to do their accidents separately once in a while, it would be something to be thankful for all my life. But I don't suppose I ever can."

Miss Marigold nodded comprehendingly, with a little laugh. The exploits, mischief, and manifold

149

scrapes of the younger Hayward children were a matter
of wonder and amusement to all the neighborhood.
A blithe, rollicking, good-natured set were they; all
bright-haired, all fresh-faced and pretty; all on the
lookout for any piece of fun, and fertile in resources
of enjoyment — resources which kept quiet Mrs.
Hayward in a continual state of mild expostulation
and amaze, and which provided their elder sister
with occupation and care enough for three girls, as
Miss Marigold often remarked, watching from her
vantage-ground at the end house.

Miss Marigold was very fond of France Hayward.
She had seen her grow up from a little child, and
had loved her ever since the days when, as a
small, yellow-haired girl in a white tier, she had been
accustomed to squeeze through a gap in the hedge to
wander among the roses and pinks on the other side,
or to present herself in Miss Marigold's kitchen with
an eye to the crullers and ginger snaps, which were
sure to be forthcoming out of the great stone jars in
the storeroom. Miss Marigold had stood by the
grave of the child's own mother, with France clinging to her gown and watching with grave, uncompre-
hending eyes as the coffin was lowered into its place,
and in the two years that followed the end house
had been a place of never-failing refuge to the motherless child. France herself could hardly remember

those days now, but to the loving heart of the little spinster their memory still brought a tender glow when she thought of them.

" She was almost like my own." said Miss Marigold to herself.

France, after the fashion of young people, understood little of the love and thought which went out to her from the heart of the bright-eyed little woman next door; but Miss Marigold's house was still a place of happiness to her, and many were the hours which the two spent together, sewing or reading, or even trying experiments in cooking in the sunny kitchen, which France always declared was the prettiest room in the end house.

This morning there was a slight cloud on the girl's bright face, a cloud which Miss Marigold recognized as having often been there of late; a look not exactly of discontent, but of absence of gladness. Miss Marigold speculated a little on its cause, as she had often done before.

" Girls have no right to look anything but glad," she thought, losing the thread of France's half-laughing talk as she meditated.

" I suppose it's because there are so many of us," the girl was saying, when her companion's wandering thoughts came back to her. " That was just why I wanted to get off with you — that is — I suppose you know what I mean."

"Not exactly," confessed Miss Marigold, looking with her soft, gray eyes into the changeful face beside her. "Go on, Francie; what did you want to tell me?"

"You always know just when anybody does want to tell you anything," said France, stooping to pick a spear of grass from the roadside and then throwing it away again. "I don't see how you can tell. But it is n't anything in particular, only — everything! I believe I'm tired of it. I wonder why you never seem tired of anything! You just enjoy life, Miss Marigold. Why, look into your yard and then into ours. Ours is just as large and just as sunny; but there's yours all running over with flowers, and you on your little seat in the middle as sweet and comfortable as — as — yourself. And then over the fence is our place; and Jack and Harry and Janie and Katy and Win and Polly and Baby — if that is n't a list for one family! — skirmishing round and spoiling the grass, and climbing the porch and filling it all up from one end to the other, and all the flowers I can have squeezed up into one corner and walked over most of the time at that. I can't make anything grow but phlox and candytuft. I think a desert island would be a good place to live on sometimes."

Miss Marigold laughed heartily.

"It's a good thing that you're where I can see

you, my dear. I might think you were in earnest, if I could n't see your face. What have Jack and Harry been doing now?"

The dimples began to show in France's cheeks in spite of herself.

" Well," she said slowly, " I did mean to make you think I was in earnest, but of course I could n't look sober enough. I don't see why I always laugh when I 'm provoked. People never will believe that I am angry. After all, I don't suppose I should like to take to a desert island *myself*, really. I might get lonely perhaps, and I might miss Janie and Baby. But if I had one near by for the boys and Katy to be sent to, when they are equal to fifty children at once " —

"It would make it quieter," said Miss Marigold. "Yes; I think it would. They *are* lively children."

" If only Katy would n't walk on the tops of picket fences, and Jack would keep out of the water, and Harry would let my bureau drawers alone," pursued France confidentially, " it would n't be so bad; but really, Miss Marigold, when Katy tumbles off twice a day regularly, and tears her skirts as no mortal child ever did before, and nobody but me to mend them — and then she 's so everlastingly good-natured, and so sorry every time, that I can't even have the comfort of scolding her. I just wonder how mother and I would feel if we ever got quite to the bottom of that mending basket!"

"So it's skirts this time," said Miss Marigold sympathetically. "Suppose you bring them over to my house this afternoon and let me help you with them. It would be just a charity, for I've finished the last bit of work in my basket, and I was just thinking I must look up something. Besides, I always like your company, you know."

"Oh, may I?" cried the girl. "How kind you are, Miss Marigold! It always does me so much good to get off with you. Sometimes I just sit and watch you and wonder — it does really seem as if you made it worth while."

"Made what worth while, my dear?" asked Miss Marigold wonderingly.

"I didn't mean to say that," said France, with a slight frown. "It slipped out before I thought. But if you want to know — I meant — you can laugh if you want to — I meant just living! There! I know it sounds dreadful, and I *don't* want you to think that I'm sentimental and think life's a hollow show and all that. It isn't that; but really and truly, as long as I've begun, it does seem to me that my own life hasn't very much substance to it. It's just the same thing over and over. Sometimes I think, if there isn't any more to it than this, if I really am not coming to anything more interesting, why it does n't amount to much!"

She cast a sidelong glance of humorous defiance at her friend as she spoke, but Miss Marigold did not appear shocked. She seemed to take the girlish confession quite as a matter of course, and walked on in silence for a few minutes, as if she were meditating a way of helping a troubled heart out of its difficulties. France, whose mood of discontent had begun to vanish almost as she spoke, was on the point of breaking out into mingled laughter and self-reproach, when the answer came.

"My dear," said Miss Marigold slowly, "are you sure you 've got hold of your life by the right end?"

She spoke so earnestly and anxiously that the girl was sobered in a moment. A shade of deeper thought settled down on her fair forehead, and it was out of the depths of her honest young heart that she answered.

"No, I'm not sure," she said; "I know I don't amount to anything. I just drift along and take things as they come, and, in fact, I'm afraid I have n't hold of any end at all. I'm just raveling."

"Then that's what's the matter," said Miss Marigold simply. "Because, of course, you know all our lives are the best for us if we only have hold of them right. Our Father does n't make mistakes when he chooses our places for us and if your part of the world does n't seem interesting, it 's because you have n't got fairly into it yet."

" I did n't exactly mean that it was n't interesting," said France, with a somewhat conscience-stricken face. " It was ridiculous to speak of it. Only it does seem a little as if — I was n't getting *at* anything. I know it 's my own fault though, of course. What difference does it make if things do get uninteresting once in a while? It 's only once in a while."

" I 'm not so sure that it does n't make a difference," said Miss Marigold thoughtfully. " I know I should n't enjoy my own life half as much if it was n't full of pleasant things to take up my mind. The thing for you to learn, Francie, is just that there *is* plenty in your own to make the world full of happiness for you, though of course things may n't be always just comfortable. It 's just as the song says. There 's a thread of gold in every pattern, and we can see the beauty of the whole thing if we only get hold of that, and just follow it out."

"Is that the way you do yourself?" said France gravely.

It was strange to her to hear Miss Marigold speak out of her heart in this way. The gentle little woman was not given to talking over the deep things of life.

" Myself?" repeated Miss Marigold, hesitating.

"My dear France, when you come to my age, you'll know that one's self isn't a very interesting thing to talk about. There isn't enough to it, at least to some of us! But if it would help you to tell you what has helped me more than anything else — though, as you very well know, I haven't any experience — I could tell you that easily enough. Only it's been my secret for a good many years now, and I shouldn't want anybody else to know. And after all it isn't anything much, only it was what I needed; and, if you won't tell, why, it's just — tithings!"

"Tithings!"

France's face fell perceptibly.

"Yes, it's just that, dear," went on Miss Marigold, with kindling eyes. "It's years and years since I made up my mind that I wasn't going to live for myself a day longer, but take a part of everything that came to me for the Lord, and I couldn't begin to tell you all I've learned since then. It fits into all your life, France, the tithing everything for him, money and pleasures and time and all, though of course I don't mean that one has to keep to a tenth of everything! And it makes living so easy and so beautiful. One comes to be just on the lookout for pleasant things from one year's end to the other, and it makes the world, as I've often said before, as interesting as any storybook!"

France's face was bright with a responsive glow as she listened.

"I understand," she said softly; "but you have more chance than I do."

Miss Marigold raised her eyes to the pine-fringed hilltop which could be seen from any street in that part of town.

"Yes, dear," she answered gently. "I have my hands free, if you mean that. I was n't any bigger than your Janie when they all went away; but I remember them, every one. There were six of us, you know, and my sister Ruth took care of me, just as you take care of Katy and the little ones. Sometimes I think I 'd give a good deal to have the chance of doing for some child what she did for me. It 's a great thing to be able to do so much as that. But they 're all gone — and I was only the youngest at any rate. I never could have had that chance. I always thought it was beautiful to leave such a memory as my sister Ruth left me."

"But I 'm not like that," said France. "I wish I were. Do you think your way of living would help with the children and all that? I suppose it would."

"It is n't my way of living," said Miss Marigold. "It 's just trying to help along a little in the work that the Lord has set all his children to do in the world — and that 's just bearing burdens, my dear.

And if you have seven little brothers and sisters at home, there must be plenty of little burdens among them for you to bear. It's just having that for the main end of your life that'll make everything come straight. If I have been saying anything that sounds like preaching, I hope you'll excuse it, France, and bring the skirts over as I said, and we'll have a good time together this afternoon. Here we are at the market, and Mr. Reese as smiling as a jack-o'-lantern; and indeed I can't help thinking of one whenever I see him, though I didn't mean to let it slip out to you."

The little market, with its fruits and vegetables outside the door, and its ruddy joints of meat within, was full of people, all in a hurry, all waiting impatiently for their turn, and all looking in a depressed way at the newcomers, as if their chance of being served was a remote one. But Miss Marigold went briskly through the throng to the round-faced butcher, who stood smiling patiently beside his meat-block, while a sharp-faced boarding-house keeper haggled over her purchases.

" If it's likely to be a few minutes before you're ready, Mr. Reese," she said, " I'll just step up and see your mother and take Miss Hayward with me."

She turned and led the way through a door at the side of the shop and up a narrow stairway, to the upper story.

" You'll enjoy her," she whispered as she went up.
" She's half blind, but as handy as can be, and so
happy if any one comes to see her. It's just a prov-
idence that you're with me, for she thinks the world
and all of young people, and she never sees them."

France was half inclined to draw back as her friend
pushed open the door at the head of the stairs. An
old, half-blind woman, the mother of a butcher who
looked like a jack-o'-lantern, was not an attractive
prospect to her. She followed Miss Marigold to the
room with almost a feeling of dread, but the next
minute stood still on the threshold, looking about
her and almost laughing aloud for sheer amazement.
Mrs. Reese's room was the most brilliant she had ever
beheld. The floor was covered with a carpet of bright
red with orange medallions; the walls were papered
with a gay pattern of poppies and birds of paradise;
the great chair by the window was cushioned with a
palm-leaf figure of the same gorgeous colors, and a sky-
blue cloth covered the little table where a Bible, hymn-
book, and photograph album lay primly about a green
vase full of many-colored Pampas plumes. It was
like walking into a broken rainbow. France was glad
when a solemn parrot, eying her from his perch beside
his mistress' chair, suddenly called out in his cracked
voice, " Ain't we beauties?" and gave her an excuse
to laugh.

"He's a wicked old bird," said the old woman, tapping him with her knitting-needle as she rose to meet them. "Is it you, Miss Prissy? But who's with you?"

She came forward, straining her eyes through her silver-bowed glasses and feeling her way with one withered hand. But when Miss Marigold drew France forward and told her name, the old woman clapped her hands and laughed like a child, with pure delight.

"A girl!" she cried; "a girl, to be sure, and me that has n't had one come to see me these ten years! And her hair so yellow that I can see it with my dim old eyes! It's better than the flowers, Miss Prissy! Sit ye down here by me, my pretty, and let me hear your sweet voice and look at the pretty hair that I can see the color of as plain as day."

As she spoke she hurried back to her chair by the window, and pulled out a hassock at her feet for France, while Miss Marigold sat down opposite. Then there was a clatter of talk, in which the old woman took the chief part, while Miss Marigold drew her out and listened with heartfelt interest to long stories of the parrot's illness yesterday, the socks that she had just begun for her son, and the sermon that she had heard on the last Sunday, with every few moments a return to France and a series of eager questions such as a child might ask about a new plaything.

"To think that you should have brought the dear child to-day," cried Mrs. Reese ; "to-day, when I was feeling a bit down-hearted, and sayin' to John, only this mornin', 'John, I would n't be findin' fault with you, lovey, that 's the best of sons, never lettin' me want nor feel the lack of anythin'; but if so be the Lord had seen fit to send me a daughter to keep me company when you 're busy in the shop!' And then you to bring her in on the top o' that! And to think she should have a red bow on, and me that can't see dull colors at all. A body 'd think she 'd dressed a-purpose!"

So the stream of talk ran on, childish and happy, while France sat, half delighted, half amused, answering questions, drinking in the simple story of a daily life that was like a bit of romance to her, and giving an interested ear to the saucy bird which filled every pause of the conversation with cries of "Ain't we beauties?" or stern commands to "Get out and leave us alone!"

"And now you 'll sing us just one song?" asked Miss Marigold at last.

"Yes, yes ; a song, surely. Was there ever a time when you asked me that and I 'd be sayin' no? An' what 'll you have, Miss Prissy? an' you too, my blossom? Though it would n't be a child like you that 'd be carin' for an old woman's song!"

" Sing Dubliu Bay," said Miss Marigold.

And the old woman, leaning back in her great chair, began in her sweet, quavering voice,

" Bay of Dublin! my heart you 're troublin'."

France listened spellbound, with the tears springing unawares to her eyes, as the tender old song went on. It was not all in the music, though the voice had once been rich and clear, and even now went straight to the heart in its wavering sweetness. There was something in the two faces opposite that spoke even more strongly than the singing. The gay little room in all its reds and yellows had faded away from them both; the old woman with her wrinkled face and darkened eyes, the gentle little lady smiling up to the calm, blue sky as she listened, both of them heard something more than the girl's ear could catch, and it was from a world beyond her that they came back as the last words died away : —

" Though no one here knows how fair the place is,
   Heaven knows how dear my poor home was to me."

France was sorry when they rose to go, and all the way home she talked about the visit, the queer room, the screaming parrot, the childish old woman who treated her as a baby, and sang as she had never heard any one sing before. She was eager to go again and quite unconscious that it was anything

more than an accident that Miss Marigold had taken
her there this morning.

So absorbed was the girl that she never noticed, as
they neared home, a face pressed against one of the
windows of the next house to her own — a young
face, with wistful eyes that followed France until she
entered her own door with a gay "Good-by!" to
Miss Marigold.

The conversation of the earlier part of their walk
had partly faded from France's mind, in the novelty
of her visit to Mrs. Reese, but it came back to her
as she opened the door of her home, and stood in the
narrow hall taking off her hat. It was a different
atmosphere in this noisy, populous place. France
stood a moment listening to the sound of Janie's
scales in the parlor at her right; to the clattering
boot-heels above, which proclaimed the fact that Jack
and Harry were having a fencing match in their bedroom ; and to the hubbub from the sitting room at the
left, where the crying of baby mingled with the shrill
voices of Win and Polly singing as they marched
about the room in the character of soldiers, and
where her step-mother's harassed voice was heard in
distressed entreaty.

"Katy, if you don't stop making Carlo bark, I
believe I shall go distracted!"

France listened, meditated, cast one glance up the

stairway toward her own room, where she could be free from interruption if she chose to shut herself up; and then opened the door of the sitting room, saying in her crisp young tones, —

"If you children will come upstairs with me, I'll tell you the longest fairy story you ever heard, while I'm starting Katy's skirts; and, Katy, if you'll put Carlo out-of-doors, and come up too, I'll let you paint with my own colors while I'm telling it!"

CHAPTER III

A NEIGHBORLY CALL.

"THEM there Ruggleses has been here," said Phebe, putting her head in at the sitting room door, as Miss Marigold came in. "Their ma wants some blackb'ry scrup that you promised her for the girl that's sick, an' they're comin' back for it. An' Mis' Stubbs, she's been arter your receipt for tea-cake, but I could n't find it, an' I told her if 't was only puddin' sauce, I knowed that off by heart, bein' you taught it to me only yesterday; but she says that would n't do, so she's comin' ag'in too. An' there's your sponge cake in the oven yet, because the fire went out while it was bakin', and I was afraid I'd do the wrong thing, so I jest let it alone till you come. Only it's fell flat, an' what be I to do?"

"And the professor and madame coming to tea!" sighed Miss Marigold. "Well, I don't suppose I ought to have left you to take it out of the oven. I thought you knew how to see to it. Anyhow, it's a good thing it's sponge cake, and no baking powder in it. You'd better kindle the fire up, and maybe it'll rise after all. And whenever the fire goes out when you're baking, the thing to do is to build it up again!"

166

"I 'll know next time," responded Phebe hopefully as she vanished in the direction of the kitchen.

" Most likely you will," said Miss Marigold, under her breath. "Only next time 'll never come, for it is n't more than once in a dozen years or so that I leave you to do anything alone, and when I do it 's always the death of it. However, as I said before, it 's lucky it 's sponge cake instead of something else."

The little woman moved lightly about the room, dusting and putting to rights as she spoke; picking up the petals that had fallen from a vase of flowers on the window sill, folding the white frock that lay finished on the workstand (a friendly lift to young Mrs. Brown with her twins), and putting away the book which she had been reading the evening before — a fat brown book from the corner of the bookshelf. She lingered a moment over this, turning it about in her hand, and even peeping into it lovingly, before she set it in its place.

"It may be frivolous," said Miss Marigold; "but if I was sick and laid up, I know it would do me good. Makes me as cool and happy in my mind as if I was in the woods by the river. It just goes flowing along."

"Sick and laid up." It was not strange that with the words should come a vision of the wistful face that looked out of the window at France Hayward

when she passed. Miss Marigold's clear eyes had
seen and caught the inmost meaning of the look that
France had missed altogether.

"Poor little thing!" she whispered to herself now.
"Tired out and lonely, most likely. I must just go
in there before this day's over."

The Winthrops had only lately moved into the
neighborhood, and no one on Beech Street knew them.
People had watched with curious eyes as they moved
in; the careworn mother in her mourning dress and
the daughter who had not been seen on the street
since she had been carried into the house from the
carriage. Jack Hayward reported that the mother
taught at the high school, and was "hard as flint-
stones when a boy was found in mischief," and France
said Jack ought to know, being in mischief every day
and all day long. This was all that was known of
the newcomers, and even Miss Marigold, who made
acquaintances with the facility of a child, had not
yet called upon them, though her heart had gone out
to the girl who had lived a life so different from that
of others of her age.

Miss Marigold could not help contrasting the two
faces that she had just seen; the one fresh, sweet,
and glowing with life and sunshine, made noble, too,
to-day, by the light of a new resolve which was to
give a deeper meaning to all the happy, careless days

through which it passed; the other pale and still,
looking silently down from a lonely window on the
gladness in which it had no share.

" If I could get France to be friends with her,"
thought Miss Marigold as she went about her work.
" If I could only get her to going there and taking
thought for a young thing like that, so near her own
age and yet shut up so, it would be just what she
needs. France does want taking out of herself a
little. Yes, she does, though a body'd think she'd
enough to take her out, with all those children. I
suppose that's just it; she needs outside things to
give heart to the home life. just *because* there's
so much of that. And that other poor child —
well, whether she's nice or whether she's sour —
which one would n't wonder at — it'll do France
good. I'll just go over there and find out, after
I've seen to the cake and taken that dress into Mrs.
Brown, and laid out the recipe for the Ruggles children, and copied that receipt for Mrs. Stubbs —
though why on earth Phebe never thought to give
her the book and let her hunt it out for herself !"

So it came about that Patty Winthrop, watching at
her window that noontime. saw a pleasant sight : a
bright-eyed, gray-haired little woman, standing on
the steps and smiling up at her with the sunniest face
in the world ; a face that made Patty's eyes brighten

and her cheek flush with pleasure, even before Miss
Marigold came in. She raised herself slowly on the
invalid chair where she lay, and turned an eager look
of welcome toward the door of the room as it opened.
If Miss Marigold had any doubts as to her reception,
they vanished completely before that greeting.

"My dear," she said as if she had known her all
her life, "my dear, I've been thinking about you all
the morning and saying to myself that it was a shame
that you should have been here a fortnight and not
had a call from me yet: so I've just come in, though
it *is* near dinner time, to get acquainted, and I've
brought some early clove pinks, because I think
there's nothing like them for bringing in the feeling
of outdoors, when one's shut up."

And Miss Marigold dropped a great bunch of the
spicy white blossoms into the girl's lap and sat down
close beside her, "looking as if she belonged just
there, and nowhere else in the world," as Patty told
her mother afterwards.

She gathered the flowers up in her hands, with eyes
that said more than words, in their grateful shining.

"How good you are!" she cried. "And they
came from that pretty garden that I can just catch
a glimpse of from my window. You see, I know
where you live. I've watched you every day since
we came here, and wished I knew about you."

" Have you?" said simple Miss Marigold in surprise. " Well, my dear, I 've watched you too, at
the window, and wondered about you. I thought you
must be lonely sometimes, these days when your
mother is at school. You must get acquainted with
us all. There are n't many young people on this
street, not counting children, I mean, and I for one
am always glad when a new girl's face comes to
brighten us all up."

Patty smiled joyously over her flowers.

" You don't look as if you needed brightening,"
she said ; " at least those of you that I 've watched
most, you and the little mother with the twins and
those children next door with their pretty sister. I
suppose they would be surprised enough if they knew
how much enjoyment I have out of them. What a
quantity of them there are ! And how ever do they
manage to get so much fun out of a day as they seem
to do? They are a real mystery to me ! "

" The Haywards? Yes ; there are eight of them,
counting France — that 's the oldest one," said Miss
Marigold, catching at a chance to speak of her favorite. " She 's a very dear child, France Hayward —
a dear child ; and I hope you 'll come to be great
friends. She will like to come to see you, I am
sure, if you would like to have her. I thought of it
this morning when I saw you at the window. · If

they can be friends,' I said; ' it will just do them good.' I'm so glad that you happened to take this house close by."

"So am I," said the girl heartily; "that is, I am very glad to be near you, and if that pretty girl will come in, it will be so pleasant. I love to watch her now. I have never had any friends of my own age, and the girls that I have seen since we came to Bentonville are like part of a great picture book to me. We have always lived in the country until this year. We lived with my uncle in a lonely place among the mountains, for he would always be where he could watch growing things and study animals and all that. Bernard has such a great collection of insects that uncle made! Bernard is my cousin — at least I call him so, for he was like a son to uncle, and every one calls him by our name. It was he that persuaded us to come here, for when uncle died, though he had thought that he was rich enough to leave us something, there was nothing, for he was always spending money in his science. Bernard came away to find something to do, and we waited till he wrote to us from this place, where he had found a situation in the great laboratory. We were so glad when he got the chance for mother to teach, and we could come and be near him ; and now that we have taken this house and he is coming to live with us, it will be almost like home again. He is so good to us — Bernard !"

" But it's a lonely life for you," said Miss Marigold, listening with interest. " And you have n't made friends since you 've been here? What do you do with yourself all day, child? "

She glanced about the room half unconsciously as she spoke, taking in every detail of the odd-looking apartment, from the piles of papers, books, and sketches on the round table to the drawings of forest scenes, flowers, and ferns, pinned upon the walls in curious confusion, wherever there was a good light; the tall bookcase, running over with books and magazines; the dainty knitting work that lay on the window seat beside Patty's chair; the microscope on a stand by itself, and the Maltese ringdove which sat pluming his creamy feathers beside it. Patty followed her glance with a little smile.

" It is n't like other people's rooms, is it? " she said. " Mother and Bernard are always reading and studying and writing, you know. I like it just as it is, though. Often, after they have gone away, I get Martha to push the table over here so that I can see what they have been doing the evening before — for Bernard spends all his evenings here. It is the funniest mixture sometimes. Last week I found Humboldt's Cosmos and Michelet's La Mer and Sir William Hamilton's Lectures, with Alice in Wonderland open at the Walrus and the Carpenter, and

Tennyson's poems with a German scientific magazine keeping the place in the middle of The Princess. Those sketches are Bernard's, and the violin is his, and the dove really belongs to him too, but they call him mine because he cares more for me than for any one else — don't you, Colin?"

She held out her hand to the bird as she spoke, and the pretty creature flew over to perch on her pillow and put up his bill against her cheek.

"Colin is my comrade," said Patty, smoothing his feathers lightly. "He keeps me company and entertains me, so that I sha'n't be lonely when they're gone. I should n't know what to do without Colin."

The bird cooed softly in response, turning his head to one side and looking up in her face with inquisitive, bright eyes.

"I wish I could understand what he says," said his mistress, smiling at Miss Marigold. "I know he understands me — at least sometimes. If he could talk, like Coo-my-doo in the old ballad, I should n't be in any danger of being lonely. As it is, it is n't half so much so as it might seem to outsiders. I can't bear to have people think I'm dismal and solitary here. Sometimes I think I have as good times as girls who can go about and do as they please. I believe there's just as much happiness in one life as another, if one only keeps one's eyes open a little, to pick it up — don't you? And then when one has n't quite so much as other people to start out with, everything that comes is just so much the pleasanter for being a sort of surprise, just as it was when you came in with your flowers after I had been watching you with Miss Hayward and wishing that I knew you. It was so good of you to come!"

The wistful look that had haunted Miss Marigold that morning was quite gone now, and the face on the pillow was as bright as France's own as the talk went on. Life had a very different look in Patty's eyes at the end of that hour of neighborly chatter and kindly good will.

" I 'm so glad we came to live on this street," she said, listening with eager interest to Miss Marigold's simple stories of life in Beech Street. " It was dull where we were before, and here there is something to watch all the time. I have come to feel as if I knew all about some people just from watching from the window. People are better to watch than the birds that I used to see in our old home, that were so tame they would come about the windows as the children here do when I smile at them. I 'm so glad you have told me about so many of the neighbors. I shall feel so well acquainted with them now, and it will be so pleasant to think it all over when I see them. It 's good to have new things to

think about — is n't it, Colin? For it *is* a little
lonely sometimes, when mother and Bernard are both
away."

"We won't let it be," said Miss Marigold, leaning
over to kiss the quiet young face that appealed so
strongly to her warm heart. "You're a dear, brave
child, and I can see already that we shall be real
friends, and we won't let you be alone so. A girl
ought n't to be. We're all neighbors here, and we
all help each other out when there's any call, and
you'll have your place among us all in no time. And
as for my France, — for she's like mine almost, my
dear, — I know that you'll enjoy each other through
and through; and when she comes in, as she will, you
must just tell her, as you've been telling me, about
the house in the woods and your being brought up
out-of-doors so, and the pets and the wild garden
and all the rest. It's all like a story. You won't
be left alone so any longer, I know that."

The sudden tears sprang to Patty's eyes. She put
up her hand and laid it on the soft old cheek beside
her for a moment, while Colin walked solemnly up
the pillow and stood meditatively surveying the visitor,
with his delicate wings outspread.

"You're so kind!" said Patty. "No one ever
came to me so before. It's just what I needed. If
I could only be with you sometimes, it will help me so

much, for I do need help now and then, and I thank you."

She brushed the tears from her eyes and drew back, beginning to talk again so gayly that little Miss Marigold, unused to such sudden transitions, was quite bewildered.

" I ought n't to speak so," said the girl, " for I really have n't had a chance to be lonely until to-day, there's been so much to see. Those children! I 've sat here and laughed till I cried, to see them climb about that yard, and tumble over each other, and invent games! If you could have seen one of the boys try to dance the Highland sword-dance with two barrel staves the other day! And the one that walks the fences and is always tumbling down and trying it over. She caught on the gatepost only last night, and hung there by her skirt, and her sister had to come out of the house and take her down ; and she did look as if she wanted to shake her. It 's as good as a play to watch them. And then there's such a queer old gentleman who comes past every day. He teaches somewhere, I think, and I must ask mother if she knows him. Do you know whom I mean? A tall, old man with a stoop, and very black eyes. He scowls fearfully all the time, and glares about him in the funniest way. Yesterday he walked over the smallest Hayward child, and picked him up as tenderly as a woman

would, and filled his pockets with chocolate drops,
scolding all he time, till I was quite enchanted, the
baby looked so divided in his mind between delight
and horror.   He evidently did n't know whether it was
an ogre or a prince in disguise."

"Oh, that's the professor!" cried Miss Marigold
delightedly.   "At least I call him the professor,
because mounseer is so hard to pronounce, and he
can't bear mister. He says it's a barbarous word.
The professor thinks almost everything in America is
barbarous. Poor man! he's had troubles, and I don't
suppose teaching French is the most calming way of
getting a living. He lives at the other end of the
street, and his wife is quite a beauty, though not very
easy in her mind, poor thing. I think a great deal of
the professor. He's as kind-hearted a man as ever
lived!"

"I like his looks," said Patty. "I wonder if I
could talk to him. Bernard belonged to a French
family, and he and mother have taught me French a
little, though not as much as I wish they had."

Miss Marigold sat up straight in her chair and
spoke out, quite unconsciously, in the dawning of a
new idea.

"The very thing!"

But then, seeing the girl's astonished look, she
made haste to cover the exclamation by hurrying into

a long story of the professor and his learning, his
queer ways, his struggles to make a living by teaching
in the high school and giving private lessons, and
"his poor wife, that's seen better days, and can't
settle down to scraping along as they have to do
now."

"There's hardly anybody that I think so much of
as I do of the professor," said Miss Marigold; "and
if folks should tell you that he is n't like people here,
and is always having ups and downs, — what with his
generous heart, and madame wanting pretty things,
and not a very regular income, — why, you must just
make up your mind that they don't understand him.
For you 'll come to know the professor, my dear; I 'm
sure of that."

She nodded and smiled to herself as she spoke,
and had altogether so exactly the appearance of a
little girl with a Christmas secret on the tip of her
tongue that Patty laughed outright.

"Do come again," she said, as Miss Marigold said
good-by. "I shall enjoy thinking over this visit all
the rest of the day."

Miss Marigold paused a moment with her hand on
the arm of the great chair, meditating.

"My dear," she said, as if she were owning a
weakness that might be received with laughter, "I
did n't ask you if you liked poetry, but if you did —

and some people do think it's good for the mind,
though I don't exactly mean the improving kind, like
Pope or Cowper, but "— she stopped with a little
laugh, and drew from under her shawl the fat brown
book which she had been reading the evening before
— " I thought, if you did, you might like this. The
Faërie Queene, it's called, and though it does go
flowing along like a river in a wood, and has knights
and ladies and shepherdesses all together, and makes
your mind seem to go floating off where you forget
the world and everything that's going on, in a way
some mightn't approve, it's just what a person likes
to have in a quiet day, and I brought it over in case
it turned out that you might like poetry. And it's
an allegory, after all," she went on in a tone of self-
defense, " and if you took pains to study it out, it
might do you good, though the trouble with me is that
I keep forgetting all about it, it winds along so and
sounds so sweet."

" She's a sort of good fairy herself," thought
Patty, taking the book with delight.

Miss Marigold looked back from the street a
moment, as she went away, and saw her sitting with
hands full of flowers, and a glow in her face that
made it almost transfigured from what it had been
an hour before.

Some one else noticed the change too. A young

man, walking up the street in such haste that he brushed against the little lady at her gate, and swerved aside with a hurried apology — an impetuous. broad-shouldered young man, with the brownest face, the brightest smile and the darkest eyes that Miss Marigold had ever seen. She watched him as he dashed up the steps of the Winthrop house, waving his hat to the girl at the window, and she said to herself with instinctive liking, " That must be Bernard ! "

CHAPTER IV.

BABY DISTINGUISHES HIMSELF.

A CRISIS in the Hayward household! Patty Winthrop, watching everything that went on at her end of the street, became aware of this fact by ten o'clock of a certain fresh, sweet morning in the week after Miss Marigold had made her first visit to the sick girl's room.

That had been a pleasant week to Patty. It was a new experience to the lonely girl to have a real neighbor close at hand, ready to smile a good-morning as she passed the door, running in at delightfully unexpected times, with a bunch of flowers for the window sill or a tempting, white-covered dish, with "Just a new experiment, dearie, that I wanted somebody besides me to try!" The days that had seemed long, in spite of the street sights which she was so fond of watching, grew short and sweet, when at any moment she might catch a glimpse of that gentle, happy face, with its crown of soft gray hair and its lovely sunny eyes. Patty looked on with a heart full of tender thoughts, while Miss Marigold went in and out, talking to the children on the street; going to and fro with the little basket that held comforts for other helpless ones besides herself; stopped on her way to market by anxious women eager to confide burdens of every description to her loving keeping, and coming home on certain days with a sort of heavenly shadow on her face that caused the watcher to decide inwardly, "It's some kind of a meeting this time. People don't have that uplifted sort of look unless they're thinking of the highest things they ever think of."

But this morning it was another kind of shadow that lay on the little woman's face as she stood with Mrs. Hayward on the sidewalk, looking down the street.

"I don't see where the child can be," Patty heard her say, and Mrs. Hayward answered despondingly: —

"I wouldn't have believed that he could get out of sight with all of us around. If only anybody had seen him go! but I've asked every one I've seen on the street and no one knows."

Patty sat up a little straighter to listen. Could it be the baby? Every one in the neighborhood knew baby Hayward, the blithest, prettiest, and most mischievous of the whole riotous brood. Patty had seen him only that morning, marching up the street in his pink gingham frock with a gay silk handkerchief floating over his shoulder by way of a flag, and all his bright curls falling about his face.

"We are little pilg'ims, marchin', marchin',"

he had sung in his silvery baby voice, and she had listened, laughing, as the last words floated back to her:

"To a country better far,
   Where our tounggan tingom are!"

Was he running away then? The naughty, brave little darling!

She leaned out of the window to attract the mother's notice; but even as they spoke the two women moved away, searching in the other direction, and the girl was left to herself. Then came a time of hurry and flurry in Beech Street. Win and Polly dived in and out of the Hayward house, searching in gutters and under doorsteps with the unerring sagacity of children. Katy, the fence-walker, having apparently taken advantage of the general excitement to forget school, explored every out-of-the-way nook in the yard, and even climbed the maple tree in front of the house to get a better view of the surrounding premises, wriggling down to the ground with unseemly haste and want of dignity as France appeared around the corner from an expedition to the candy store, where it was supposed the recreant baby might have been tempted to go. Mrs. Brown and Mrs. Edwards came out and joined in the search, and every passer-by was eagerly interrogated. Even Mr. Hayward came up from the office presently with an additional wrinkle in his anxious brow, which already seemed to have fulfilled the old prophecy of " a line of care for ilka bairn."

All this time Patty sat at her window, unable to catch the attention of any of the hurrying seekers, quite forgotten by them, and ready to weep for vexation that she, the only one who knew which way the child had gone, should not be able to speak out. It was not until M. Dubois came slowly up the street on his way from the morning lesson at the high school, that she found some one to hear her. Patty knew the keen-eyed, frowning face of " the professor " so well by this time, that it seemed quite natural to her to call him appealingly by the name Miss Marigold had given him.

" O professor ! " she cried, and the old man stopped, looking curiously into the flushed young face, with its tearful eyes and trembling lips.

" Can I serve you, mademoiselle ? " he said, with a grand bow and a face studiously devoid of surprise at this unceremonious greeting. But Patty was too eager to think of formality.

" It 's the baby that 's lost," she said hurriedly. " Don't you know, the one you knocked down one day, and gave him chocolate drops to make up for it? And they 've asked everybody but me. and they look in the wrong direction, for he went up past here, and

out the next street above. I saw him just after
mother went to school. Oh! won't you tell them,
so that they 'll go that way?"

M. Dubois dropped his dignity in a moment.
"The baby? The little one?" he cried; "and lost?
Ah! you were right to stop me! A young lady of
kind heart! And where is this poor mother? Ah!
I know what it is to lose a child!"

He whirled about and hurried off, his white hair
streaming behind him, and his loose coat flapping as
he went. The flock of hunters gathered about him,
Mrs. Hayward and France, pale and frightened, in
the midst. Then there was a brief consultation under
Patty's window, another scattering of forces and more
hours of hurrying back and forth, the old professor
joining in the search with his frown deeper than ever,
while the older Hayward children came loitering home
from school to be sent hastily out on errands of
inquiry, and the neighbors began to shake their heads
and whisper forebodings as the day wore on without
news. But Patty was not left to herself again. Mrs.
Hayward and Miss Marigold, France, Mrs. Brown,
and the professor, one and all stopped to speak to her
and tell her of their progress as they passed the house.
That anxious, watching face, with the dark eyes that
looked out so eagerly for a stranger child, drew them
all to her, half unconsciously, and Patty made more

acquaintances in that day than in the whole year before she came to Bentonville. There was a sort of exhilaration to her in the very sensation of being "counted in" as one of the interested members of that busy, neighborly community, and when Mrs. Winthrop came home from school at four o'clock she found her daughter, with Win and Polly Hayward on either side of her, keeping them out of mischief and "off their mother's mind" with stories and picture books, while France's anxious, grateful face appeared through the window, as she stopped the twentieth time that day to say that there was no news of baby, though her father had just gone off to see the tenth lost child at the central police station.

"I'm beginning to be so afraid," said France, with a sudden break in her voice. "There's the river — and he's heard Jack and Harry talk about it so much! But oh, you can't tell what a relief it is to have Win and Polly here! I don't see what we should have done without you to-day!"

France could not understand the wave of glad color that swept over Patty's face at the words.

Meanwhile the cause of all this commotion was engaged in proving a triumphant exception to the rule that "the way of transgressors is hard." That day was long marked with a white stone in baby Hayward's mental calendar. From the moment when he had set out " a-maying," lured by the dim memory of woods and fields which he had visited long before on a drive, success had followed his erring footsteps. The very street car which he had entered under protection of the draperies of an unconscious lady had landed him on the outskirts of town, with only a green field between him and a paradise of tangled woods that were the delight of every truant in Bentonville. Baby laughed aloud for pure joy when he had wriggled through the fence and stood knee-deep in the young, sweet grass that showed blue patches of beauty all about him — patches which first revealed to his soul the origin of violets.

"Tumbled out of 'e sky!" he said, looking critically up at the deep, calm azure overhead.

He filled his hands with the flowers and let them drop again in a misty trail behind him as he pushed on toward the woods. There were streaks of lilac and purple over yonder that were prettier than blue, he thought, though when the shadows of the trees were reached the wild crane's-bill was quite forgotten for the gray rocks crowned with nodding columbine a little farther in. Oh, the columbine! How it danced and swayed from every mossy stone, and flung up its red lanterns in a carnival of elfin beauty! Baby clapped his hands and danced too, tossing his yellow head like one of the flowers. It seemed to him that

he had found a new world — a place full of treasure,
and all for him.

Deeper and deeper among the trees he went, now
stopping to look into the heart of some new wonder,
now sitting down to rest, now gazing with innocent
sweet eyes up the line of some great elm, flecked with
golden lights and crowned with shimmering young
leaves. " 'Way up!" whispered the small explorer.

Here and there, in the sunny places, early butterflies
hovered about the blossoms, or flitted like gleams
of sunshine before his face, as if to lure him farther
into this wilderness of beauty. Once, with a cry
of joy, he pounced upon a great globe of clear
yellow, hanging, like a baby moon, under the shade
of a far-spreading oak. It was not half so pretty
when he brought it out to the sunshine, but he carried
it carefully in one hand, and called it " my lamp,"
calling out to the butterflies, " Come, I'll show you
the way!" as he plunged into the deep glooms again.
But long before he began to grow tired of the en-
chantments of this palace of springtime, the young
monarch discovered that he and the butterflies were
not alone in the woods. Toiling up the side of a
tiny hollow, full of young fern leaves, just unfurling
their furry scrolls, Baby caught the sound of a clear
voice singing.

" Mon cœur joyeux, plein d'espérance!"

it rang out, filling the woods with the swinging melody, and though the small listener could not understand a word, he caught the gladness of the strain, and hurried on to find the singer. There he was, sitting under a tree, with a pile of green leaves and flowers about him, and a notebook on his knee in which he was busily sketching: a tall, broad-shouldered young man, with brown face and keen, dark eyes that opened wide in amazement at sight of the yellow-haired invader of his solitude.

He lifted his hat ceremoniously and bowed low as Baby stopped and surveyed him with leisurely independence.

"Good-morning, your majesty!" he said. "I take it for granted that I am speaking to the spirit of the orchid that you carry in your hand. I hope you are not offended at seeing me in your grounds."

"That ain't the way to talk!" said Baby scornfully. "Nobody knows what it means. Can't tell what the singin' means either. What's your name?"

"Bernard Winthrop, at your service," replied the stranger with a twinkle in his eyes. "May I ask yours?"

"*Not* Baby!" said the young hero decidedly.

"Baby! Of course not! Babies don't go exploring through the woods by themselves. But I suppose you *have* a name? Most people have. I have four myself."

Baby stopped and surveyed him with leisurely independence.   Page 190.

" Badyady," said Baby in a wild attempt to pronounce his rightful title, and the young man dutifully pronounced it after him with becoming gravity.

" And where do you live, Mr. Badyady?"

" In my house."

" Probably. How did you come here?"

" On 'e street cars."

" Hum!" said the stranger thoughtfully; " and so you 're lost."

" No!" said Baby with emphasis. " I 'm findin' flowers. Don't want to go back."

The young man sat thinking in silence for a few moments. Then he spoke out meditatively.

" Well, I don't suppose you do. But I do suppose your mother 's half wild about you. Now, look here. It 's noontime now, and I 've got to stay out here till I find a certain plant that they say grows in these woods. I must have it to-day. Now, I can't go back with you yet, because, don't you see? I was sent out here to do a special thing. It 's just where I belong, which is more than you can say. Now you stay with me a while, for you 'll be dead tired before you know it. You 're miles from home. I 'll give you some dinner and take you home the minute I get my work done. Don't you know what street you live on, or anything about the house? Who lives near you?"

Baby's spirits, which had begun to droop under the explanation, grew bright again at the last question.

" Miss Marigold," he said succinctly.

A sudden light broke over the stranger's face.

" Patty's fairy godmother! Beech Street! Of course!" he said. "That's fortunate! Now I'll be bound you're one of those children that Patty talks about so much, next door. Now we know where we are! Eat your dinner, Mr. Badyady, and I'll hunt while you're at it, and we'll make quick time home, as soon as we can." He drew a small package from his pocket, and opened it on his guest's lap, laughing at the speed with which the last crumb disappeared. Then followed a few hours more of woodland roaming, while the two dived into dell and hollow, gathering flowers and leaves, peeping into an occasional bird's nest, now and then stopping while a sketch was made, and again pushing on, baby riding high and triumphant on his new friend's shoulder, and listening with comfortable immunity from anxiety to his careless singing.

The shadows were beginning to deepen under the trees before the object of Bernard's search was found and placed in his botanical case, with a whoop of exultation which caused his companion to regard him with patronizing wonder from his perch on his shoulder. Baby was even then hardly willing to bid good-by to the woods, but the moment the specimen was secured his protector broke into a hasty march toward home, and the short period of complete liberty, toward which Baby always looked back as the golden age of his childhood, was over.

It was twilight as Bernard came down Beech Street, with his little charge nestled asleep in his arms, a picture of rosy peace and happiness, with not the slightest shadow of guilt on his smooth baby brow. To-morrow he would melt into tears at the reproaches of his mother, and the brightness of his sunny memory would be dimmed by the inevitable result of childish wrongdoing; but to-night his sky was clear and serene. There were lights in Mrs. Winthrop's parlor as they came to it, and Bernard saw Patty's face pressed against the window, and caught the sudden pleasure that flashed across it at sight of him with the child in his arms; but the next moment he had forgotten her, for out of the next house came flying another figure — France, with her shining hair and startled glad eyes, with parted lips, and hands outstretched to take her little brother.

"You have found him! O Baby! Baby!" she cried.

In a moment they were all about him — Mrs. Hayward sobbing for joy, the father shaking Bernard by the hand and forgetting to stop till one of the children pulled his arm; the younger ones bursting into a babel of talk; Miss Marigold laughing and crying together, and Mrs. Winthrop, from next door, forgetting reserve in the excitement of the moment. But while he answered questions, parried thanks, and gave an account of the proceedings of the small prodigal, Bernard's eyes turned again and again to one of the party, and even after the evening was over, and he sat in his own room spreading out his specimens by lamplight, the same picture rose unaccountably between him and his work — an open doorway, with the light streaming into the dark street and falling full on one lovely figure, a girl with shining hair and wide gray eyes, and arms clasped about a rosy child who lay asleep with cheek close to hers.

CHAPTER V.

THE professor and his wife lived at the upper end of Beech Street, in one of the most unattractive of the commonplace brick houses which filled that part of Bentonville. There was no attempt at a garden before it, not even the bed of geraniums or the gypsy kettle of lobelia and wandering Jew with which most of the neighbors decorated their grass plats. Far be it from M. Dubois to imitate the custom of an American street, even though it were one which secretly pleased his critical soul. The old Frenchman looked upon the inhabitants of the New World as a race of barbarians, with only here and there a scattered spirit, like a rough diamond among pebbles, capable of appreciating the glories of Europe and of sitting at the feet of France, as the light-bearer of the nations. So the professor's flowers were banished from the front of the house and only secretly cultivated in the corners of the back yard and in the windows of the little sitting room, where he and his wife sat together this evening, the one trifling with embroidery and the other pacing up and down the room with nervous haste and impatience.

The monthly accounts always occasioned a disturbance of the domestic atmosphere at the professor's. There was a pile of papers in the old man's hands now, and the lines between his eyes grew deeper and deeper as he looked at them. Between worry in the class room and anxiety over the " wherewithal " of home life, those lines were becoming very deep indeed as the professor grew older. His hand shook slightly as he grasped the papers, and his ceaseless march about the room showed plainly the stoop in his shoulders and the droop of the head that had evidently been carried proudly enough in bygone days.

Madame Dubois, meanwhile, sat calmly at work, with an expression of studied carelessness in her eyes, and with one foot restlessly tapping the little velvet hassock before her chair. Madame Dubois made it a point not to be interested in the monthly settlement of affairs. What business was it of hers if the bills were larger than the professor expected! Did not he do the marketing himself, and was not he the house-provider? Madame stitched away at her embroidery and looked out of the window in superior silence.

" He grows old day by day," she thought within herself.

" It will take almost the whole of this month's

money, and what shall I do for the robe she must have for the warm weather, and the fruit that she needs now when the springtime comes on?" thought the professor, casting an appealing glance around the room as if he expected an answer from the ivy-covered wall or from the St. Cecilia who looked out with calm, rose-crowned forehead from over the fire-place.

It was a pretty room, this household chamber of the Duboises. The neighbors, who were so fond of laughing at the odd ways of the foreigners, would have been surprised if they had passed the bare exterior of the house and come into this one little nook of comfort and beauty, with the luxuriant vines, the pictures, the soft chair where madame sat at the window, the dainty work-table, with its bit of a faïence vase, always filled with flowers, and the tiny bookcase with its red silk curtains and its shelves crammed with worn volumes in half a dozen languages.

The professor used to stand in bookstores and dream pleasant dreams over the treasures to be found there — dreams of additions to his little library, and of large bookshelves full of beautiful editions, with the place of honor reserved for his old friends in their cracked binding; but he never brought new books home. Madame did not care for reading. The truth

was that madame cared for very little in these days.
The tired professor, with his anxious eyes and weary
heart, could remember a time when his wife had been
gay and happy from morning till night; the gayest
and happiest, as she was the prettiest, in the far-off
town where their home had been.

That was long ago. Sometimes the memory of
those days came back to him like a beautiful dream
that had never been true. Across his eyes would
flit the vision of a vine-covered hill, crowned with
gray towers that gleamed rosy in the setting sun; of
a quaint old town climbing halfway up the height,
with red-roofed houses standing fair against the misty
green of the trees; of a rocky beach, where the waves
were always dashing in wild jubilee, and of the pier,
with all its cheerful bustle, as peasants in clattering
sabots, and bourgeois serene in conscious respecta-
bility, gathered to watch the ships that floated up
the harbor like white-winged birds, or went sailing
away like clouds across the limitless sea, bearing —
The professor broke away from the pleasant dream
with a wrench when it reached this point, and turned
again to his classes, with eyes and voice made sharp
by inward pain. The mischievous boys and girls,
always on the lookout for cause of laughter in their
daily lessons, were sure to spend a part of their
recess in hilarious reproduction of " monsieur's tan-
trum," after such a vision had come to him in class.

Sometimes, sweeter still, came faces smiling at him across a mist of troublous cares — faces of little children — the children who had once been his. He saw them, his brown-eyed boys, with their smooth, dark heads against the cheek of their young mother. Could her fresh, joyous face be that of the faded, fretful woman who sat in the easy-chair at the west window? Sometimes his little daughter came dancing to meet him, with chestnut locks flying in the wind, and arms outstretched to clasp his neck ; little Didine, the first to fly from the nest to the heavenly country, where her older brothers so soon followed her. Their father thought of them with tender longing, even now, when the last of them had been sleeping for twenty years on the green hillside across the ocean. The same words sprang involuntarily to his mind whenever he thought of them : —

"Les reverrai-je un jour? Mon Dieu, reviendront-elles,
    Ainsi que le ramier qui traversa les flots,
M'apporter un rameau des palmes immortelles,
Et me dire, la-haut est un nid pour vos ailes,
    Une terre, un lieu de repos?"

There was no bitterness in the memory of these innocent darlings of his heart ; but a deeper shadow fell over his brow at thought of another face which rose beside them : the face of his other child, the silent boy who was left behind when the shadow of death fell over his father's house; the youngest son, almost forgotten by father and mother in their grief over the lovelier ones who were gone; the boy who grew up, carelessly watched and tended, while his mother grieved her heart away and lost the light and beauty from her face in fruitless pining, and his father shut himself up with books, or studied in vain the problem how to retrieve his failing worldly fortunes; the boy who spent his days among the peasants, on shore and hillside, or deep in the boundless forest, learning to know and love every plant and blossom within miles of his home; drinking in knowledge from brooks and trees and wildwood creatures, and poring over books of travel and adventure, until at last, while still a child, he disappeared, — slipped away into the great world, — leaving behind him empty hearts and longing love that he had never known were his. The professor's voice, always gentle as he spoke to his wife, grew more tender when the memory of this deepest sorrow was bitter in his thought, and it was at such times that the flowers in the faïence vase were renewed most often, and that he ransacked his slender purse for the little luxuries which might bring a smile to that worn, unsatisfied face.

Only one of the Beech Street people had access to the professor's house. That one was little Miss Marigold.

" Mees Marigold," said the professor, " is not Américaine ! She is above America — she is — Christian. Mees Marigold is an angel of God — a messenger ! She does me honor in calling me friend — though the perfection of her charackter might still be enhanced if I could prevail upon her, even at this day, to receive a course of instruction in the French language, that she might be introduced into the glories of that tongue the most elevated — that literature the most sublime ! "

Into the midst of the painful atmosphere of monthly accounts and harassing cares came Miss Marigold, on this evening; tripping up the street with her work in her hand, as her wont was when she dropped in for a " real visit " at one of her neighbors' houses. That there was some especial purpose on her mind just now was made evident by the light in her eyes and the air of secret delight mingled with anxiety which pervaded her whole presence. The fact was that the little lady, after a fortnight of meditation over the two young hearts which she had made up her mind must be brought together, was ready for the carrying out of her plan, and in her own light-hearted fashion of complete absorption in the fortunes of those in whom she was interested, was brimming over with eagerness to consult the professor and discover if any obstacles lay in the way of her desire.

Her face was so happy as she entered the room
that even madame's grew bright in spite of herself,
and she gave gracious thanks for the bunch of pansies
that was laid on her table, though madame's conver-
sations with Miss Marigold were rendered constrained
by the fact that she had resolutely resisted the learning of English ever since leaving her own home, so
that a few detached sentences were all that she could
be prevailed on to utter.

"To understand the tongue hideous is sufficient,"
said madame, with appalling frankness.

The professor, on his part, welcomed the little
woman with a beaming face, and began suddenly to
perceive the cheerful side of certain experiences of
the day, which had rasped his sensitive soul almost
to the point of frenzy.

"See, then, mademoiselle," he said, in answer to
his friend's inquiries about lessons, "of what use
is the French to these sheep of infants in your
schools. *Écoutez!* This morning one young girl
frightful, with hair about her brows and what you
call—bangle?—on wrists, asked me how to pronounce the name of Chopin. I tell her, amazed that
one should ask the question of a name so illustrious—
and then, mademoiselle, what think you was the
succeeding question—this girl, this demoiselle in the
School of Music? 'But, monsieur,' she said (ah,

so sweetly!), 'how do you pronounce Chopin in English?'"

" And what did you answer?" said Miss Marigold, with interest.

" I looked upon her!" responded the indignant teacher, with a glare of the eyes which called forth a sudden peal of laughter from his sympathetic listener — " I looked upon her and answered with irony, as she deserved. ' Mademoiselle, how do you pronounce Washington in French?' But she answered, ' I — don't — know, monsieur'; and I turned my back upon her in despair. Of what use is it, I ask you, mademoiselle, that such young girls should go to school?"

" Well, I don't exactly know," responded Miss Marigold, " but there might be worse things, you know. And after all, I do wish, myself, that some of those names were a little easier to pronounce. You see, when they end in *n*, professor, they sound so very strange, that there are a great many men I've read about that I never dare speak of just because of that, and if one only *could* just say them in the easiest way! But then of course you know best."

" Worse things!" replied the professor, with grim humor — " that I well know. There is a youth of fifteen in my college class who gave me, in an exercise on Rome, the names Palestine, Philistine, and Quarantine, as three of the Seven Hills! Yes, mademoiselle, there *are* worse things. If one should people a colony of dunces from your public schools, one would take Master Reese before Mees — I will not mention the title of the young girl. One should be tender of the young ladies."

Miss Marigold sighed gently over her knitting.

"Well, I'm sorry if Johnny Reese is so stupid," she said. "His father is my butcher, you know, and his mother is dead; he has only an old grandmother who is almost blind, and so proud because Johnny goes to the high school! They are saving everything they can to send him to college and make a minister of him. Poor Johnny! He's so good at home. I'm sorry if he can't get through."

The professor's keen eyes grew soft as she spoke.

"It is true that goodness is before learning, mademoiselle. Perhaps I can help the boy a little. His worthy parents should not be disappointed — though Master Reese in a pulpit!" The old man threw back his head and laughed a laugh that did Miss Marigold's soul good to hear; while madame smiled again her quick, restless smile over her embroidery. Miss Marigold took advantage of the clearing away of the clouds that hung over her friends as she entered, to slip into the story of Patty Winthrop and her lonely life. The little woman grew quite eloquent in telling her simple tale, and M. Dubois sat down and listened with face growing gentler and gentler as the story went on.

"I've been there every day, nearly, for the last two weeks," said Miss Marigold, "and the poor little thing takes right hold of me, professor. I can't help thinking about her, making the most of everything she has, and living along in that brave way, feeling guilty if she gets lonely, and just longing for a chance to be of use in the world. And the only young friend she has is that cousin of hers, that's off at his botanizing, day in and day out — not but what it's his business, and he brings her home handfuls of wild flowers, and sings and talks like a magpie, and makes the house lively of an evening when he can be at home; but he is n't like a girl, and she ought to have something to do with girls. Now there's France Hayward, next door. You know France, professor, for you taught her in the high school, and she's so pretty that one does n't forget her. Besides, you were there when that mischief of a baby ran away last week. And France is as sweet a girl as ever lived, but just tied down at home with all those children, and her mother not strong; and what she wants more than anything else is something to take her out of the grind a bit. She wants to *reach out*, you know," Miss Marigold said with simple

wisdom, " and anything that will bring her close to
Patty will do her good. So I was thinking that
if they had something regular, something to keep
them at work a little together, why that would be
just what they need, both of them. They're beginning to take to each other already, with Patty persuading the little children to come in there to stay
with her, and France seeing her at the window every
day so. So if you *could* just tell me what you charge
for giving lessons, professor, for I 've sounded 'em
both and they know about the same amount of it,
and it would be just the very thing!" concluded the
little woman with a sudden burst, as if she had kept
her plan to herself to the last moment of her power
and now let it out regardless of consequences.

The professor straightened up in his chair with
involuntary relief. Two more scholars! The robe
for madame should be forthcoming now. It never
entered his simple mind that this very result of the
arrangement had been a part of Miss Marigold's
deep-laid plot. He entered into the idea with enthusiasm.

" For Mees Winthrop," he said eagerly, "that
young lady of so kind heart, who looked out so weel
for the neighbor child — ah, I shall teach her with
delight! I will show her the treasures of our language. My books — she shall read them all, she and

the other. But for the price—and her mother a teacher—and she a child of sorrow—and I too have seen sorrow—mademoiselle, the custom is not that one teacher should ask of one teacher the price of an outside one! Half the price is sufficient!"

He said this with eyes on his wife's face, and his apparent expectation was justified by a glance of well-directed surprise and a slight elevation of madame's delicate eyebrows.

"And the accounts, my friend?" she said in a low tone, looking at the pile of papers which still lay on the table.

The professor flushed slightly.

"But they cannot pay the whole, Julie!" he said, with a faint touch of irritation in his voice.

Miss Marigold made haste to change the subject, and for an hour or so the talk ran on gardening, needlework, and the like safe topics, while madame's face gradually lost its usual discontented expression and grew calm and quiet as it always did while with her gentle little neighbor. But when Miss Marigold said good-by, the professor followed her to the door and there in a sudden whisper stated his mind on the subject of the lessons.

"She does not see! she does not know!" he cried, with an emphatic gesture toward the door they had left. "You see, my friend, she is not what she was!

It is the grief! But as for me, the price will be
nothing! nothing! It is all I can give. I will teach
the poor sick one for the sake — ah! mademoiselle,
for the sake of the good God who gives us all. But
to her say that it is as a fellow-teacher! that also is
truth. We are friends, you and I — we will help the
dear children together."

And Miss Marigold, going out into the moonlight
with Phebe for protection, thought with a glow of
pleasure at her heart, " I have n't the right to say
no to him. And now it 's my part to fix it for France,
as he 's done for Patty — for the sake of Him who
gives us all."

CHAPTER VI.

YES, she's to home, but she ain't to be seen."
    Phebe stood in the back doorway uncompromisingly regarding a discouraged-looking small boy who sat on the lowest step with a fat baby in his arms, looking as though he had dropped down the moment that he could take advantage of an opportunity to rest.

"Why ain't she to be seen?" he responded gloomily, propping up the baby against his shoulder.

"She's shut up in the press room, up garret, and I ain't goin' to rout her out for no Ruggleses nor nobody. She says to me, 'I'm a-goin' up garret, and I'd like to be left to myself a while;' and she's a-goin' to be," said Phebe, setting her lips with evident enjoyment of her authoritative denial.

"Sit up, will ye?" muttered the small boy, regarding his charge with contempt. "Much good you be for a baby! Bill Jones' baby, it can walk. Great fun it is to lug you round and then not see anybody after all. Now I s'pose I've got to lug you home again!"

"Think likely," said the unsympathizing Phebe.

209

"I'd like to know how you'd like it yourself," said the boy, transferring his resentment from baby to girl. "Jest s'posin' you had to keep house and cook the dinner and everythin' as if you was a girl, —might as well be named Jemimy as Jedediah,— with your mother off washin' and Mary Jane sick and the other two young ones a-fightin' and a-squallin' and a-knockin' the best teacup off the sink, which I had n't got no chance to wash it up yet, and ma that'll blame it on to me! And if I'm big enough to see to everythin', seems to me I'd ough' ter be too big to get a whippin' for everythin' what gets broke when I'm a-lookin' after 'em!" concluded the young housekeeper misanthropically.

"Well, did you jest come traipsin' up here to tell Miss Marigold all that yarn?" asked Phebe.

"No, I did n't. I come to ask her about the rice," said Jedediah, fairly melting into tears over the head of the unmoved baby.

"There was ma, she told me to put on a half a teacup of it in the water for Mary Jane, and Mary Jane she says she knowed it war' n't enough and she was sure she'd want about all there was in the bag, and I put it on, and it comes up and comes up and comes up, and biles over, and sozzles out, and there's the dipper and the tin pan and the potato dish full, and the bottom beginnin' to burn and nothin' to put

any more in, and what ma 'll say I don't know. How
was we to know it 'd spread out like that? Worse 'n
umbrellas! There 's five times as much now as
there was when I put it in, and it 's comin' more all
the time; so I set it off and come up to ask her, and
now she ain't to be seen, and how 'll I know what to
do when I get back?"

"You can't do *nothin'*," said Phebe solemnly.
"You 'll jest have to live on rice till it 's used up,
that 's all; and next time you better do as you 're told.
I 'll tell you what I 'll do, though. I ain't a-goin' to
call Miss Marigold, but I know she 'd give you
somethin' to help you out, and I 'll jest take the
considility and give it to ye myself."

She vanished into the pantry, and Master Ruggles
devoted himself to meditation with a faint gleam of
comfort dawning in his troubled countenance.

It was a lovely, sunshiny morning, and the little
garden was looking its very best in the sweet light.
The last violets and the first pansies were smiling together from their border, and the tulips were all ablaze
with crimson, gold, and dazzling white. A bed of nar-
cissus lay full in a beam of sunshine that fell through
the pink-wreathed boughs of the one apple tree, and
a couple of pigeons were walking about near it, their
burnished throats gleaming softly as they turned their
heads. Overhead the sky was blue and clear, and

the wild, sweet song of a wren floated down from the topmost boughs of some neighboring tree. Across the fence could be seen the yellow heads of the three younger Hayward children as they chased each other like butterflies about the yard, and through the window came the voice of their elder sister, singing at her sewing, —

"Sweet Wicklow Mountains, the sunlight sleepin'
   On your green banks is a picture rare.
You crowd around me like young girls peepin',
   An' puzzlin' me to say which is most fair —
As though you'd see your own sweet faces
   Reflected in that smooth and silver sea.
My blessin''s on those lovely places,
   Though no one cares how dear they are to me!"

But the lovely air had lost the hint of sadness that had thrilled through it as Mrs. Reese sang. In France Hayward's blithe young voice, it sounded only sweet and glad, like the glow of a golden memory in a sunset sky.

Presently Phebe came back through the kitchen with a paper bag of sandwiches in her hand, and a red apple, which she stuffed into Jedediah's pocket, standing on the steps to watch him as he went away, with the cares of life still printed on his brow and the baby hanging over his shoulder, making futile snatches at the flowers as they passed.

" If she 'd a-known there was one of them young ones here she 'd 'a' be'n down in quick time," thought Phebe, with a chuckle. " Queer what makes her take such a shine to every ragged boy and girl that comes along."

Meanwhile, up in the storeroom under the eaves, Miss Marigold sat before an open trunk with a pile of soft white within it, over which she was leaning in a sort of daydream, forgetting to lift it out or to wipe away the tears that dropped upon it as she gazed.

Memories of the sweetest and saddest time of all her tranquil life were shut away in that little trunk, and while she looked into it, and touched the soft mull at the top with tender fingers, thirty years had slipped away from her, and she was young again : a fair, soft-eyed girl, standing, all in white, on the steps of a rose-covered porch, and watching for a form that was sure to come up the street before the twilight deepened into darkness.

That pretty gown with all its dainty embroidery and falling lace had lain out of sight ever since that summer, taken out and aired occasionally by its owner's careful hand, and thought of with a sort of tender warmth of heart, as holding the joys of that bygone time, even now when the roses of those days lay withered in the ebony box, and when Miss Mari-

gold had grown old alone. But now there had come
a call for it, her heart was thrilling with soft excitement as she looked it over and thought of its coming
out into the everyday world again.

" Just as good as new," she decided, fingering the
delicate fabric, " and just what she wants. Queer it
should come so hard to get it out. Prissy Marigold,
I hope you are not growing selfish, when you know
as well as can be that you can't give that dear child
the money, and that if they can save the price of
a new summer gown they'll jump at the chance of
giving her the lessons. What good is it to you now,
you lonely old woman? No, not lonely, not lonely,
thank God!" She lifted her head and looked out
beyond the dark old rafters — was it into the heavenly
kingdom? Into Miss Marigold's face came a light
and gladness that made it lovelier than it had ever
been in the days of its young sweetness. She lifted
out the dainty gown and carried it to her own room,
laying it on the bed and turning it over to make sure
that it was quite in order.

" France will be as pretty as a picture in it,"
she thought. And then before leaving the room the
simple little woman fell on her knees at the bedside
and hid her face in her hands.

" Lord," she said softly, " any one would think
I was the most foolish old woman in the world, to go

on so over an old dress ; but thou knowest all about it. And I do thank thee that I have it all to look back to, and that this one little piece of that happy time is n't all I have of it. I thank thee that it is all here safe in my heart, and that I have a chance to give a little tithing of that joy to help one of thy children, even in such a small way."

Mrs. Hayward and France sat together at the mending that morning, talking confidentially over the decreasing pile of worn garments. They were planning out the summer's expenditures and rejoicing over the fact that father's salary was to be slightly raised, and that the prospects were fair for a pretty summer outfit for the girls.

"If I can have a new dress myself," said France, holding up a forlorn pinafore to decide on the best place for beginning a darn, " if I can, — and I must have something, you know, mamma, — why then I shall just make over my blue muslin for Janie. It will be so becoming to her, the dear little thing ! and there 'll be enough left for a slip for Polly."

Janie was France's favorite among all the children ; a clinging, affectionate child, with gentle ways and soft voice, the only quiet one among them all.

"It 's just a delight to work for Janie," said her sister fondly ; " she 's so happy when one does anything for her. I 'll look up the patterns to-morrow, so as to be ready when the warm days come."

"If you can spare the dress," said Mrs. Hayward thoughtfully, "it would be pretty for her. And there's poor Katy. We must think of something for her too, France. She does enjoy pretty things, even if she does spoil them the first thing."

"Oh, Katy! If we could only have a sort of mold for her and pour her into her clothes to stay till they wear out," said France, laughing. "But we 'll think of something, mamma; don't be anxious. White piqué wears forever, and can't be torn very easily. We shall be as fine as a flock of humming-birds when we go out together; and, after all, Katy is the prettiest of all us girls. It's rather a pity, too, I think, considering she's such a flyaway. Do you know, on Sunday, when Dr. Wylie baptized that poor baby Sir Walter Scott, Bart.. she giggled out loud and set the boys off, so that when the doctor looked over our way every one in the pew was in such a broad laugh that he actually smiled himself as if he couldn't help it. Every one but me, I mean. Even father hid his face. I suppose a pew with seven in it, and every one beaming, is rather a funny sight."

"Your father told me about it," sighed Mrs. Hayward. "Well, I was ashamed enough; but I suppose Katy can't help her laugh being catching; and people ought not to baptize their children by such ridiculous names. To be sure, nobody ever did in our church before. Well, then, we'll buy her a new piqué, if we can ; and then there's only Jack to think of, for Harry must take his last year's best suit, and we can cut over Harry's for Win. I don't see what I should ever do without you, France."

France leaned over and kissed her stepmother's cheek.

"I don't do half what I ought," she said lightly. "To tell the truth, mamma, I'm only just beginning to understand what a chance I have to help in the world by being one of a family with plenty of people in it. If Miss Marigold hadn't talked it over with me, I don't believe I should ever have found it out; but since she told me the aim she has before her in her life, I've been trying a little myself; and I'm getting glimpses all the time into a new world — or rather this world is a great deal better and lovelier than I ever dreamed it was. And I declare, there the blessed little woman comes through the hedge this minute."

France sprang up as she spoke and ran out of the side door to throw her arms around her friend and draw her into the sitting room. Miss Marigold wore a look of delighted self-consciousness and she carried in her arms a heap of white mull, which she deposited on the sofa with an air of triumph.

"Try it on, Francie," said Miss Marigold with a

radiant face. "My dear, it's a dress that I had when I was a girl, and so pretty that I put it away and kept it bleached, and never thought how the fashions were coming round till just last night, and here it is as good as new, and real India mull, and you only a bit taller than I, dearie, and a little letting out would fix that. Try it on, France."

"Miss Marigold, it isn't for me?" cried the girl, taking the dainty fabric in her hands. "You don't mean — And you've kept it all this time! Oh, I never had anything so pretty in my life!"

She fairly clapped her hands and danced like a child, in delight, while mother and neighbor looked on with faces shining at sight of her pleasure.

"It's too much!" said Mrs. Hayward, the tears springing to her eyes for pure gladness. "O Miss Marigold, if you'd any idea how I've wanted to get France some such gown as that; something so sheer and soft, to set off her face as it ought to be! You needn't look so, France! You know you're pretty as well as any one, and though you don't seem to think of it at all, I can tell you I do. And I'd been turning it all over in my mind, and just feeling so disappointed over not being able to get as pretty a one as I wanted. And now to have it just come!"

Mrs. Hayward waved her hands in speechless appreciation of the gift, regardless of the fact that one held a darning-needle, while over the other was drawn a flame-colored sock.

" It 's nothing at all," said Miss Marigold, parrying the thanks which both mother and daughter poured forth. " It 's only that I had it, and thought it would be pretty for France and was glad to bring it over. But try it on, France, and let us see ; and then, if it has to be altered, I 've brought my needlecase, and I 'll help a bit with the mending, and then we 'll rip it out, and work it over together."

So France slipped off her pink gingham and appeared in flowing white, to the delight of the two older watchers, and the intense admiration of Polly and Baby, who strayed in from the garden with hands full of leaves and grasses, and faces which showed plainly the propensity of all babies to grub in the earth.

" All pretty," said sententious Baby, backing off to regard his sister with round gray eyes, while Polly walked about her and privately determined to have a gown of the very same pattern as soon as she should be grown up.

" I 'll have mine trimmed up with gold, though," said Polly, " and there 'll be red roses down the front of it, and I 'll wear a crown with shiny glass stones in, and so I 'll be a queen."

Then there was an eager consultation as to the

alterations; and presently the three were seated together again, with the mending finished, and the transparent breadths of mull between them, as they ripped and talked.

Diplomatic Miss Marigold let the conversation run on many intermediate subjects before she approached the matter of lessons. Street affairs were discussed in kindly gossip, the last ailment of the twin Brown babies, who were objects of interest to all the neighborhood; the new carpet which Mrs. Edwards had just bought, at such a bargain that the shopkeeper had begged her not to mention the price; the heap of wild flowers which Bernard Winthrop had divided between France and Patty the day before, because France happened to go in there after Win, just as he came home; the last visit which France had made to Mrs. Reese, and the songs which the dim-eyed old woman had sung over her knitting; all this and more still were discussed, before Miss Marigold introduced the matter at her heart.

When she did so, Mrs. Hayward caught at the idea with enthusiasm.

"It's just what would do France good," she declared. "Just exactly. I was always sorry that we couldn't afford to send her away to school. I wonder we never thought of it and he right on the street. And we can do it as well as not this year"—

with an unconscious glance at the new gown which
had paved the way so conveniently. " Would n't you
like it, France? And then sometimes you could
teach Janie a little, you know. You always like to
have Janie with you."

" I should be so glad," said France with sparkling
eyes. " The dear, old professor! I always liked
him in school."

" And it 'll be good for him," said Miss Marigold,
with eagerness. " You don't know what a hard
time he has, France, with poor madame always ailing
and pining for her own country and the children she
lost so long ago. And then in school and even in the
private classes there 's hardly anything to make life
pleasant for him. He just gives up all his life to other
people " — Miss Marigold would not say to his wife —
" and nobody does anything for him. I shall be so
glad for him to have you to teach. It 'll be a bright
spot for him, I know, and I 'm sure you 'll think of
little ways to show that you appreciate him. Poor
professor! He told me one day that he seemed to
be out of his place somehow, and he was afraid he 'd
never find it till he got into the New Jerusalem."

" Poor professor!" echoed France softly.

" And there 's Patty," went on Miss Marigold.
" How pleasant it will be for her, poor child, in these
long days! You must do your studying in there

sometimes, France, for she's as lovely a girl as
ever was, and brave as brave, and watches you and
wants to be friends with you so much. And I know
you'll like her; and besides, it's just another chance
to help some one, and some one that's brought right
to your door on purpose, this time."

" I wonder if I shall ever be as clear-sighted as
you are in finding out chances," said France, laying
down her finished seam.

But before Miss Marigold could answer, a great
bustle and clatter were heard outside, a wild whoop
rang through the house, a strap full of books was
flung through the half-open door, and after them with
a hop, skip, and jump came Katy, with curls in bright
confusion, Jack and Harry engaged in a friendly
scuffle, and Janie walking staidly, with serious face
looking out from the shadow of her broad straw hat.
And as France went hastily to meet them, sweeping
Katy off to brush her hair, straightening Harry's
collar with good-natured speed, taking Jack's torn
coat to mend before dinner, and dropping a kiss on
the upturned face of her favorite little sister, Miss
Marigold slipped away to Patty with a heart full of
loving satisfaction.

Before that night the matter was all arranged, and
a general congratulation was held in the pleasant
after-supper hour, when the Haywards were accus-

tomed to gather in the parlor to sing, play games,
and indulge in what the boys called " a good time
all around," in which France was the leader.

" I'm glad you think it's fun," said Jack over the
chessboard after the little children were gone to bed.
" I think it's nice for you to have it, Francie, and
that gown is stunning; but I don't believe you'll have
near such a good time as you think you will. Lessons ain't any fun with the old professor. There
was me, to-day; just making one or two little mistakes in a rule and then making up a sentence to
match and forgetting what 't was about; and did n't
he hear me all through and then drop his book as if
I'd taken all the strength out of him, and shout out
as fast as he could jabber, · *Ah-h-h-h!* eet *ees* such
a beautiful day! It rain, it snow, it is so warm
because it is so cold! *There* is your sentence!' and
all the fellows roared. You wait till you miss your
lesson once and see how you like it. You'll be sorry
you tried it, I can tell you! "

CHAPTER VII.

LESSONS IN FRENCH.

VICTOR HUGO, mademoiselles," said the professor, lifting an impressive forefinger, "Victor Hugo is like two matches rubbed together. Sometimes one gets a bright light; sometimes one gets a bad smoke, and sometimes one gets — two sticks."

France and Patty being just on the eve of an introduction into the works of the great Frenchman, received this announcement without dispute. They were sitting close together with the soft June breeze playing around them and filling the room with fragrance from a vase of blush roses on Patty's table. The two girls had come to be warm friends in the past few weeks. Hardly a day passed now that France did not run in to see her neighbor, sometimes with a bit of mending or a scrap of the embroidery which she kept for " catch-up work," sometimes with a new book to be shared together, sometimes to sit resting with folded hands for a good talk, with perhaps Baby's sleepy head on her shoulder. The girls knew all about each other by this time and were never tired of comparing memories : the busy life of the one and the quiet days of the other possessing a mutual fascination for them,

Patty told of her mountain home, with its grand forest climbing upward from the very edge of her uncle's lawn, its myriad birds, making the air ring on every side, flying fearlessly about windows and veranda, or perching on the shoulder of the old man who loved and fed them day by day; its garden where no foreign flowers found a place, but every wild flower in the woods was made at home and carefully brought to perfection under the care of uncle and Bernard: and its windows looking away down the mountain side and over the little white village below, to the green hills that rolled like a sea of glory as far as eye could see, melting away in tender purple at the far horizon.

In return, France had her simple story of stirring home life; the frolics and small sorrows of her brothers and sisters; the planning out of work and play for them; the birthday festivals; and those merry evenings in the crowded sitting room, when the children gathered about the old piano and made the air ring with "Bonnie Dundee" and "Over the Water to Charlie," or set the windows rattling with their romping games. She told of her visits to Mrs. Reese, and Patty sent many a message to the quaint old woman, causing her childish heart to flutter with pleasure and her voice to tremble with delight as she talked of her "two young folks."

Patty puzzled out patterns in knitting and busied

her brain in reducing them to plain wording for Mrs.
Reese to learn from France, or chose bits of verse
to be read aloud to her, with what joy in the pleasant
work only those can tell who have long been waiting
for a chance to be of use. It was a new life opening
to the lonely girl ; a life full of gladness and sunshine.
Patty lay on her couch with eyes that daily grew
more calm and bright, and a face whose look of
wistful patience was beginning to change for one
of hope and courage, pleasant to see.

As for France, the substance which had seemed
lacking in her bright young life was found at last.
She had found the right thread and was following
out the golden pattern. All her busy days, with her
little cares and duties. seemed full of a new inspiration. Often she went about her work singing the
lovely hymn of George Herbert which holds in a
few verses the key to a treasure-house of Christian
experience : —

> All may of Thee partake:
>   Nothing so poor and mean,
> Which with his tincture (*for thy sake*)
>   Will not grow bright and clean.
>
> This is the famous stone
>   That turneth all to gold;
> For that which God doth touch and own
>   Cannot for less be told.

But it was not only France and Patty who gained good from their friendship. Mrs. Winthrop's care-worn face grew bright at sight of her daughter's happiness; the old professor looked forward to his semi-weekly visits as the brightest spots in his toilsome, anxious life; and one other, coming on the girls sometimes at twilight, used to linger with them, almost forgetting the specimens and tables of figures which awaited him in his own room. Bernard Win-throp's bright dark eyes were coming to be a familiar part of France's life, and many were the talks which the two had at Patty's side, and the songs in which they joined at " the other house."

The Hayward children had all learned to know him as one who could tell the most delightful stories of birds and squirrels and flowers, who could climb a tree better than Jack himself, and whose company on a walk was the most desirable privilege within their range of desires. Tired Mr. Hayward turned from his ledger with enjoyment to listen to his breezy out-of-door talk, and among the neighbors who dropped in every day at the Haywards' the young man was rapidly becoming a general favorite.

It was a revelation as new to Bernard as to Patty, this pleasant bustle of family life, the open-hearted chatter of children, and the frank neighborhood gossip; above all, the bright-faced girl who seemed the center of it all, with her gay manner and tender heart always showing in little actions of help and kindness to one and another of her home circle.

" She watches for her chances," thought Bernard, looking on with observant eyes from his corner beside Mr. Hayward, as France settled disputes between the boys, helped Janie with her examples, or marshaled the three juniors to bed, bringing them to father and mother, and even to himself, for the good-night kiss from their sweet, dewy lips.

Bernard often heard the girls speak of their old teacher, and now and then lent a helping hand in the preparation of their lessons, laughing gayly at their blunders and overwhelming them with floods of rapid French by way of practice in comprehension. He had looked interested when he first heard the professor's name, and had asked several questions, relapsing into indifference on hearing the account of the white-haired old scholar with his bowed head and wrinkled face.

" Dubois is as common a name as Smith," he said. " I 've known many Duboises, but no old man like this."

He had never yet come in contact with the professor, the visits of the latter being during the daytime, when Bernard was always at the laboratory with his herbariums. Once France asked if he would

like to call at the Duboises' with her, but it was on
a lovely moonlight evening when Jack and Harry set
their hearts on a row down the river after the first
water lilies, with Bernard and their sister for company; and the old man was forgotten in the delight
of the sweet air and the beauty of gleaming water
where the folded lilies slept. France sang as they
floated down, and afterward Bernard began to hum
softly to himself and then to let out his clear voice
in the same song that had charmed Baby in the May
woods : —

"Mon cœur joyeux, plein d'espérance!"

"My mother taught it to me when I was a little
child," he said softly. It was the first time he had
ever spoken of his own people in France's hearing.

"Some time I should like to tell you about my
old home," he said after a moment, while she looked
at him with gentle, inquiring eyes. "I have never
told all about it to any one; not even to the dear
old man who became a father to me. May I tell
you?"

"I should like to hear," said France, in a low
tone. "Is it long since — you lost them?"

Bernard knit his brows slightly as if in pain. "I
can't tell you to-night," he said; "it is too long
a story. Some other time — and then I want you
to tell me what I can do to — atone."

The last word was spoken so low that France hardly caught it. She looked up quickly in surprise; but he had already turned away and was reaching out over the side of the boat to gather a half-open lily.

France had often thought of that talk since, but it was seldom that she saw Bernard alone, and he had never attempted to renew the subject. Nevertheless, there had always been an especial bond of friendly feeling between them since that night.

There was one member of our little circle who watched the unfolding of friendship, and the opening out of the lives of the two girls with a glad thankfulness of which they never dreamed. Little Miss Marigold, standing at her vine-covered gate or passing in and out of Beech Street houses, laughed inwardly for pure joy to see France flying out of one door and in at the other, or Patty leaning out to watch her as she went by on one of her many household errands.

"To think that it should have come about so beautifully," remarked Miss Marigold to the roses by her front door. "They only needed to have the way opened to be the greatest blessing to each other that could be. Think of my little Francie doing so much in the world — helping the poor, sick girl that's never had a friend in her life, and bring-

ing real sunshine to Mrs. Reese, and getting hold
of those boys till they never think of doing anything
without her knowing all about it; asking Johnny Reese
to come to see Jack, and entertaining the poor, stupid
fellow till he thinks their house is like heaven — the
poor boy that has his life worried out of him with
trying to keep up in school, and knowing that every
one calls him stupid. France is working it out sure
enough, and a blessing she'll be in the world as long
as she lives. And Patty, that has the heart to do
anything, and never knows that she's of use, poor
child! I wonder if she knows what she's doing for
France? It was just some one to help that she
needed, and the braver and sweeter that one was, the
more France would learn," said Miss Marigold wisely,
nodding to the professor as he went by from his
lesson.

"How are the lessons doing, professor?" she cried
out; and the old man stopped, with his ceremonious
bow, and the rare smile that always lighted up his
face like sunshine.

"Excellent, my friend," he answered. "They are
young ladies of brain and heart, these two. I teach
none others such. Look!" and he pulled from his
pocket a little parcel and opened it with a beaming
face, spreading out the handkerchief it contained upon
Miss Marigold's gate post. "Do you perceive, made-

moiselle? a handkerchief, embroidered with my initials
— L. D. ! Do you comprehend? It was worked for
me ! Mees France — ah, the beautiful name ! — Mees
France has procured the kerchief, and the other, the
poor sick one, she has worked it for me herself, for
my fête. Mademoiselle, it is long years since one has
remembered my fête — not since my little ones" —
He stopped short. with trembling lips. "See, then,
Mees Marigold. When I have finished my lessons
to-day — and all through it my young ladies they are
smiling at each other, and at me. and I comprehend
not, since we are beginning the works of Victor
Hugo, and I have chosen some passages the most
pathetic for the day — after it is over they smile the
more, and Mees Patty she draws from under her
pillow — this. They have asked me once the day, and
I thought nothing. I have been taken back, as you
say. I could say nothing. Ah, mademoiselle, those
are young ladies of heart!" He folded the handkerchief with careful hands, while Miss Marigold uttered
congratulations with eyes as beaming as his own.

"I'm so glad, professor! And so it's your birthday! I shall just pick you an old-fashioned nosegay
to honor it. Sweet peas and boy's love and lemon
balm and honeysuckle. Wait just one moment, till
I bring them :" and she flew lightly down the garden
walk. coming back with a hastily-gathered bunch,
which the old man took with delight.

"I wish I'd known it myself." thought Miss Marigold. "I'd have made a cake, I declare, for the dear old man. To see how radiant his face is! Those children are working it out together, just as I was saying, and building themselves up with every chance that comes to them. It isn't any little thing to make one of the Lord's saints as happy as that."

Patty and France, left behind in Mrs. Winthrop's sitting room, would have been surprised to see the difference that their gift made in the professor's home. It was a pity that they could not have followed him into his house, and seen him open his package again, on his wife's knee, telling the story with many enlargements and gestures, and dwelling, with moistened eyes, on the fact that Patty had worked his initials with her own hands. It would have done them good to see madame's face reflect the light in her husband's, and to hear her ask question after question about them, with an interest which she had not shown for a long time in anything outside her own dwelling.

"If Mademoiselle Hayward can speak French with me, I shall be pleased to receive her here," said madame, finally, to the surprise and delight of the professor. Truly that little birthday token was laden with a blessing of which the givers did not dream.

After that, it was only a few days before France "took her life in her hand," as Harry wickedly whis-

pered, and went up the street to call on the dreaded
French lady whom no one knew but Miss Marigold.
There had been a little struggle of mind, a little sink-
ing of heart, and considerable consultation with Miss
Marigold and Patty, before she could make up her
mind to accept the professor's eagerly-given invitation.

" I'm afraid of her, that's the honest truth," said
France, laughing at herself as she spoke. " If it
were only you, Patty, or if you were well enough to
go too ! "

" I wish I were," said Patty, with a touch of the
old wistfulness. " It's lovely to be able to do such
things, France. Just think of the poor woman all
alone, and not able really to talk to any one but her
husband. And to think that she has never asked for
any one to come to see her before ! "

" I'm so thankful that I could almost cry over it ! "
said Miss Marigold. " France, my dear, if you had
any idea how dismal that house is, and how it will
hearten madame if she can only come to get interested
in something outside herself — not that I mean to
blame her, poor thing, after all she's gone through,
and in a strange country — but if she only *could* get
away from herself a little ! And she *wants* you to
come, France ! "

So France went, persuading Polly to keep her
company, " as a means of self-defense " ; which

arrangement proved the best that could have been
devised for making the acquaintance, as madame,
who had watched all the Beech Street children with
hungry eyes since she had lived there, welcomed the
little creature with warmth, and sat with an arm
about her during the whole visit, even exerting herself to rise and find her a box of bonbons before
the two went away. To France she talked little,
except with regard to Polly; but she looked at the
girl with kindly eyes, and graciously asked her to
come again.

"And bring me once more the little one," she
added, dropping a kiss on Polly's rosy, sunburnt
cheek.

This was the beginning of a curious, fitful intercourse between France and Madame Dubois; an
intercourse which could hardly be called friendship,
and yet drew the two together in a way of which
they were hardly conscious. Madame sometimes met
the girl kindly, sometimes with coldness, sometimes
almost with silence. Now and then she would grow
animated in talking of old times, and tell her young
visitor long stories of balls and assemblies where
she had been gayest of the gay, thirty years ago.
Sometimes she talked of her mother, or of the con-
vent where she had been educated, and occasionally,
but very rarely, she alluded to her children.

France never dared ask a question about this part of madame's story, but her heart grew tender toward the lonely, fretful woman, at thought of those little graves on the green hillside across the sea, and the thought of them strengthened her in the resolve to continue the visits which made the professor so happy, which gave her such a varied story to tell to Patty, and which, Miss Marigold insisted, were slowly " rousing " madame herself.

So the June days deepened into midsummer, and the roses passed away from the gardens, and the vacation days began for the children. But France and Patty kept up their study, and along with it the deeper lessons which the great Teacher was setting them from day to day.

CHAPTER VIII.

" PARTNERS."

THE summer wore on, hot and sultry, settling down over Bentonville with an oppressive weight as July began. Rain seemed to have deserted the country; the streets grew parched and dusty, the trees stood with drooping leaves, and all through the town people began to watch the clouds with longing eyes, and to say to each other from day to day, "No rain yet!"

Miss Marigold and Phebe were kept busy carrying water for the flowers that withered in spite of their care; the trim green yards of Beech Street came to look brown and dry, and even madame's ivy lost its rich color. News of illness began to creep into the papers; items concerning the increasing death rate; funeral notices of little children, and hints that in the poorer portion of the city was suffering such as Bentonville had never known in summer weather. Miss Marigold came and went with a slight cloud on her sunny face, and the ebony box on her table was emptied again and again, as she made her journeys into the alleys and byways. More than

once a weeping woman or girl came to the end house
and went away with hands full of white flowers from
the garden; and one morning Miss Marigold was
found sewing, and crying over a little cambric gar-
ment, which she held out, saying through her tears:

"Such dear little children, and both gone! Twins,
just as old as Mrs. Brown's, and their mother working
in the factory and not even with them when they died,
because of the other three that's left to work for.
And nothing to use for a shroud, so I said I'd have
these ready to-night."

Patty Winthrop grew paler and thinner as she lay
in her chair through these July days. Sometimes she
was not able to be moved to the window at all, and
could only lie with closed eyes and silent lips, "keeping in" the fierce pain that seemed to drop from
those burning skies. Occasionally the professor's
lessons were interrupted for a week, and many times
during the summer the plan of study was laid aside,
while the kind old man sat in Mrs. Winthrop's parlor
and read, in his gentle voice, poems or stories that
might make the invalid forget her suffering.

"The knowledge of the literature glorious pro-
gresses as well in this way," he said, with his rare,
sweet smile, looking up from Molière or Pascal to
see if the listening face on the pillow showed signs of
weariness. And Patty never failed to smile back.

These were hard days at the professor's house. The two girls who were learning to love that noble, careworn face saw the lines of trouble deepen and deepen as the summer passed. Very few people cared to keep up their French lessons in that heated, sickly season.

"How the professor manages, I can't tell," said Miss Marigold, to France, with tears in her eyes. "If only anybody could help him! But it's no use to try; and there he is, working away all alone, trying to write articles for the papers, and worrying over the marketing and everything, and ready to break down under it all, and madame never noticing, poor thing! Not that I mean to blame her; but it seems to me that if I was in her place, I'd manage to do *something* to help him, as long as nobody else can!"

"If she only would think about him a little," returned France; "but to see him come up the street as he did last night, with his head down and his face all lined; and then, when he came into the room where we were, smiling as he always does when he comes home, making his grand bow to us both and complimenting madame on her rose-colored ribbon that I'd persuaded her to wear, just because I knew it would please him. I couldn't help wheeling up his chair to the window, and though he does appear so shocked to be waited on, usually, he dropped into it as if he were worn out. And madame just sat and embroidered and said 'Thanks,' when he laid a flower on her work. To be sure it was a frock for Polly that she was doing, for she'd just taken my breath away by telling me so, and I need n't be finding fault with her on account of it."

" It 's habit," said Miss Marigold, reaching out to gather a faded geranium leaf, for the two were in the garden. " It 's just because it 's always been so since the troubles came on them. Poor madame! It 's better to have the burden of it all than to be as she is. But when once the warm weather is over and his lessons begin again, it will be different. I shall be so glad when this hard season is past ! "

" Is n't it wonderful for madame to care to do anything for our Polly?" said France. " Just think of her embroidering that dress for her; and she talks to her more than I ever heard her talk to any one in English, and even tries to teach her French and laughs at the work she makes of it. Polly takes her dolls in to visit her, and makes herself at home as if she belonged there, and madame lets her do anything she chooses in the house. Mamma tries to keep her at home, but when she does n't go in every few days madame is sure to send me a note inquiring where the little one is, and Polly marches off to see her triumphant. It 's the oddest friendship ! "

" Their little girl was just Polly's age, the professor says," answered Miss Marigold. " He is so happy about it, France. He says that madame is brighter than she has been since they lost their last child, fifteen years ago. Polly's doing more for her than anybody else can. Perhaps she may come out of herself yet, after all."

" I hope so, I'm sure," said France, with a laugh, which was followed by a sudden, fleeting blush of surprise as the garden gate clicked sharply near them and Bernard Winthrop's tall figure was seen standing among the rose bushes as if doubtful whether to advance or retreat.

" Bernard, how strange to see you at this time of day!" cried the girl frankly. " I never knew you to come home before evening!"

Bernard did not answer. Instead of coming toward the garden seat he drew back slowly to the house.

" Miss Marigold," he called from the steps, " I wish to see you. Give me one moment, if you please. Let me go inside. Miss France will excuse you, I know."

" Oh, certainly!" cried France, with a touch of pique in her voice. " Go in, Miss Marigold, and I'll run over to Patty, so I wish you a pleasant visit, I'm sure."

She ran through the hedge, with a saucy look over

her shoulder at the doorstep where the young man had stood, but he had already stepped inside.

"Very odd," decided France inwardly. "What private business can he possibly have with Miss Marigold?"

Bernard stood on the threshold of the sitting room as Miss Marigold came in. He was very grave and quiet as he spoke to her.

"Miss Marigold," he said, "I've come to you because you are the only one I know who can tell me just what to do. I know you go about where sick people are, and you're alone in your house, and — I'm sure you're not afraid. I thought you could tell me. It's a boy in our laboratory. You know what a settlement of working men there is around our place, and how crowded and disagreeable the tenements are. I saw you in Brown's Alley last week, or I would n't have come to you now. But this boy, he's been working under me, off and on, and I've taken a little interest in him because he was a bright little fellow, and devoted to me; so when I missed him I went to see. And Miss Marigold, it's low typhus, the doctor says. And so close and crowded there! He can't be moved either, and there those poor things are, in the house with him and all about, and what they'll do I don't know. Of course I did n't come from there here. I've changed everything, and all that, so that

there really is n't any danger to you, I suppose, if you
did n't want to do anything " —

" Do anything ? " cried Miss Marigold almost sharply.
" Bernard, are you crazy ? Of course I 'll go. You
knew I would when you came, did n't you ? What
else am I alone in the world for, if it is n't to be
ready in an emergency ? "

" Well, I hoped you would say so," said Bernard,
with a look of relief. " You see, the poor little
fellow is boarding by himself, and there 's no one
to look after him. Of course I can take care of
him myself. It 's a dull season now in the botanizing
line, and I can take a vacation as well as not. Besides, I 'm rather fond of him. But the others in
the house — and there are a number of families — will
need so much talking to, and helping along to keep
it off them. The doctor says he 's afraid they 're in
for a regular run of it, starting in that place so,
where it 'll spread. And so if you can go down " —

" I 'll be ready in a few minutes," said Miss Marigold, beginning to fold up her work. " I 'm glad
you came to me, for I think I can help the poor
creatures. Perhaps it won't spread after all ; but
I may as well keep away from here a little while
till we see. Just wait till I put up a few things and
we 'll go back together."

" If you can as well as not," assented Bernard ;

"and I thought perhaps you would leave a little note for Mrs. Winthrop or Patty. I did n't quite like to go in there because of the questions they would ask, and it's no use making them nervous. If you'd just tell them that I'm going to help with a sick boy belonging to the laboratory, and that you're with me, they need n't know anything more. It might n't be good for Patty. I'd just like to have them know that I have n't run away."

He laughed gayly as he spoke, and Miss Marigold answered him in the same light-hearted way as she went out of the room.

But when, in a quarter of an hour, she came back to him, serene and quiet, with the "uplifted" look in her face which Patty had already noticed now and then, Bernard took her hand in his a moment, looking into her eyes with grave tenderness. The young man had grown fond of the little lady of the end house, like all other young people who saw her from day to day.

"I don't want you to think because I came to you now," he said earnestly, "that I don't think about the risk to you, Miss Marigold, or that I don't care. It's only that there's nobody else that seems all ready for people to come to. And when I saw that poor little fellow and thought about the others, I could n't help coming. I'll do everything in the world to help you, though a man is n't good for much at such a time; only you must n't think I don't care." He stooped and kissed the hand he held as if it had been a queen's.

Simple Miss Marigold blushed like a girl with pleasure.

" You 're very good, Bernard," she said, smiling up at him as they left the house. " I 'm sure the risk to me is n't worth thinking of a moment. If I was nervous, you know, it would be different, but I 'm not at all afraid. We 'll just be partners for a little, you and I, and see what we can do for Brown's Alley together."

France and Patty saw the two pass up Beech Street, talking earnestly and gravely as they went, and wondered together what could be the object of their expedition. Weeks went by before they saw either of them again, except once or twice in the early morning, when France, looking down into the garden at the end house, caught a glimpse of its owner slipping in or out from the carriage that waited for her at the gate.

Those weeks were the strangest and saddest that had ever been known in Bentonville. People spoke of them long after as the fever season, looking back almost with a shudder to that time of dread and suffering. All through the crowded district where the disease had broken out, men, women, and children

lay dying, or slowly struggling back to life, to take up
burdens of toil and trouble, all the heavier for the
weeks of pain that had laid them aside.   Doctors and
nurses went about with careworn looks that spoke of
sleepless nights and overworked days; the hospitals
were crowded, and even the dwellers in the airy, open
streets of the upper part of the city were struck with
a panic which opened the way for the approach of the
very enemy they dreaded.   There came a time when
more than one house in Beech Street was overshad-
owed by the mighty wings of that angel of pestilence ;
when France Hayward went about pale and worn
with watching by her little brothers and sisters, and
when poor Madame Dubois shed hot tears of impatient sorrow over the danger of her rosy-cheeked
baby favorite.

" It is so with all whom I love — all ! " cried madame,
burying her face in the little finished frock which
Polly might never wear.   " I will love no more in this
world.   It is all hard and without pity ! "

" Yes, that is true, *ma mie*," said the professor,
laying a gentle hand on his wife's head ; " but love
is not of this world.   That is of another life, my
Julie, and deathless !   But for the dear little one, we
will speak to the good God for her and he may spare
her ! "   And the old man took up his hat with trembling fingers and went slowly down the street to ask

at Mrs. Winthrop's for the latest news from next door.

Once, as he stopped outside the gate, Bernard Winthrop, coming out of the Hayward house, met him face to face. Something in the erect figure and keen, dark face, somewhat worn and softened now, by long watching at many sickbeds, caused the old man to stop and look after the young one as he passed swiftly by, on some errand for his friends within.

"My sons might have grown to be like that," thought the professor, with a pang.

As for Bernard, hurrying to the doctor's office, he had hardly noticed the white-haired figure at the gate. There were other and tenderer thoughts to fill his mind and heart. France Hayward's face was before him, pale and quiet, as he had seen it when she came down from Polly's bedside with the message for him to carry. It was a long time since he had seen her last; a time filled with memories, both sweet and painful, that made it seem like years since he had gone down to Brown's Alley with Miss Marigold. Bernard had given himself up heart and soul to serving the suffering people among whom he was thrown. His face was known in all the "fever district," and more than one dying boy had breathed out his life in those strong young arms that never seemed to tire.

"I'm the next thing to a doctor, anyhow," he said gayly, when Miss Marigold tried to persuade him to rest. "I take to it naturally, and I'm not going to stop while there's such need of help as now. I'm not the only one that's doing the same thing, and the doctors are pressing everybody in that they can get. Besides, why should I give up before you? I'm stronger than you are, and I haven't anybody to prevent my coming here, more than you have."

"But I'm old and you're young," returned Miss Marigold, stirring the broth which she was making. "It isn't so natural. Not but what it's a happy thing that you're here just now, for what on earth we should do with Max Spindler in those delirious fits I don't know, if you weren't by to quiet him down again."

"Poor Max!" said Bernard, rising from the chair where he had been resting, with his head on the table. "I must go back to him. Do you know, he called me Saint Martin last night, and said over and over, ' Holy Saint Martin, pray for us!' till I came near breaking down entirely over the poor fellow. To take me for a saint!"

"I'm afraid there's little hope for him," said Miss Marigold. "I'll come up and see him presently, when Emmy Bergmann is comfortable. But as for taking you for Saint Martin, — that was the one that

divided his cloak, was n't it? and I suppose he 's
Max's patron saint, — that is n't so strange. But,
Bernard, I 'd think a little about the rest of that
legend while you 're working over him up there. Do
you remember what Saint Martin dreamed in the night
after he had shared his cloak? That part of the story
is true, anyhow — as true as any allegory that ever
was written."

Bernard blushed as deeply as Miss Marigold herself
had done on the afternoon when they started out
together on their errand of help.

"If I ever got to be any kind of saint at all," he
said hastily, "it would only be poor old blundering
Christopher. If I ever accomplish anything, it will
be when I don't know it, like him! Good-by, Miss
Marigold."

He went away, going lightly up the stairs so as not
to disturb the sick girl whose room he must pass, and
Miss Marigold heard him soon afterwards singing
softly to the boy who was never so quiet as when
Bernard's voice was in his ear.

CHAPTER IX.

"LONG AGO."

IF it is n't good to be at home again!" said Miss Marigold, with heartfelt enjoyment, as she sank into the easy-chair in the sitting room.

"It's middlin' good to see ye, too," responded Phebe from the kitchen door. "Be'n sort o' lonely round here, me an' Carlo, all alone. If ye had n't 'a' come home pretty soon, we 'd 'a' left, I guess."

Miss Marigold smiled, as in duty bound, at this joke.

"I suppose everything 's gone all right?" she said, with an inward doubt unconsciously pervading her voice.

"Yes, *ma'am!*" said Phebe triumphantly. "I ha'n't broke a thing but the student lamp, an' I 've kept the flowers up real well. Did n't you notice the asters as you come along? Never see such heaps of 'em at a time before, an' more white an' gold ones than you could shake a stick at. I was real tickled to see 'em comin' out, bein' you liked them kinds best.

"I took a bunch of daylias over to Mis' Reese one day, as I knowed you 'd do if you was here, an' law!

you'd ough'ter seen her go off. Big red an' yeller
ones, you know, so's't she could see the color. Says
she, 'Miss Prissy's the sunshine of my heart!'
Thought I'd tell ye so you'd know what she meant
when you go in to see her, an' she talks about 'em.
Them there Ruggleses come one day, Jed an' the baby
an' Mary Ann, an' I jest let 'em stay round, they
seemed to like to be here so much. Queer none of
them caught the fever. Then there's be'n Mis' Brown
after you half a dozen times, to tell her what to do
for the twins to keep it off 'em. Poor little young
ones! Seemed too bad they had to be divided, did n't
it? I felt real sorry about the one that died."

"Poor Mrs. Brown!" said Miss Marigold, with
a sigh for the proud young mother whose babies had
been a never-failing subject of chat to the Beech
Street people for the last year.

"An' there was Katy Hayward," said Phebe,
looking out of the window in the direction of the
next house. "Last day she was out walkin' our
fence as fine as a peacock, an' tumblin' off, right into
the pansy bed an' smashed it flat before she could get
up. An' now there they are, she an' Polly an' Jack,
an' nobody knowin' how they'll come through. Makes
it kind o' worse, comin' jest at the end of it all, seems
to me. Poor Mis' Hayward's got her hands full this
time, if she never had before."

"They're better, all but Katy," said Miss Marigold. "I stopped in there as I came home. France looks worn out. She's too excited, now that they're beginning to have hope for Polly, and Jack and the baby and Janie are out of danger. I told Mrs. Hayward I'd make the beef tea for them after this, Phebe, so you may as well go over to market after the beef now."

Miss Marigold laid her head back against the soft cushions, looking about her with a feeling of comfort which could hardly be dispelled even by the thought of the shadow which still hung over her friends.

It seemed strange, after the days and weeks of confusion and watching which had passed, to come back to this fresh quiet place, with its dainty furnishings and restful order. These were very different quarters from those where Miss Marigold had been housed lately. Even Phebe's face of mingled dullness and serenity was a relief after those sharp, pinched ones which still rose before the mental vision of her mistress as she rested in the great chair.

"Thank God that it's passing away!" said Miss Marigold, as she dropped quietly asleep in the stillness.

The twilight was just falling, and the first stars were beginning to burn like tapers in the clear amber

sky along the western horizon. Here and there in
the street lamps were being lighted, and sending out
long beams of yellow radiance as if in answer to
the " pale candles " of the sky. Bernard Winthrop,
coming through the dusk, with his pocket full of
oranges for the Hayward children, caught glimpses
of more than one brightly-lighted room, showing like
pictures in the half hour before the curtains were
drawn and the outside world shut out. He saw Mrs.
Brown with the tears falling on the soft curls of her
living child, while she rocked him to sleep and thought
of the other, lying, in dreamless peace, under the
churchyard pines ; he saw, through Mrs. Edwards'
window, a cluster of boyish heads bending over some
new game that lay spread out before them on the
table ; at one door a young wife stood peering out
into the shadows and singing softly to herself as she
waited ; at another a white-haired old man was letting
himself in with his latch key. It was all as calm and
peaceful as if the city were not just emerging from
the shadow of death. Bernard nodded to one and
another as he passed, and stopped a moment at
Patty's window to go through a series of pantomimic
performances, expressive of grief at not being per-
mitted to enter, and admiration of the scene within,
where Mrs. Winthrop sat reading to her daughter,
with the lamplight falling softly over them through the
rose-colored shade.

"Bernard would laugh if he were going to everlasting banishment," said Patty, laughing back across the pile of bright worsteds in her lap.

But the young man's face grew grave again as he passed on to the house where danger still threatened the lives of the children with whom he had frolicked so often that spring and summer. The door was on the latch and he stepped quietly in without ringing, pausing a moment in the hall to listen for any sound from above. There was nothing to be heard but a faint, wailing cry from little Polly, which was echoed still more softly from the sitting room at the right. Bernard stepped into it and looked around him.

It was almost dark here, but in the dim light he could see that the pretty room was disordered and desolate; the piano was open and scattered over with loose sheets of music; Mr. Hayward's coat lay on the table, and Harry's bat and ball were on the floor beside it, where the boy had dropped them the day before when he came in from a forlorn attempt to amuse himself without his constant comrade, Jack.

"I may as well see what I can do here," said Bernard to himself, picking up the coat and depositing it in the hall.

The faint sobbing which he had heard as he entered ceased as he opened the inner door; but as he came in a second time and turned to the chimneypiece to strike a light, he stumbled over a small heap on the floor, which uttered a smothered cry by way of greeting.

" What you 'bout?" remarked Win, with unnecessary sharpness, as the young man picked him up and sat down in the armchair, holding him on his knee.

" I might ask you the same thing," said Bernard calmly. " It seems to me that you 're not in very good business for a young man of your age. All alone, are you? Where is everybody?"

" Upstairs, or else lying down in mamma's room, or gone on errands," replied the boy, resigning himself, with a final sob, to his captor's embrace. " Papa, he 's taking care of Jack, and there 's the nurse with Katy; and Polly and baby, they 're in the nursery, and France staying with 'em. Don't seem to be no place at all for me 'n' Harry. Don't see why I could n't have got sick too, or something. 'T ain't any fun, standing round this way!"

Bernard laughed under his breath.

" Poor little fellow!" he said. " Well, I don't wonder. I 'll keep you company for a little and see if we can't get up some comfort in this corner of the house. I suppose if they want to send for anything we 'll hear them coming out and I 'll be on hand. Did I ever tell you about the time I saw four bears at once, out in Colorado? No? Then listen." And

Win, leaning back against his friend's shoulder, forgot his troubles in drinking in the story.

France stopped at the door a moment to listen when she came downstairs a little later. It was a relief, in the midst of the strain of grief and foreboding which she was undergoing, to hear that cheerful voice talking gayly on as if illness and fatigue were nowhere in the world. It had seemed to France lately that the whole earth was full of them. Win's stifled laugh at the end of the crisis of the adventure struck her heart with a sense of comfort which brought the tears to her eyes.

"So when the bear came trotting up," said Bernard, "the mother turned around and looked at him, instead of seeing me; and then she put up her great paw and brought it gently down on the baby's head, as if she were pretending to box his ears; and they went straight up the side of the spur and left me behind the juniper bush, ready to give them a vote of thanks, only not a rising one, just then! And if you had seen me the moment after they disappeared —I can tell you, young man, you never ran so fast as that in your life."

"That was fun!" said Win, with a wriggle of enjoyment.

"More fun now than it was then," said Bernard; "for if ever a man was frightened, I was. I say,

Win, let us see if we can't pick up this music and make things cozy a little for your mother and sister when they come down. I can pile up things as neatly as a lumberman. We'll have everything like a ship's deck when they come in."

"You need n't do that," said France, coming forward, with a faint smile. "It is n't very pleasant, that's a fact; but to-morrow I shall have more time. Did you light the gas yourself as well as make poor Win comfortable? You are very kind."

"You don't seem to have much faith in my powers," said Bernard, standing on the hearth rug, and looking comically down as she dropped into a chair beside him. "I can dust most beautifully, if you only knew it. Botanizing men can always do those things. However, I won't insist on having my own way. I'm too well-behaved for that. How are they all upstairs?"

"Better," replied the girl wearily. "That is, all but Katy. We can't tell about her until to-morrow, the doctor says. Poor little Katy! It's dreadful to see her so, she has always been so full of life and fun. And there's nothing to do for her."

"Can't you go and lie down or something?" said the young man anxiously. "You look all worn out, Miss France. Did n't you come away to rest? I'll go away if you would rather be alone here. I only came to see if I could help."

"No, don't go," answered France, choking down a sob as she spoke. "I'm as bad as a child to-night. I can't be quiet without growing almost wild with thinking of them all. Even now that they are all doing well but Katy, I can't help going all over what it would be like, if — if "— She hid her face in her hands a moment and then looked up, struggling for composure. "Tell me something, as you did Win," she said. "If I could forget about it for just a little while I could go back so much stronger, I believe."

Bernard sat down and drew Win to him again.

"I can sympathize with this little fellow," he said, taking no notice of France's nervous emotion. "I remember the time when I had the same 'left out' feeling that he seems to have."

"When was that?" asked Win, on the lookout for another story.

"That was long ago," said Bernard. "When I was a child in France. How you would have liked to see my home, Win! I can remember it as plainly as if it were yesterday, though it was fifteen years ago that I — ran away."

"Did you run away?" asked the child in an awe-struck tone.

"Yes, I did. Sometimes it seems like a dream that I ever lived there, but I can see it all so clearly:

that odd little town, with all the red roofs among the trees, and the great castle at the top of the cliffs. I 've climbed those towers often, when no one dared follow me. There was ivy all over them, and I found an owl's nest in it once, with three little fluffy owlets. I remember I took them home, and old Marie would not let me keep them, and I cried till my mother heard me and came down in her black gown, and said that I should have my way."

" Did you have brothers and sisters?" asked Win.

" When I was very little, I can remember my two brothers, handsome boys, tall and strong, and my father teaching them to fence, while I stood in my white frock and looked on. My father was an army officer, and so straight and handsome! What dark eyes he had! I was proud of him always, but after my brothers died I never used to see him much. He was always shut up among his books and I used to steal into the library and find what I wanted to read without speaking to him. Now and then he would talk to me, and then I was so happy! He was away in Paris a great part of the time, and my mother used to go and come with him; but I always begged to stay with Marie and Jacques, where I could get out to the woods and the beach, and they let me have my way."

" And your mother?" asked France, softly, from the armchair.

Bernard raised his eyes to the girl's face, with the same knitting of the brows which she had noticed when he spoke of his mother in the boat.

"My mother was very beautiful," he answered. "She was always singing and laughing about the house, as I remember her when I was a little child. That was before the others died. She used to come into our nursery and play with us. I can see her quite plainly in the firelight, with her shining dark hair all pulled down about her and my sister in her lap. My sister was the first of all who died. She was always singing and dancing, like *maman* herself. It must have been pretty to see them together, if I remember rightly. It was in those days that my mother taught us all the song that I sang to you. I should not have remembered it, for she never could bear to hear me sing it after the others died, but Marie used to make me sing it to her in those evenings when I was alone with her and Jacques. Marie was very good to me. My mother never seemed to care to have me with her after I was the only one. I suppose it only made her long for the others. Sometimes she used to come up to my room at night and cry over me there, and sometimes she would take my part, as she did about the owlets; but that was all. So I used to slip away from home, where it was so still and sad, and go out to the mountain. There

were peasants there (some time I'll tell you all about
them, Win, an l their queer huts and the goats that
they kept and the charcoal that they burned), and I
was as gay with them as I was quiet at my father's
house. Oh, what woods those were! I've dreamed
about them many a time, as I have seen them in the
moonlight, when Marie thought me asleep in bed, and
I had stolen out with Victor Clargis, one of the for-
ester's sons. How they waved — those great beech
trees, with the white light all about them; and how
the nightingales sang there! We used to tame the
squirrels and feed the birds, and when we were tired
of wandering we would drop down under the trees
and tell stories, if it were evening; or, in the daytime,
I would read aloud from some of the books of travel
that I found in the library at home. We always
planned to go off together some time, to seek our
fortunes, like the knights we used to read about or
the travelers whom we made heroes of; and at last,
when we were nearly twelve years old, we did run
away. It was when my father and mother had gone
away to Paris on one of their journeys. My father
had seemed more than usually silent and anxious for
a day or two before they went. I think he must have
been in some trouble about money, though I can't be
sure, of course. I did not see them to say good-by,
for I was up at the castle with Victor, and we were

planning to slip away the next day and go on board one of the ships and hide until we were well out at sea. We chose a strange vessel, and took all the money of our own which we had to pay our passage. We had no idea but that those few francs would take us through. I hate myself when I think of it," said Bernard, breaking off suddenly in his story. "But. Miss France, I was like a child in it all. We were going to make our fortunes and find out knowledge in strange countries, and — it was years since I had known much of my father and mother. It was only afterwards, when memories of them came crowding back to me, that I knew they must have cared for me through it all. We came to America, and there was a year of misery — it's of no use to talk of that. Victor — poor Victor — died, and I was left alone. Once I wrote to Marie and once to Victor's father, but the letters must have been lost, I suppose, for I never heard from home. Then, when I was ready to despair, I found work with a nursery gardener, and at that I was quick and clever, because of the great love that I had for everything growing. And there Patty's uncle found me and took me to the mountains with him. Dear old man! how good he was to me and how I loved him! He taught me everything he knew and sent me to college, only persuading me to take his name in return. He had never married, and I think he felt as if he had found a real son in me. You know all about the way of life in our home; the wild, free mountain life that I have always loved. I have been very happy. Sometimes I feel as if those first twelve years were something I had fancied, it has been so different since; but there are times when my mother's face comes up before me so plainly — and always as it was when she sat by the nursery fire and played and sang with us, and cared for me with the others."

"But you have never tried to find them?" cried France wonderingly.

"Oh, yes!" he answered. "Mr. Winthrop and I both wrote, but we could hear nothing of them. I think they must be dead, my poor parents! My father was not young, even as I remember him. Some time, when I am rich, I mean to go back to the old home and try there to find some trace of them. Perhaps I may find their graves with those of my brothers and sister. If they are gone, I think they will know how I repent of the grief I must have caused them — and they will forgive!"

There was a long silence in the room as Bernard ceased speaking. Win slipped down from his place and went away, and France sat thinking over the story until the young man spoke again.

"I've wanted to tell you this for a long time.

Somehow, I wanted you to know all about me: to know how badly I started out in life, and to tell me if we can be friends all the same. You don't know what it has been to me, the coming here and being with you all; and yet it has made me feel somehow as if I were n't what you thought me. I don't mean that I think it was a crime to run away; but when one has brought trouble like that on the people that he belongs to, and when there's no way to make atonement, one can't help having a sense of guilt. At any rate, I wanted to tell you, and I've just waited for a chance until now. Does it make a difference with you?"

He held out his hand in the frank, winning way which was peculiarly his own, and France laid hers in it with hearty good will.

"Of course we are friends!" she said. "How could we be anything else, after this summer, and all the kindness you have shown us, and especially after these days when we could n't have got along without you at all? I am only so sorry for you and for your poor mother!"

"Thank you," said Bernard, softly.

"I must go back to the children now," said France, turning to the door. "You are going to Miss Marigold's to-night? Give her my love, and tell her that I am rested and strong again. The dear little woman looked quite worried when she was here this afternoon. And thank you so much for telling me, Bernard."

"Good-night," he answered, and went quietly away.

CHAPTER X.

IT'S the greatest chance that ever came in my way!" said Bernard, walking about the room excitedly.

Miss Marigold and Patty looked at each other with eyes kindling in answer to his own, yet with trouble plainly visible amid the surprise.

"But, O Bernard!" said Patty, "what should we ever do without you?"

Bernard stopped in his walk to look absently out of the window. He evidently saw something more than the quiet street, lying still and pleasant under the October sunshine. The young man's eyes were full of a great light and gladness which hardly clouded even at sight of the shadow on his friends' faces.

"Of course that part would be hard for us all," he said; "though I'm not vain enough to suppose I should make such a difference as you think, Patty. You're always putting your friends in the high places, you know. But just think of the advantage to me! One year away, and then — then" — He broke off suddenly. "Why, Patty, think how I have always

266

wanted to see those tropical countries! and what a chance this is! I may come home really famous. Would n't you like to have a cousin with half a dozen medicinal plants named after him and with his articles in all the scientific journals? Not that I expect to have them there, but it 's just as well to suppose that I do!" He laughed a joyous laugh, in which Miss Marigold and Patty joined in spite of themselves.

"I don't doubt that they will be there, Bernard," said Miss Marigold, with calm certainty. "I 've always thought you 'd be famous some day, and this is n't any surprise at all. When anybody knows every plant in the woods for twenty miles around, and can tell what anything is just by looking at the leaf — I always knew they 'd offer you something or other soon. But to send you to Brazil! My dear boy, I can't bear the thought of it."

"It 's just where I 've always wanted to go," said Bernard, coming round to sit beside the little woman. Bernard and Miss Marigold had been great friends since their partnership in Brown's Alley. "Why, Miss Marigold, I 've thought about it for years, though I did n't expect to be able to get there so soon. I 'm sure that there must be numbers of valuable plants in those forests that have never been discovered; and that I should have the chance to explore there is such good luck as I never dreamed would

come to me!—to say nothing of the advanced salary
and the promotion that will come when I get back!
I can just imagine myself wandering about there."

"So can I," said Patty, somewhat dolefully.
"You'll be as happy as the day is long.

> "Gil Morris sat on Huntly bank;
> He whistled an' he sang!

"I suppose that's what you'll be doing, with boa-
constrictors and jaguars and apes standing around,
and fevers and agues and every other sort of disease
prospecting for you while you're discovering the
plants to heal them. And here we shall be, just
living along, and watching you. I wonder what on
earth mamma will say!"

"And"— Miss Marigold stopped at the very
beginning of the sentence, casting a sudden glance
out of the window. France Hayward was just passing and turning toward them to smile at Patty, her
beautiful face framed for an instant against a square
of brilliant blue sky as she paused. It was only
lately that people were beginning to call France
beautiful.

The three friends within looked after her as she
went down the street, leading Baby, and smiling back
at them from under the scarlet maple trees.

"My dear child!" said Miss Marigold, with unconscious tears in her soft eyes. "What will she say?" was the thought in her mind, but she did not utter it.

"Somehow France is different since the fever," said Patty. "That — or something — has changed her. She did n't use to have that clear, shining look. I love to look at her nowadays, though of course she always was pretty. What do you suppose she 'll think, Bernard?"

Bernard said nothing. He was standing at the window and watching the last flutter of the girl's gown as she turned the corner above. When he turned again, it was to plunge into an eager discussion of his opening prospects as if France Hayward were nowhere in his thoughts. But when Miss Marigold rose to go the young man followed her out, and even went with her to her own gate, standing by her among the chrysanthemums and asking question after question concerning outfit and preparation, with an eagerness which made the kind-hearted little woman smile to herself as he lingered, apparently unable to come to an end.

"My dear Bernard," she said at last, with a sort of tender amusement in her face, "you want to say something to me: it 's plain to be seen, and I 'm all ready to hear it. Don't you think it would be as well to begin at once? It 's something about — France, is n't it?"

A sudden wave of color rose in the young man's face.

" Yes, it is," he said, with a sigh of relief. " I do want to tell you, Miss Marigold. There is n't any one else that I can tell, somehow, until I know from herself — but I 've thought of her for weeks and months, and wished ! — Miss Marigold, you don't know ; I can't tell you how I 've wished that I was in a position to ask her if she would care for me ! But I would n't when I had so little. It would n't be fair. And now, the one thing that makes me so glad is just that I can ask her ! In a year, if I go, I shall be able to settle down here and make a home for her, if she will come to it, and then " — He drew himself up joyously, looking beyond the gray-haired woman before him into a world of pleasant visions in which she had no part.

No part? Miss Marigold's face was all alight with changeful feeling. One would have thought that the beautiful future of which Bernard was dreaming was her own ; and yet there was compassion in the gentle eyes that met his.

" How little he knows what it will be — this year ! " they said. But if Miss Marigold's eyes spoke of sadness, her words were as warm and glad as the young man could have wished. Whatever memory of suffering his little story had brought to her heart, she said nothing of it as he followed her into the house, talking fast and eagerly, now that the ice was broken, and pouring out the tale of his hopes and fears with a boyish ardor which set his listener's heart beating in a flutter of sympathetic happiness.

" I shall be so glad!" she cried, " so very glad, Bernard! To think of a wedding here in our street; and the very girl I love best in the world! If it only comes out all right, — as it will, please God, — I shall be the happiest old woman in Bentonville, to see you two brought together."

And as the young man went away, his simple-minded confidante plunged into a delightful whirl of daydreams, in which the wedding outfit, the house furnishings, and even the place of abode of the future bride, were settled with a promptness and disregard of expense only to be found in such airy moments of outlook, and from which Miss Marigold was only recalled when Phebe in her lank calico dispelled the vision of France in bridal white, by a call to dinner.

It was hard to come down from the clouds to matters of everyday life that afternoon. Miss Marigold's mind was in a tumult of pleasant emotions, wandering from France to Bernard, and back again to France, with ever and anon a journey unawares into the long past, where her own youthful joy awoke and smiled upon her as if in response to the vision of new happiness which was before her eyes to-day. She went upstairs and sat in the afternoon sunlight for a long time, with the ebony box before her, and the faded roses in her hand.

"Till a' the seas gang dry, my dear," she murmured, as she laid them away once more.

"The perfessor's downstairs," said Phebe, breaking in on her mistress' revery; and Miss Marigold rose with a half sigh and went back to the sitting room.

The old man stood by the window, with head bent over the box of plants which had been set there as cool weather drew on. He was looking strangely worn and old, in sharp contrast to the bright young faces which had moved through Miss Marigold's dreams all day. A sudden pang of pity shot through her heart as he bowed with his gentle smile. Life was very hard at the professor's house this fall. The accounts had fallen behind in the summer, and the fever season had prevented the opening of classes at the usual time, so that the monthly balance was an affair of greater difficulty than ever. Miss Marigold, watching with an aching heart, had seen the old man steal out in the twilight more than once with a small square package under his arm, and had noticed at her next visit that the books in the little case were carefully arranged so as to fill up the vacant spaces and present the usual appearance of full shelves.

"One needs not many books when one grows old," the professor was wont to declare when any one noticed his little library. "When one is young, one wanders through all lands of thought — as your poet says, —

"In the lands of gold,

and through the islands of the sea; gathering up flowers everywhere, or poison too often. But when one grows old one keeps a few writers, and reads them again and again, and digs the riches out of them — out of their very heart. My few books are enough for me."

But in these days the declaration was made in an uncertain voice, and the professor's eyes grew wistful as he glanced at the empty places where his old favorites had stood. The world would have been very gray indeed to those brave old eyes but for little Miss Marigold and the two girls whose blithe voices and eager young minds brightened so many hours for the overworked and anxious man.

A look of rest came over his face now as he sat by the window in the gathering twilight and watched the lights in the next house while he talked over the events of the day, recounted the last effort of schoolboy intelligence in the historical line, and enjoyed the laughter of his neighbor over the "two-jointed kings" who were reported to have governed Lacedæmonia, and the Spartan mother who, according to Johnny Reese, "commanded her son to return from battle bearing his sword, or borne upon it!"

The sound of music stole presently forth from next door, and they paused in their talk to listen. The curtains were not drawn in Mrs. Hayward's sitting room, and they could see France at the piano, straight and slender in her gray gown, with her hair shining in the lamplight, and her brothers and sisters standing about her. Only one of the golden heads was absent; one of the gay voices was missing as they sang the merry chorus. The children had mourned in their passionate, childish fashion as Katy was laid away to sleep, dressed in the new white frock that would never be worn out. They had said over and over that they would never forget her; and they spoke of her often in awed, hushed voices, whenever they were particularly quiet and solemn. The heavenly land seemed nearer and more real to every one of them since this mischievous, blundering, light-hearted little sister had entered it, but the thought of death could not long cast a cloud over those joyous hearts. Even their older sister looked like a creature

"Of sunshine and the dancing dawn,"

as she led the song, though the tender grace that had begun to blossom in her fresh young presence of late shone in her eyes, and made her like one set apart, among the childish faces that surrounded her. Miss Marigold could see from where she sat another figure, standing partly hidden behind the piano, and Bernard's voice was plainly to be heard above the children's. The professor leaned forward to hear more clearly.

"It is sweet and glad, is it not, my friend?" he said, smiling.

"That is a pretty picture, the young children with their sister. How fresh her voice is and how the words ring out — 'The Birks o' Aberfeldy!' That is a song of Burns, is it not? How they are joyous, the Scottish songs!"

"It's good to see them happy again," said Miss Marigold. "What a little time it is since they were all in such trouble! What should we ever do in this world if it was n't that trouble is the thing that passes away and the happiness of our lives is the real groundwork of them? I 've thought of it often as I have grown older."

"Is it so?" said the professor, half doubtfully. "Yes, we do count from gladness to gladness rather than from sorrow to sorrow. But sometimes there comes such a long time of cloud that one forgets that it is only a vapor that vanishes. If one could but remember, it would make the darkness bright, often."

"I was worried about France through all that illness," said Miss Marigold. "It was hard for a young girl to bear. Every one depends on France so much nowadays. But to see her to-night one would think that she had never known anything but happiness. What a beautiful wife France would make!" sighed the gentle dreamer, speaking out of the depths of her conscious soul.

"Ah! she should never know care and trouble," said the professor with a sudden cloud on his face. "No, my friend; she who is like the dove with silver wings of which one reads in the Psalms, she should never leave her nest. She should rest and be sheltered and know nothing of the care that comes when one is in a home of one's own." And in contradicting this heretical opinion Miss Marigold forgot to watch her favorite or to listen to the young man's voice, which brought with it an excitement such as she had not felt for long years.

France and Bernard, meanwhile, sang calmly on as if neither had an idea in life beyond the amusement of the twilight hour with the children. Bernard had told of his new prospects when he first came in, and the matter had been discussed in every light by the entire family; the little boys clamoring to be allowed to go too; Janie and Polly reveling in accounts of the flowers and birds which Bernard would see; Mrs. Hayward appalled and wondering at the idea; and France keeping her opinion to herself in a way that caused her mother to glance at her with incipient anxiety in her eyes. But after the singing was over, and Mr. Hayward too had had his say on the all-engrossing subject, Bernard came over to France, where she sat working at the table, and spoke in a low voice : —

"You have hardly spoken about it at all," he said. " I want to know what you think, only not now. To-morrow I have set my heart on taking you all out to the woods by the lake, you and Miss Marigold and Patty and the three children. This Indian Summer weather is so warm and still that it will be beautiful, and Patty is so much better that the doctor says she may go. Poor child! she has not been in the woods for two years. I have thought about it for a week or two, but I would n't speak till I was sure. It will be the last expedition that we can have together before I go away. And out there in my favorite place I want to tell you something more about myself and hear what you think about it. You will come?"

"Of course," said France quietly. "It will be beautiful for Patty — and us all. I shall enjoy seeing her out there. And the little ones — they will never forget it. It was kind of you to think of it,

Bernard." She flushed slightly as she spoke, but did not raise her eyes as Bernard stood looking down at her before he went away.

So on the next day, among the beautiful autumn woods, France's happiness came to her. Patty, lying among cushions and rugs at the foot of a great elm, with Miss Marigold sewing near her, saw the two coming toward her out of the deep forest where they had gone to hunt for ferns, and knew by the look in their faces that a new life had begun for them. Patty and Miss Marigold never forgot that picture — the glorious sun-lighted trees in all their splendor of color, the still, blue lake and the shining hills beyond, the showering leaves that fell like a rain of gold about the two figures in the midst, and, lovelier than all, France's face, grave and sweet, with lips trembling in their new gladness and a look in the clear, gray eyes which brought a rush of happy tears to those of the old watcher and caused her to whisper in her heart : —

" It 's my own story over again, and, O God, grant it may be as sweet and without the pain at the end ! "

The homeward drive was very still that afternoon. Even the little children caught the infection of happy silence, and sat quietly looking out on the hills and vales bright with rainbow colors. Patty lay back among her pillows, gazing from the beauty about her to her friend's fair face with the strange, new light upon it; Bernard and France were lost in a maze of mingled joy and sorrow, thinking now of the year of separation before them, now of the beautiful unknown world of love that had opened for them both to-day; and Miss Marigold, watching with tender, glowing heart, sang in her soul the sweet refrain of a song of love that had never died out of her life, though to outward seeming she had been alone in the world for thirty years.

"I'm glad that it came in the autumn," thought Miss Marigold, smiling up at the billowy hills in the distance, "just when everything is at its loveliest and the world looks like the foundations of the New Jerusalem. It will all come back to France like a lovely picture, in this long year that's coming."

It was almost dusk when they drove down Beech Street, and the lights were beginning to gleam in some of the houses, as they had done on the evening when Bernard told his story to France, just before Katy died. To-night he saw none of the household pictures which he had watched then.

The world about him was blotted out with fairer visions, and he cared little for Beech Street sights. But Miss Marigold, looking out from a rosy mist of love and memory, caught a glimpse of one picture that brought a heartache with it — the professor's room, with madame listless in her easy-chair, and the old man at his desk, his white head dropped in his hands, his face hidden, with an air of utter weariness and discouragement sad to see.

CHAPTER XI.

HOPE DEFERRED.

A FEW bright, never-to-be-forgotten weeks of love and gladness; of planning for the months of waiting to come and the fullness of joy to follow; of walks and talks in familiar haunts transfigured by the new light which had dawned upon them; of songs sweeter than any sung before: of farewells said again and again; with silent prayers put up from trembling hearts, — and Bernard was gone. A stillness seemed to settle down on his friends when the parting was over and they had taken up their usual life again. The days and weeks slipped by in strangely quiet fashion, now that there was no tall figure to come springing up the street with arms full of woodland treasures and suggestions of expeditions by land or water, in sublime disregard of household arrangements. The girls missed his teasing comments as they prepared their essays and translations for the professor: Bernard had insisted on their studying in the evening so that he might " see the fun"; and the choruses in Mrs. Hayward's parlor had lost half their charm now that his clear tenor had gone.

"I never would have believed we should miss him so." sighed Mrs. Hayward, as she sat in the corner with Miss Marigold and looked on with inured calmness while the boys rolled about the floor at their usual evening romp.

"I did n't take it in myself," the little spinster would respond, knitting with all her might at the stockings which she always had on hand as winter drew in. The children at the Orphans' Home were accustomed to look forward to those stockings with inward longings and to regard with jealous heart-burnings those who became possessors of them. People who sent in stockings did not ordinarily make them with an eye to artistic effect, and Miss Marigold's soft scarlet and blue ones were as desirable in the eyes of the orphans as they would have been in those of the most "stylish" of small aristocrats.

"I like to knit pretty things better than dull ones," said Miss Marigold ; "and as long as the babies like them, why should n't I do it?" To which certainly there was no answer to be made.

There was other work in which Miss Marigold took a delighted part during that winter and spring. There were lengths of delicate embroidery and bits of dainty "fagoting," which grew day by day under her skillful fingers, and found their way one by one to the drawers where France was gradually laying away her pretty, home-made bridal finery. Such work had to be done bit by bit in that busy, overflowing household, and the girl was already counting the time until Bernard should come and she should step with him over the threshold of her old life into the new one which was to be so full of blessing.

"In September," she murmured in her heart, making of the words a quiet song, which sweetened all the time of separation that lay between. France's dreams of the time to come were very secret and timid, in these days, yet full of sweetest meaning to her own heart.

> "Her whole thought would almost seem to be
> How to make glad one lowly human hearth."

A little spot of light in the world which they said was dark — that was what her home and Bernard's should be — a life of love and joy and service. The fairest future that thought could fashion stretched before her like a green meadow full of flowers, lying under the silver mist of early morning. The sun would scatter that light veil after a little, and they would enter hand in hand. The thought blossomed afresh in her heart with new sweetness when, night by night, she knelt to thank the Father for this fairest gift of her life, and to ask like a little child that he would take care of Bernard and bring him safely home. In the meantime her days were full of duties, cares, and pleasures which made them pass swiftly.

" I 'll live the time between as I want to live all my life afterward," thought France ; and in that thought the time between grew transfigured.

But if the girl's deepest hopes and dreams were shut away in the silence of her own heart, there were others in which those about her shared. Father and mother, Miss Marigold, Mrs. Winthrop and Patty, all knew and delighted in the plans for the coming year. There were joyous consultations by Patty's side, over laces and gowns, simple though they were to be, over house plenishings, furniture, and carpets to be purchased in the future. The very house which Bernard hoped to take was chosen, a bright little cottage at the further end of Beech Street. Miss Marigold and Patty had furnished it half a dozen times in imagination, and had laughed again and again over the fine vagueness of France's own plans, she having said in answer to some questions on the subject of furniture : —

" We must have a low bookcase and an oyster-broiler. Bernard likes broiled oysters so much ! "

Bernard's own letters were full of air castles, oddly erected in the midst of gay descriptions of his life among the forests, his discoveries, and his experiences with Indians and wild beasts ; a life so different from the quiet existence he had left that such bits of his letters as France would consent to read aloud were pronounced equal to Robinson Crusoe by Jack and Harry, and were asked for again and again when entertainment failed in the children's hour after supper. Outside the home circle were others who shared in the girl's happiness. Old Mrs. Reese had laughed and cried with sheer excitement when France had told her the news.

"My dearie! my dearie!" she had cried, "it's myself that can't be telling you how pleased I am! To be married! Oh, the winsome bride it'll be, and me that'll be hearing all about it beforehand, for I know you'll never leave telling me, the kind heart that you are! You'll let me work for you, dear? I'll just start an African this very day if John'll get me the right colors. Only there's none pretty enough for the like of you, that's brought more brightness to a blind old woman than I'd tell you in a year."

Accordingly she was engaged in knitting a gorgeous blanket of scarlet and green, which was triumphantly produced at every visit of France and Miss Marigold, and was dutifully admired by both, to the rapture of its maker.

Even Madame Dubois grew interested and affable in discussing the girl's prospects, and gave the benefit of her "French taste" in matters of doubt with the most charming readiness, even helping with the sewing in a manner that caused the neighbors to open their eyes in wonder, and brought sunshine to the tired face of her husband as he watched her across the piles of exercises which it was his fate to be always correcting.

"She is aroused at last, my poor Julie," he thought, listening with dreamy pleasure as madame talked to France over the work, describing her own marriage and dwelling on the glories of her bridal robe with a dignified patronage of the inexperienced American girl which would have vanished in wrath if she had guessed with what joyous secret laughter of soul it was received. It was wonderful, Miss Marigold and the professor thought, to see how France "got on" with madame.

"It would be sad without her visits this winter," the old man confessed, as he watched her down the street, a vision of youthful freshness and sweetness, with her golden hair shining under her little scarlet "cloud." "It would be dull. The winter season is a time of dullness in this so dreary climate. It is well for madame and myself that Mees France has pleasure in our household."

The days certainly needed brightening for M. Dubois. A time had come this winter which had long been dreaded in his home: the time when he could no longer keep from his wife the struggle for daily bread which it had been his care for long years to endure alone. The little maid whom he had managed to keep to spare madame the household labors was sent away now, and her mistress' hands were beginning to lose their dainty smoothness over the kitchen work. Madame seemed to care very little for this, but her husband looked on with piteous eyes while she moved about the stove or set the supper table, passing to and fro, a proud and graceful figure, with her delicate, faded face and restless eyes.

"It is not fitting, my poor friend," said the professor sorrowfully. "It is I that should do all, since I can no longer win the money to pay for the service. It is not for thee, this labor. Tell me, then, how I should do, and go thou to thy broidery for the dear child whom we love."

But though madame might utter sharp words of blame for failure in worldly prosperity, and might go about the house with no smile or word of comfort for the husband, whose care was an old story taken as a matter of course, she lifted her share of the burden which he could no longer carry alone, and went on with it bravely enough, with perhaps a brighter face for the effort. The loyal professor would have shrunk with dismay from the suggestion that his wife was happier now that there was real work for her, but he found a ray of comfort in seeing the lines smooth out of her forehead and in hearing an occasional song hummed over her sewing.

"It is Mademoiselle Marigold and France," he said to himself. "It was the young life that she needed, my Julie, and Mademoiselle Marigold has brought it to her in this dear child. May the good God bless them both!"

But if the shadows were beginning to pass away from the heart of Madame Dubois, they seemed to settle down more and more deeply over her husband. People were strangely apathetic this year toward the French language. The professor inveighed in eloquent terms against those feeble and flippant minds who dared to assert the superiority of the German literature over that of "la belle France." German was the favorite study in fashionable circles just now, and more than one of the old man's pupils had forsaken Corneille and Molière for Goethe and Schiller and the legends of the Rhine.

"It is inconceivable!" cried M. Dubois, standing in Miss Marigold's sitting room and gesticulating fiercely across the workstand. "Do you comprehend, mademoiselle? That the German poets are superior to those of my illustrious country — it is this which these student *bêtises* dare to assert! Superior to that list of names glorious and unparalleled

of which you, mademoiselle, have the misfortune to
be ignorant save in translation. A young lady has
even ventured to ask of me with concealed derision
this afternoon, ' Professor Dubois, do you really think
France is the foremost nation of the world in everything?' I met her with scorn!" cried the excited
professor, shaking his white head like a lion, " with
scorn! I replied, ' No, mademoiselle! I claim not
for my country the foremost place in all; but observe
that in arts, in literature, in music, in military glory,
in philosophy, and in science, no nation can approach
to her! I wish you a good-day, mademoiselle, and
congratulate myself and you that my engagement with
you is at an end!' She is to join a German class,"
he added, with a curious break in his voice. " The
American mind is singularly fickle, Miss Marigold. I
have lost many pupils in this way, of late."

" It 's a shame!" said Miss Marigold as indignantly
as if she had been acquainted with every claim of
both languages. " I don't see how they can! The
idea of liking German better than French! I 'm sure
I only wish I was a little younger, to study with you
myself. How anybody can want to change, when
there are such funny things as those plays you
translated to me, and such heart-breaking ones as
poor old Jean Valjean, that France made me cry my
eyes out over only last week! But people are apt to

be foolish in this world, professor, and so I've often thought."

" The truth is, my friend," said the professor, with an approach to confidence that brought a sudden mist before his listener's eyes, knowing his life as she did, " the truth is that this year I cannot so well afford to lose my pupils as in any other year. It is sometimes difficult to plan one's expenses when one's income is uncertain."

" I know it is, professor," said his friend heartily. "It's just a shame and nothing else. Yet you do manage so beautifully, and madame is so much better. Besides, the winter is almost gone now, and spring always makes things easier. It's been hard times everywhere, this winter after the fever, but it won't last long, I know. It's a long lane that has no turning, you know, and yours 'll turn soon I'm sure."

" Yes," he answerd, smiling absently; " and yet, my friend, sometimes I almost fear that my lane will only turn when it leads into the fields of Paradise. Sometimes it seems a very long time since my little ones went away and the troubles began that have led me here. Now and then — only now and then — it has been hard to keep a brave heart, as you say. Sometimes one feels a sting when one cannot provide as one should; and yet, as we all know, one should not murmur at what comes from the heavens. I say to myself that I have no faith if I cannot take what is sent to me, and then it seems to me there comes a voice from heaven — the voice that Pascal heard in his prison : ' Be comforted ! Thou wouldst not search for me if thou hadst not found me.' " The old man looked up with a bright smile. " I can follow that voice, my friend."

Miss Marigold turned away to her box of mignonette to hide her face. She had never heard the professor speak in this way before.

" If I could only do anything ! " she murmured ; " but there is no way to help them."

She gathered a bunch of flowers and sent them to madame, watching with tear-filled eyes as the professor went away with slow footsteps.

" His lane must turn very soon, or it will be as he says," she thought with sad foreboding.

But the turning was not reached yet. Week after week, month after month, the winter slipped away, bringing no change for the better to the Duboises. The gaps in the bookcase could not be hidden now, and even madame's vase sometimes stood empty for weeks. Now and then the professor remarked with guarded carelessness that he should not come home to dinner — there was work to do at school which would take up a part of the afternoon. Madame need not provide for him. He would take care of himself down town. Madame did not approve of such arrangements. It made the day lonely, she said, and the day was sufficiently lonely, at best. The professor sighed half impatiently as she said so.

"There are worse things than loneliness," he said, almost with a touch of bitterness in his voice.

But the bitterness never lingered. The professor's step might grow slower and his face more worn, the "tantrums" which gave joy to the hearts of the irreverent youth of the high school might come with increasing frequency, and the thought of home and children might pierce his heart with longing, day by day; but the flashing smile still illumined his face, and the treasures of his books and the interests of his pupils still furnished food for discourse and laughter among his few friends. The professor had never heard of Lady Grizell Baillie, but the words of her pathetic song of sorrow would have mirrored his heart as face answers to face in the water: —

"Were na my heart licht, I wad dee!"

Once, in the April twilight, France sat with him and his wife near their window. There was no light in the room, and a slow, soft rain was falling outside; such a rain as brings with it the thought of the "coming musk-rose, full of dewy wine," and makes one listen in the stillness to hear the violets growing in the damp, cold meadows. It was very quiet in the room. France and Polly had been spending the afternoon with madame, and the little one sat nestled in her friend's lap, with her soft, round cheek pressed against madame's thin one, and her clinging arms about the childless mother's neck while she whispered some baby confidence with regard to her plans for the next day.

"It's my baby Bella's birthday," murmured Polly, "and I'm going to have a party for her in the playroom, and all the dollies will be there, and you may come, madame, if you like."

Madame smiled graciously and thanked the small hostess, with a light kiss on the rosy cheek. Madame's face was quite calm and peaceful to-night. The professor, on the other hand, sat silent, with his head bowed. He had been telling France about the day at school in answer to her questions, and had broken off suddenly in a way that she thought strange. She could see that his face was very pale, and he looked straight before him with a curious, unseeing gaze, which made the girl wonder what could be in his mind. Could he have heard bad news? France grew silent herself as she pondered. She knew a little of the straits in which her friends were placed this year, and had seen that look on the old man's face once or twice before, when he had been brought face to face again with the bills which he had been unable to pay.

But to-night it was deeper and darker than ever before, and the girl felt her heart go out in desire to do something to lift the cloud from the brave heart that was groping in darkness. She began to sing softly, with a sudden impulse. France's voice was sweet and pleasant to hear, with that rare quality which causes one to forget the singer in the song. She had laughed often because people never complimented her singing, but only her songs.

"Now don't be sorrowful, darling!"

sang France, with her happy face, and the professor raised his head to listen, wondering. Softly it stole through the room, the tender air with the beautiful soul of comfort in the words. France saw the old man's lips quiver and the tears roll down his cheeks as she went on : —

"Taking the year together, my dear,
    You always will find the May.
We've had our May, my darling,
    And our roses, long ago.
And the time of the year is come, my dear,
    For the long dark nights and the snow."

Madame's hand stole over in the dusk to find her husband's. It was like the voice of his own heart speaking to her.

The tears were in her eyes as she watched his face in the faint light of the street lamp. For once madame had forgotten her own troubles. "Poor Louis!" she whispered.

The professor smiled back at her, brushing away the unbidden tears. He straightened up in his chair and his face was as bright as France's own while she sang the last stanza: —

"But God is God, my faithful,
Of night as well as of day,
And we feel and know that we can go
Wherever he leads the way.
Ay, God of night, my darling,
Of the night of death so grim;
And the gate that from life leads out, good wife,
Is the gate that leads to him."

"I am a man foolish and unbelieving," said the professor to himself, rising. "It is a song the most pleasant, my dear mademoiselle, and we are grateful, madame and myself, for it. Come, then, and let us light the gas, and I will do my part in return by reading to you from whatever volume you shall choose. It is not yet time to go home."

Nothing more was said about the song. Only madame's face still wore the softened look which made it so much the sweeter, and the professor still smiled at her across the book which he held. But when France and Polly were gone, and madame was busy over the supper table, she heard her husband humming to himself the words that had touched him, and listened with a pang of fear : —

"The gate that from life leads out, good wife,
Is the gate that leads to him!"

CHAPTER XII.

THE IMMORTAL PALMS.

THE summer had come and gone, bringing France nearer to the time when her girlhood would be left behind and the little dream-home would become a reality. Bernard's joyous letters dwelt more and more on the home-coming, and his friends were beginning to reckon the days and hours till he should arrive. A pleasant air of festive preparation hung over the Hayward house, and France was always running in to show Patty some new triumph of needle-work or sample of dress goods. They were to be married almost as soon as Bernard came, and France was resolved in her own mind that the bustle of preparation should be over before his arrival, so that they might be free to enjoy the last few weeks together.

Just when the arrival would be, no one knew. Bernard had gone on a last expedition farther into the forest than he had before ventured; and there would probably be no letters until just before he started for home. Meanwhile, there was a time of waiting which began to grow wearisome as September

passed into October, and nothing had been heard.
Mr. Hayward watched newspapers with an uneasy
anxiety, and many were the secret consultations
held by his wife and Miss Marigold, as well as the
Winthrops.   But no one spoke of the matter to
France.

" We won't make her anxious, poor child ! " said
father and mother pityingly ; and although Miss Marigold, at least, suspected that the girl understood
everything in their minds, she agreed with the rest in
ignoring any cause for anxiety when with her.

There was another interest to fill the minds and
hearts of the little circle this fall.   In a quiet
chamber at the other end of the street lay the professor, worn out at last by the ceaseless struggle, and
waiting in vain for strength to enter on the round
of work.   He had fainted in the classroom one
day, just after the opening of school, and had been
carried home to rest.   The rest had lasted for a
month or more, now, and though he still spoke
cheerily of returning to work in a few days, his
friends were beginning to look at each other with
grave, pitiful eyes when they spoke of him, and to
say in their hearts, " His rest will not end when he
thinks."   Miss Marigold spent a great part of her
time at his house, helping madame with the care
of him and busying herself in household matters.

Madame herself seemed at first to have no thought of danger to her husband.

"He studied too much," she said. "A learned man is always intemperate in study. For my part I would like to lock the books away from him until he is able to return to work. Miss Marigold and France are foolish to sit and read to him as they do. What he needs is to think of nothing."

But week after week went by and the old man grew no better. The readings were dropped, with no words on the subject. Sometimes he lay for hours quite silent, with closed eyes, too weak to think of what went on about him. Sometimes his mind wandered and he talked of the friends of his youth and the red-walled town by the sea, or thundered out some hasty rebuke, as if he were in his class, rousing at the sound of his own voice and looking about him with a bewildered smile of apology. Little Polly was often in the room, and he liked to have her sit beside him on the bed and tell him about her small joys and sorrows, though once or twice he passed his hand over her yellow head as if puzzled, murmuring, —

"But it was brown. It should be brown."

Poor madame sprang up and hurried out of the room as she caught the faint whisper.

Once, as Miss Marigold sat by him alone, he fixed his eyes on her, as if trying to recall the thoughts that would wander, and spoke, with an effort, quite clearly.

" You have been my friend, mademoiselle," he said, " and the friend of my poor wife. Tell me, then, it is not that one who is needed for the life of another is taken away? One stays in this life until one's work is done, is it not? I have not a mind quite clear. Is it not that the Lord does not call one away when one has work that must be done?"

" The Lord always lets us finish the work he wants us to do, professor," said Miss Marigold steadily. " I would n't worry about that. But if you do think about it, try to remember that madame will never be left alone while I 'm here to help her. I 'm alone in the world and I 'll stand her friend as long as I live, and be a sister to her if ever anything should happen, which I pray the Lord there won't."

" No: one must finish one's work," murmured the old man, a look of contentment coming into his anxious face. " One must do one's work, and the Lord will never call one away from it till it is done. I felt that it was so, but I cannot think now. And you are madame's friend and will never leave her alone."

And he closed his eyes and fell away into a long sleep.

Madame's face began to wear a look of still fear and grief terrible to see, in these days. She went about the sick room with noiseless steps, scarcely speaking, and turning away from every attempt at comfort with dumb anguish. Even Polly met with more than one harsh repulse from the desolate woman.

"You are not my own! not my own!" cried madame, in a tempest of mingled French and English, as she pushed the child away from her knee. "Ah, when was it ever known that one should be so left alone! alone! that the children should depart, and my Louis should be stricken down and I should have no help! Where is the good God to whom he speaks in his wanderings, that this should be?"

But the professor had passed out of reach of grief and longing. He had slipped away with the passing days into a pleasant region of sunshine and flowers, the land of his childhood, where he roamed joyously, talking in his own tongue of birds' nests in great trees which he was climbing; of frolics with long-dead brothers; of walks with mother and father along the sunny beach across the sea. The long, hard day of toil was over, and the tired heart was at rest, even now.

Day by day came messages from the outside world that could not reach him now. The professor had never known that so many people cared for his welfare. Pupils from the high school stopped morning and afternoon to ask how he was, and to say with somewhat conscience-stricken faces how sorry they were that he was ill.

"You see, we got so in the way of laughing at him that we really did n't take it in how much we all thought of him," said Jack Hayward, with honest, boyish tears in his eyes. "He was so quick to come down on a fellow that we sort of enjoyed it, and used to stir him up. I wish I had n't ever done it now. Is n't there anything a fellow could do for him?"

Johnny Reese hung about the door of the house with pathetic patience, waiting for some chance to be of use. The professor had lent a helping hand many a time to the slow-witted boy since Miss Marigold had told him of his circumstances, and Johnny's heart was full of gratitude. Miss Marigold treasured up with sorrowful pride the cards and messages left by fellow-teachers and acquaintances.

"Madame will like to think of them afterwards," she thought; "but, oh! why did n't they ever think to be so friendly before?"

It was strange and yet sweet to France Hayward to be in this peaceful chamber of death. She passed in and out daily, doing little offices of kindness and watching with loving eyes the dying flame of life as it flickered lower and lower. There was a certain sense of rest in that unconscious presence. The happy old man, roaming among the long-faded flowers of his childhood, knew nothing of the secret anxiety which was wearing her heart away. Others looked at her with pitying eyes, and avoided speaking of Bernard in a way that gave her a frantic desire to cry out to them that they had no right to think of what could not be true. France said constantly in her own thoughts that it was only a fancy, the unspoken fear which made them all so tender to her. Bernard must be safe. Had she not prayed daily, almost hourly of late, for his safety?

" Nobody shall make me believe that he will come to harm, until — *unless* — I hear it in a way that no one could mistake," she said defiantly.

The others wondered to see with what apparent freedom from doubt she still talked of all the happiness to come, and planned for what should be done "when Bernard comes." It was easier to rid herself of the haunting fear which would not be quite silenced when she was at the old man's side, and it gave her a vague feeling of comfort and strength to see that he smiled at the sound of her voice and liked to have her near him.

So the days went by, until, one clear, beautiful evening, just as the sun went down in a sea of amber flame, the professor opened his eyes and looked about him with childlike wondering gaze that did

not take in the faces around his bedside. His wife
was close to him with white, yearning face against
his very pillow, but he looked beyond her into the
radiant sky.

"You have been long away, my children," he said
in a quiet voice. "Thy hair is blown about by the
wind, Didine. *Maman* must arrange it. Kiss me,
my little brown dove."

The wind rustled softly in the dead woodbine
branches outside the window. There was no other
sound in the room. A strange, wonderful light was
dawning in the professor's face. "You must go to
your mother," he said gently. "She has been lonely
without you. It is hard for a mother to miss her
little ones. Come, let us find her and tell her that
you are safe." His voice died away in a whisper,
but a smile — the last smile — stole slowly over his
face.

"Louis! Louis!" sobbed madame, with her lips
against his cheek. "O my Louis, listen to me!
Speak to me, not to the children. Let them go, only
stay thou with me. We can bear all if we are
together, thou and I. Louis, speak!"

Too late, poor heart! The light in those weary
eyes is not for you. The sunshiny smile will never
dawn for you again. He is beyond your reach, with
the children whom he loves. Listen: from the gates

of the other world his voice steals back, sounding calm and clear through the quiet chamber.

" *Les palmes immortelles!* " said the professor, and so, still smiling. grew silent.

" It is over," whispered Miss Marigold through her tears.

CHAPTER XIII

TITHING THE MEMORIES.

FRANCE opened the door of Miss Marigold's room and came quietly in. She had knocked very softly, as if she did not wish to be heard by any one besides the occupant. The little white room was bright and cheerful, with a wood fire in the Franklin stove. The winter sunshine lay full across the window sill, and rested on Miss Marigold's lap as she sat with her Bible in her hand, close beside it. She looked up with a half-surprised welcome as the girl came in. It was not often that any one but herself entered this room.

"Come in, my dear," she said, holding out her hand to her visitor. "I'm glad to see you, if it is Sunday afternoon and up here. I came away to be quiet for my reading, you know, now that madame is with me. Why — France, what is it?"

For the girl's face was pale and startled, and her lips were parted in excitement. She came swiftly over to Miss Marigold and dropped on the hassock at her feet.

"Miss Marigold, I've found it out!" she cried.

"Madame — Bernard — Oh, how was it that we never knew? O Miss Marigold, she is his mother!"

Miss Marigold dropped her book, in excitement equal to France's own.

"What do you mean?" she cried — "the little boy who ran away? You can't mean that he is our Bernard! France, do speak. Tell me how you know. I can't believe it!"

"I have just come from her," said France, struggling to be calm. "I came over to talk to her and keep her company while you were by yourself, and I found her crying down there, in that quiet, heartbroken way that almost breaks one down to see. So I tried to get her to talk about other things, and gradually she came to speak of her children, as she does so often now, and — and — she told me about little Raoul. I never knew that he was lost before. I thought they were all dead; but she told me about his wandering in the woods and how she and his father were always saying to themselves that they must not let their hearts cling to him as they had done to the others, for fear of losing him, and Bernard had told it all to me before. I could hardly believe it when she talked about the old castle, where he used to climb about, and the mountains beyond the town, where they thought at first that he had gone. Then she spoke of Jacques and Marie, and I began to wonder more and more, for Bernard had told me that his father was an army officer, and it did not seem possible. And then she spoke of his singing, and began to hum the very hymn that he had sung to me, over and over; and, O Miss Marigold! she told me his name — *Bernard Raoul!*"

" But how — how — It does n't seem possible!" cried Miss Marigold, with a bewildered face. "My dear France, I can't take it in. The professor was in the army once; you knew that, did n't you? But Bernard! how is it possible that they should live eight months in the same street and never find it out? Though, to be sure, the professor never cared to meet people, and Bernard was hardly ever home except in the evenings. But I can't take it in! Oh, his poor father!"

There were tears in both their eyes, at the thought of the brave old man who had trodden his path of sorrow to the end without knowing.

" Does madame know?" said Miss Marigold.

France dropped her head on her friend's knee, in a sudden, uncontrollable fit of sobbing.

" How could I tell her?" she asked, with choked utterance. " Now, when Bernard is — is — It would only be cruel! It all came over me as I was going to speak, and I could only come away to you. I — Oh, where is Bernard?"

Miss Marigold put both arms around the shaking form and drew the bright head to her breast, as if she had been the girl's mother.

"Thank heaven she has spoken it out at last!" thought the loving woman.

Miss Marigold had watched with anxious eyes during the past few weeks, and no news came from Bernard, and France still maintained her silent self-command. It was two months now, since the time when he had expected to return. The wedding preparations had been quietly laid aside, with no explanations. Patty and France had ceased to discuss the furnishing of the little house up the street. Indeed, Bernard's name was seldom spoken now, at least before France, though at every mail time members of both households were sure to meet, with questioning eyes and guarded words about the uncertainty of all postal systems and the probability of letters being lost between South America and home.

But France resolutely turned from all discussion of the subject. Bernard was probably on the track of some important discovery, she always said, and was too far away to send letters. They would hear from him in time. She went about her daily duties, a little paler than before, a little quieter and graver, but that was all. It seemed as though she were afraid of the least deviation from her usual way of life, lest it should be taken as a confession that there was cause for anxiety. She sang and told stories to the children as before, sat over the mending with her mother and discussed neighborhood matters as if there were nothing more absorbing in the world, and made her visits to Mrs. Reese and madame with the same regularity. But Miss Marigold shook her head in secret as she looked on.

" It 's not natural," thought the wise little woman. " I 've been through it all, and I know."

Now, when the pent-up suffering suddenly burst forth, Miss Marigold made no effort at consolation. She sat quite silently, with her cheek against the golden hair, until the girl's passionate weeping grew still.

Then she spoke, very gravely and gently. " My dear, you are right not to tell madame. She has all she can bear already. I 'm glad you thought. We must keep it from her until some news comes. And, France, I 'm as sure as one can be of anything without really knowing, that it will be good news. Of course no one knows what our Lord may see fit to do, but it seems to me he means to give you and Bernard the chance to make that poor woman happy in her last years. Think what she 's borne and lived through, and how she 's changing and growing gentler and softer in these last months, and especially since the

professor died. It seems to me she's just ready for
happiness, and it will come with her son. I can't
believe the Lord means to bring comfort so near her,
and then let it slip past. We'll hear good news soon,
I'm sure."

France smiled faintly in reply.

"And think of the joy to Bernard," went on Miss
Marigold; "and, O France, that you should be the
one to find it out♠ It will be something to be thankful
for all your life."

"If he only comes!" breathed France, with a long
sigh. "But how *can* I wait? You don't know."

Miss Marigold sat quite silent for a few minutes,
thinking, with her soft eyes fixed on the ebony box
beside her. She drew it toward her at last and opened
it slowly, lingeringly.

"Dear," said Miss Marigold, "look here."

She set the open box on France's knee, and raised
the pale blue handkerchief which covered the faded
flowers and the rosy shell. France looked wonderingly from them to the sweet, grave face beside her.

"What are they, Miss Marigold?"

"They are what is left from the happiest part of
my life," said Miss Marigold gently. "I have never
shown them to a soul before, France, but I want you
to know that I know all about it. I've kept it all in
my heart just as those have lain in my box, along

with the Lord's money that's in the other part, shut
up where nobody knows. I never thought to talk
about it again, but I've no right to keep back the help
that came to me, when I can give it to you. My dear,
it was long, long ago, when I was younger than you,
that it began. I was the only one at home, you know,
after I was a child, and the house was still and lonely
for a girl in those days. Father was always ailing,
and mother was busy with him, and I was left to my
own ways more than some girls, though I was always
happy. I only spoke of that to tell you what a difference it made when Reuben came. I could n't begin to
tell you the difference," said Miss Marigold simply.
"When I saw you and Bernard so happy last year I
seemed to be living it all over again with you, though
you never knew. Often and often I could hear Reuben
singing 'The red, red rose,' as he did on the night
that he brought these roses to me, 'Till a' the seas
gang dry.' It's strange how people's voices come
back to us after years and years. I've heard Reuben's voice as plain this last year as I ever heard it
thirty years ago, singing that line. He was a sailor,
and just as brave and warm-hearted and honest as a
sailor should be. I used to be so proud of having
him care for me, for I was always an insignificant
little thing. But poor father could n't bear to give me
up. He was losing his mind in those days, and he

would cry and beg me not to leave him, and so we
agreed that we would keep it all to ourselves and wait.
A few years out of our lives would n't matter, we
said, as long as we were sure of each other. So
Reuben went away on a three years' voyage, and I
waited here. I did n't hear a word in all those years,
though he wrote at every chance, he said. They were
lonely years, for father died before he came back;
and yet I never felt quite alone, I was so sure of
Reuben. When he came at last it was only for a few
weeks. He wanted to be married before he sailed
again, and I was all ready." The quiet voice faltered
for a moment, and then went steadily on. "We had
thought that it would be a comfort to us both, for we
knew better than before how hard it was to be apart.
And Reuben had made up his mind to buy this house
and leave us in it, so that he would know just how to
think of us; for you know mother and I were n't very
well off then, and we did n't own it until uncle Asa
left us his money. We were very, very happy. But
just then, only a fortnight before he sailed, he came
here one night all broken up and half distracted. His
sister's husband was dead, killed in an accident on the
railway away out west, and there were four little children, and his wife had nothing in the world to support them on. So, of course, I told him to go to
them. Somehow I had a sort of hope that something

might come to help us, but when he came back, only two days before the ship was to sail, he had nothing new to tell me. My poor Reuben! he would have given me back my promise altogether, now that there was no hope of our being married for years to come, but, as I told him, we belonged to each other for good and all, and it was only a little longer waiting. So he said good-by and went away — and — that was his last voyage."

Miss Marigold stopped to brush away the tears.

"That was all, France. We never heard from him again, until, four years afterward. one of his shipmates came up here to find me and tell me how my poor boy died of fever, and how they found in his chest this handkerchief and shell, in a packet with my few letters. It was kind of the man to bring them to me! I think a great deal of them," faltered Miss Marigold, touching both with her tremulous fingers. "And so I wanted to tell you," she went on after a little, "that I know just how it is with you better than other people could, perhaps. And I wanted to say, what you'll find out for yourself some day, if you have n't already, that even if the very worst you can fear should come true — though I don't feel as if it would, as I was saying — but even if it should ever be with you as it has been with me these many years, the gladness of the love is something that can't be taken away, even by — death. When one loves any-body with all one's heart and soul," said the little woman, smiling through her tears, "when one has anybody safe in one's very life, like that, one can't lose him. Somehow, the older I grow, the surer I come to see that whatever is in God's keeping is n't so very far off from the hearts that want it. I don't feel as if Reuben was quite taken away from me, even now, and it is so with you and Bernard, my dear. Living or dying, if you 're given to each other you can't lose each other. Our Lord takes care of that; and I 've learned it through and through, in these years that I 've been alone." She bent over the girl and the two kissed each other with silent comprehension. Then she closed the box again and set it in its place, while France watched her with loving, grateful eyes.

" Come now, we 'll go down to — Bernard's mother," said Miss Marigold, rising; and they went hand in hand.

CHAPTER XIV.

ON CHRISTMAS EVE.

"YOU need n't be afraid," said Polly, standing with her back to the kitchen door and regarding with critical eyes the quintette of small Ruggleses who stood eying the passage to the sitting room. "There is n't anybody there but Miss Marigold and those mission school children and all of us and Mrs. Reese and Johnny, and Patty and her mother. An' that noise is only just everybody playin' 'ki yi yi.' They 've got handkerchiefs on their heads and they shake their hands and march round. France shows 'em how. I don't play, 'cause me and madame we 'd rather sit in the corner and look on. Why don't you go in? I came after you a-purpose."

The small Ruggleses huddled together and looked at each other in dismay.

"There 's heaps and piles of you," said Jed, after a moment's pause. "That room 's chuck full. Did n't I see it a minute ago when you opened the door? An' every one a-jumpin' an' a-roarin'. Wish t' we 'd waited for ma. *I* don't want to march in there."

" Then what did you come to a Christmas party for, if you was n't goin' to be in it when you got there? " asked indignant Polly. " Miss Marigold, she said, ' Polly, you run out an' get 'em, that 's a dear ; ' an' now you won't come ! You have to mind the lady that gives the party, *always*," went on the perplexed messenger. " Besides, how are you goin' to see the Christmas tree if you ain't there when the door is opened ? "

Mary Ann made one bashful step toward the door and then drew back. The Christmas tree was a strong inducement. Mary Ann had never seen a Christmas tree. They did not grow in Brown's Alley. " I wisht we could peek at it out here," she whispered, pulling Jed's sleeve.

But in the midst of Polly's silent displeasure and the growing embarrassment of the guests, the door opened, and a lady came out of the sitting room, a pale, quiet lady in a mourning gown. She had grave dark eyes, and there were bands of silver in her black hair. The children looked at her with doubt changing to relief as she lifted the smallest Ruggles in her arms with a little smile.

" For what then do you fear? " asked madame in her slow, broken English. " Come then with me. I s'all take you to Mees Marigold, and if you s'all not wish to take part in the *ronde*, I s'all show to you *des gravures.* The Christmas, it is the day of children, and you must not have fear. Come."

The children followed shyly without a word. Children were not often afraid of madame. The little one whom she carried surveyed her with round, judicial eyes for a moment and then pushed his fat hand against her cheek and laughed.

" Christmas comin'," he said.

It was bright and warm and cheery in the sitting room. Outside a whirling cloud of snow was driving about the windows, and the wind was wailing in the chimneys, as if it would like to get in to share the fun in the fire-lighted room.

" It 's going to be a white Christmas, sure enough," Miss Marigold had said that afternoon, as the first flakes began to fall. "A white Christmas ; and that means a glad New Year. It's a blessing that I arranged for Patty to come early and stay all night. She 'd never have come if we 'd waited till now to bring her."

" A blessing " it did seem to Patty, as she lay or. the wide, old-fashioned lounge opposite the fire, look · ing about her with bright, pleased eyes at all the pleasant pictures. Miss Marigold and France had made a green bower of the place with pine and holly : the plants in the boxes were in full bloom, and a nasturtium vine had run up to the very top of the east window, tossing out its yellow flowers like gay little festal lanterns. The professor's bookcase stood in one corner, and the St. Cecilia hung over it. His wife had draped her ivy in a graceful curtain around them both, and a single white hyacinth stood in pure, plume-like beauty against the dark background of the old volumes.

Madame's eyes turned often to that corner, as she sat with a child on each side, turning over a picture book furnished by scornful Polly for the two bashful infants who still declined to join the circling game which went merrily on in the middle of the room. Madame's worn face was strangely softened since her last overwhelming sorrow. Patty wondered silently at the change as she watched her now.

"Is it because there's nothing in the world left for her that she's beginning to forget herself?" she thought, as madame turned from one of those lingering looks to smile at the little boy who was pulling at her sleeve, and answer some question about the book in her lap.

But Patty was not allowed to watch the others without interruption. Close to her couch, in the great cushioned chair, sat old Mrs. Reese, her childish face glowing with delight and her busy chatter filling every pause in the general confusion. It was an occasion long to be remembered in the old woman's life, this Christmas party at Miss Marigold's.

"I've been through scenes and unseens, as they say to meetin'," she cried with a happy laugh, "since I've been at a Christmas time before. It's just like Miss Prissy to think of a poor old body like me! Hark to them, Miss Patty, my dear! Did you hear my Johnny laugh? What are they singin'?

"Round and round this ring doth wander!

Eh, but it's a fine tune!"

She joined in with her sweet, trembling voice, nodding in time as she sang. Miss Marigold and the other guests looked around to listen, as they caught the sound, and laughed to each other for pure pleasure in her enjoyment. Even madame's sad face lighted up in response.

"We must have a song from you alone," said France, coming over to perch on the arm of the old woman's chair. "Come, children, we have played till we are tired. Sit down and listen, and then we'll have our Christmas carols before — the tree."

A broad smile of anticipation ran around the circle of childish faces at the word, and France smiled back brightly. France's face had gained something in the past three months of anxiety which it had not had even in the beauty of its crowning joy. It was graver and stiller, perhaps, but ennobled and glorified by the unconscious light of faith and courage

shining out from the inner chambers and making a
sunshine in the shady place.

"'Tribulation worketh patience, and patience experience, and experience hope!'" thought Miss Marigold,
watching her to-night. "It's all unfolding like the
twistings of a rosebud. There'll be the flower of
love and joy at the last, whether it's in earth or
heaven. Thank God, I'm sure of that, this Christmas eve!"

"Sing us a Christmas song," said France; and
Mrs. Reese sat up in her chair with simple pride at
being asked to sing to such an audience.

"God rest ye, merry gentlemen!"

she began, and the talk and laughter died into silence
while the joyous carol went on.

"And now we must have

"Waken, Christian children,"

said France, starting the tune in her clear voice,
while the children joined in one after another. The
twilight was failing and the fire cast flickering, dancing shadows over the room as the happy voices filled
the air. Carol after carol, ringing out with a joyous
will, as one and another called for favorites, they
sang through the dusk hour. Even madame took her
turn and sang low and clear a plaintive little French

hymn about the child Jesus in the manger, with the snow on the thatch overhead and the angels singing " Noël! Noël!" above the low roof. Mrs. Ruggles and Phebe came to the kitchen door to listen, and wiped their eyes in unison as the French lady's voice died away.

" Don't know more 'n week after next what it all means," said Phebe, " and 't ain't the time to be cry-in', on Christmas eve, with all them oysters jest in the oven, and Miss Marigold and France a-lightin' up the tree this minute, but *I* can't help it; it ketches holt of me!"

But thoughts of a pathetic nature were successfully banished a few minutes later, when the doors of the best parlor were thrown open, and the event of the evening took place. That tree! Was there ever one equal to it in Bentonville? Polly and Baby held a solemn consultation with Mary Ann and decided not.

" There was n't never *anything* so pretty *anywhere*," said Mary Ann with weighty emphasis. " I jest wish t' all the folks down our alley could see it. Never s'posed there 'd be a live workbox an' a red hood an' all them nuts an' candies for me! Did n't even think our young ones would have them playthings! Won't it be easy times takin' care of 'em when ma 's off washin'! How 'd anybody know what to put up there for us, I wonder, an' have it just what we wanted?"

"Miss Marigold always knows what to do for folks," said impressive Polly. "And next time you'd better do just what she tells you to, when she says come in anywhere. Where'd you been if you'd stayed out in that hall all this time?" To which inquiry Miss Ruggles had no reply.

"I'm so happy!" sighed Miss Marigold to herself as she sat watching her merry guests, who filled parlor and sitting room in delightful confusion, "so happy that I can't seem to thank the Lord enough for bringing me around to this Christmas and giving me the means to have this party and France to help me out with it. To see them all frisking about, and making the house ring as it hasn't since the old times when we were all together! I wonder I never thought of it before this year. I believe if we could hear from Bernard I'd be perfectly happy to-night!"

But it was pleasanter still a little later when the poorer guests were gone home, laden with gifts and overflowing with Christmas gladness, and only the Haywards and Winthrops remained for a final chat about the fire. The children clustered in a corner to discuss the afternoon's fun and the rapture of the mission children, with an important sense of having helped to entertain them. The elders drew close to the hearth and talked gently and happily of other Christmastides, with a soft shadow over their faces as they spoke the names of one and another who were keeping the feast this night in the " upper chambers " of the King's palace. France dropped on the rug beside Patty and sat with an elbow on the edge of the couch and her head on her hand, resting, as she watched the faces around the fire. " Dear little Miss Marigold," said Patty, " how happy she looks! I'd like to paint a picture of her and call it Peace. It's no wonder she makes everybody happy who comes near her, when she is so happy herself."

" No," said France ; " and yet it is n't because it happens so with her. It's just that she's near enough to the heart of things to — know. She's got into the inside of the church like Hawthorne in the Italian Notes, and what looks like a great ugly pile of stones on the outside is like a gallery of jewels from where she sees it. It's more than just *seeing* that things work together for good," the girl went on, with a thought of the hidden treasures in the ebony box upstairs : " it's being so sure that everything that comes to her *is* good, that she never stops to think about it at all. I wonder if I shall ever get as far as that."

" Into the church?" said Patty with a smile ; " well, I don't know, Francie ; but, somehow, it seemed to me lately, that — if you were n't in the very middle of it, you'd got inside the door at any rate. I suppose the next thing to being at the heart of it all is the knowing that the heart is there."

"And that we're all under the same roof, some- how," said France brightly, "as it is in the Te Deum, you know. I wish you could go to church with me to-morrow, Patty, to hear them chant it.

"The Holy Church in all the world doth acknowledge Thee!

It does bring every one so close together."

Patty put up her hands to touch lovingly the shin- ing head beside her without answering. A silence fell between the two — a silence full of tender, sad, and sweet thoughts, which made it hard for either to speak again. It was a strange Christmas for those whose hearts were still watching and waiting for news from beyond the sea. Presently Madame Dubois rose from her low chair at the fireside, and went slowly over to the little bookcase. Madame spent a great deal of her time in that corner in these days, training her ivy, or taking down and putting back one book after another from the shelves. Sometimes she would try to read them and sigh as she laid them up. Miss Marigold often wondered what the professor would have thought to see her with puzzled brows knit over Bossuet or Pascal. Poor madame! France rose quickly now, and went over to where she stood

alone. Patty looked after her with sympathetic eyes.
The hearts of both girls were very tender toward
Bernard's mother, who did not know that he was hers.

"Strange that France should know just how to
take her, always," thought Patty, as madame turned
with a slight brightening of face at France's touch.

Some one else, standing on the steps outside, saw
them so; the girl's fair face and golden hair standing
out in strong contrast to the dark robes and sad
eyes of her companion. The watcher stood a moment gazing eagerly at the little picture before he
rang the bell; the snow whistled around as he
waited: a tall young man with bronzed face and
joyous dark eyes.

"Christmas eve!" he said to himself with a
bounding heart; "and what a Christmas day it will
be!"

Miss Marigold went to the door a moment later,
wondering a little that any caller should come on
that evening. France remembered all her life the
look of the familiar room at that moment; the
wreaths of evergreen, the flowering plants, the floor
strewn with bits of pine and scraps of bright paper
dropped by the children, the blazing fire that made
every corner warm and ruddy, the unconscious faces
about her; she remembered the touch of madame's
cold hand in hers, the very breath of keen, snowy

air that swept through the house as the door opened —and then the sharp, startled cry — " *Bernard!* "

He was in the room in a moment, with strong arms about her, and glad, loving eyes flashing light into hers, in the midst of a whirlwind of laughter and tears, of confused, eager voices and astonished faces! Her heart was beating in a joy keener than pain. Were these tears on her cheeks? the room was reeling before her eyes; some one was telling her not to faint; they were hurrying out of the room in a little huddled crowd; madame's face was before her, lonely, wondering, in the midst of all the gladness. France would hardly have known her own face, white and shining, as she turned from Bernard himself to throw her arms about his mother. Miss Marigold and Mrs. Hayward swept the amazed children away. Mr. Hayward caught up Patty in his arms and carried her out of the room followed by her mother. It was only a moment, the time that had seemed to France an eternity of bewildered, overwhelming happiness, before she was alone with the two whom it had been given to her to bring together on Christmas eve.

Miss Marigold and Patty, sitting in breathless silence across the hall, a little later, heard a sudden wild cry of eager, unbelieving, rapturous joy. Could that be madame's voice? They looked at each other with tears raining down their faces, the two who were yet not in the happiness of those three.

" God bless them!" sobbed Miss Marigold, with her face hidden in her hands. "What a Christmas this is!"

In the hush that followed, the air about seemed to ring with responsive gladness, as it echoed to the ringing, dashing, joyous chords that the Hayward children were singing as they ran homeward through the snow: —

> 'And all the bells on earth shall ring,
> On Christmas day, on Christmas day,
> And all the bells on earth shall ring,
> On Christmas day in the morning!
> And all the angels in heaven shall sing,
> On Christmas day, on Christmas day,
> And all the angels in heaven shall sing,
> On Christmas day in the morning!"

www.ingramcontent.com/pod-product-compliance
Lightning Source LLC
Chambersburg PA
CBHW020939030726
47496CB00005B/1262